'The thing is, Cyn, I shouldn't be here.'

'I know,' I say tartly. 'You should be at home, in your cot, with your parents.'

'I don't mean that. I mean, I shouldn't be here, period. In the world. Not now, anyway. I was born . . . by mistake. You see, I'm what you might loosely call a guardian. An angel, maybe. One of many souls whose job it is to watch over the Earth and observe its state of balance.'

'You're saying you're some sort of *alien*?'

He considers. 'Hardly. Just from a different dimension. There are many of us around the planet all the time. You just can't see us . . . well, not unless we inadvertently become flesh, as I have. And we're worried about this planet. Once it was beautifully balanced, but now it's overworked. Its energy web is being squeezed and pulled and pushed, bulbous here, frail there. It's not in good order, I'm afraid.'

Angel Baby

Lindsey Dawson

CORONET BOOKS

Copyright © 1995

First published in Great Britain in 1995 by Hodder and Stoughton

First published in paperback in 1996 by Hodder and Stoughton
A division of Hodder Headline PLC

'A Coronet paperback

The right of Lindsey Dawson to be identified as the Author of
the Work has been asserted by her in accordance with the
Copyright, Designs and Patents Act 1988.

10 9 8 7 6 5 4 3 2 1

All rights reserved. No part of this publication may be
reproduced, stored in a retrieval system, or transmitted,
in any form or by any means without the prior written
permission of the publisher, nor be otherwise circulated
in any form of binding or cover other than that in which
it is published and without a similar condition being
imposed on the subsequent purchaser.

All characters in this publication are fictitious
and any resemblance to real persons, living or dead,
is purely coincidental.

A CIP catalogue record for this title is available
from the British Library

ISBN 0 340 65749 9

Printed and bound in Great Britain by
Cox & Wyman Ltd, Reading, Berkshire

Hodder and Stoughton
A division of Hodder Headline PLC
338 Euston Road
London NW1 3BH

For Ken and for Jim – and for Pete, who is my rock.

"Marama [the moon] divides the waters of the mind. Marama releases the tides within. Marama opens the way to the trails of the wairua, the wondrous spirit we gather from the stars. Sometimes a child is born with a wairua that is older than old and knows a deep wisdom beyond its years. And sometimes it is too young to journey far in this world and stays but a short time before returning to the stars." – from *Song of Waitaha: The Histories of a Nation*. Published by the Ngatapuwae Trust, New Zealand.

PROLOGUE

The angel hovers, caressing his favourite planet – awesome globe, so green and blue. He touches its web, the glistening threads of energy encircling its ripeness. A bloomy plum, alight in space, wreathed with mist. He thrills to its song. Feels its hum.

And gets too close.

He doesn't mean it to happen. He is merely patrolling the web as is his duty, assessing its energy, soothing weak spots, when he is distracted by the sounds of imminent birth. Babies are squeezing forth all the time, of course, all over the globe. Their tiny trumpetings constantly fill the sky. But this particular one is putting up an unusually strident squawking as it emits its soulcall, its come-to-me bugling. An empty vessel, yearning to be filled.

And he sees, arrowing in to inhabit the body, a most appalling spirit. Malevolence writhes within it, and greed and overweening pride.

'Begone!' he shouts at it. But still it comes. And he zooms in closer, so close that when the soulcall goes out again, the yearning cry claims him whole. He pushes aside the dark soul, sending it spinning, and in that unguarded moment is drawn helplessly into the flesh, slipping into that pink, permeable space called human.

Oh, the tightness. Such aching pressure. Such an ache-filled bundle of bones and fat. He hears a howl, feels its effort reverberate in his surging muscular prison. It is her. This woman. His mother? 'I don't need a mother!' he screams.

And in an explosive, slithering wet rush, he is out between her thighs. Lights make his eyes hurt. People try to make him breathe. Hurtful squirtings and suckings in his nose and mouth. He is mewling, lungs pumping. The shocking taste of air fills his sea-swamped lungs. He cries, high-pitched, 'Ah, ah, ah'. Oh, Lord, he cannot speak.

A nurse leans over him with beatific smile. 'You're just fine, aren't you?' she beams. 'Such a dear wee soul.'

He feels such a fool.

ONE

ONE YEAR LATER

'Look at my sole!' I hold my shoe up to Robert at the desk next to mine, flicking the loose piece with my finger. 'I've only had the damn things a couple of weeks.'

He looks. Shrugs. 'Take them back,' he says.

'But I shouldn't *have* to,' I grit back at him.

Then, just to add to the joys of the day, my phone rings. And it's not someone inviting me to lunch. It's Louisa. My boss. Editor of *Maggy*, New Zealand's best-selling glossy magazine. Fashion, style, profiles, hot issues . . . you know the sort of thing. I don't want to talk to her because I know it'll be about the boring story she's been pressing me for. A profile on yet another visiting French fashion designer. I trudge to her office, limping in my stupid Italian imports.

'So how was he, Cyn?' she asks.

'Hopeless,' I say.

She gives me her sceptical look. It's one of her top

expressions. She's a big woman, Lou, trying to ignore middle age. She has lots of tangerine curls and more mascara than is good for her. She sits, arms folded, expression unforgiving. 'How come he was so dull?'

'He just wouldn't give. Deadly bland.'

Louisa makes a doubtful noise. 'Have you got enough stuff for a thousand words?'

'I think so.'

Louisa sighs. 'Christ, pull your finger out! You're supposed to be my star writer. What's wrong? Do you have a problem?' She often asks that. It's a way of denying she has any glitches in her own life. And it works. Bitch. 'No,' I tell her.

'Good. Got something else for you.' Louisa's bracelets clatter as she opens a folder. 'I know it's not your thing, but Sally can't do it because she's come down with some damn flu bug.'

I can guess what's coming. It gives me no joy. Sally is producing a special one-off parenting section. *Maggy* is a sharp glossy, you understand. Children have not been part of its ambit. But Lou's suddenly getting interested. It's quite alarming. She seems to feel she should acknowledge the cocooning trend even if she has no intention of doing anything so daft as getting involved in it herself. I make doubtful noises.

'Don't panic,' says Lou. 'There's just one piece outstanding.' It's for the *Superbaby* section, she explains. I remember now. Sally's been seeing mothers of precocious brats, asking them for tips on raising gifted kids. Louisa sniffs as she hands over an address. 'This one's barely a year old, for God's sake. Poor little bastards don't even have time to muck about with their Lego before they're being enrolled in violin class.'

'But I don't know anything about kids,' I whine. 'I don't even like them.'

'Who does, darling? Off you go. Quick-smart. Whack out your fashion piece first, huh?'

So three hours later I'm parking in front of a shabby little house in a boondock suburb. At the front door the chimes do the usual bing-bong. Down at knee level two pink starfish-like shapes appear, pressed against the inside of the mottled glass. Baby hands, patting at the panes. Then there are quick adult steps, the door opens, and a woman bends to pick up the kid and tuck him against her hip. The child sits, soggy finger in mouth, staring at me with grey eyes. His hair is golden brown. I have to admit to a degree of cuteness.

'Philly, don't suck your fingers!' scolds his mother. Her name is Shirley Preston. She darts a nervous smile my way and leads me into a small living room that's sour with old smoke. Yesterday's paper is crumpled on the couch, creased open at the TV programme page. There's a playpen on the floor, building blocks tumbled in its corner.

'Would you like coffee?' Shirley asks. She looks shockingly young to be a mum. Her limp blonde hair is loosely pulled back, exposing an ear lobe encrusted with a curving row of silver rings and studs. A small tattooed seahorse swims on her right upper arm. Her eyes are wide and hopeful. Vulnerable. She wears a flowered muslin top and faded blue jeans.

I offer an encouraging smile, and then wish I hadn't

for she bundles the boy into my arms and heads for the kitchen. He's heavier than he looks. I try to hook him on to my hip and he clamps his legs around me and leans back against my arm. He looks curiously into my face. I feel exposed. Just for a second, it's as if this kid sees into my soul. He chuckles.

'Hello, little one,' I say. My voice comes out in that silly twittering cadence that people lurch into when conversing with the very young. And I suppose because I've seen it done before, I stroke his soft cheek.

He takes his finger from his rosebud mouth and grips mine, pulling it away from his face. 'I'd really rather you put me down.' he says. 'You make me feel insecure and I'd hate you to drop me.'

I nearly do. Kids his age don't talk, do they? I lower him to the grubby carpet, where he sits down amongst the clutter of toys, one foot tucked comfortably against his other knee. I go on gaping.

He picks up a garish yellow bunny and straightens its bow tie. 'Are you going to write an article about me?' he asks.

'Philly, you can talk so well!' I sound daft, like Little Red Riding Hood. My, Grandma, what big ears . . .

'I'd rather you called me Philip. Shirley calls me Philly, but it always makes me feels like a diminutive cream cheese.'

'Uh?'

He grins. 'Where did you hear about me, anyway?'

'Your mother wrote to us.'

'Oh dear,' he says, mouth pursed like an elderly tutor. 'I do try not to sound too erudite in front of her. She's so young, you see, in herself – I don't think she could cope if I showed her the real me. What did she say?'

'She thinks you're special.'

'And what do you think?'

I hear the squeak of Shirley's sandals. 'Here we are!' she trills, carrying in a tray. Philip begins to build a pile of blocks. And as his mother bends to cut the cake, he flaps a broad conspiratorial wink at me. Come on. Is a kid that age supposed to have such motor skills?

'So,' says Robert, watching me suck at my Chablis, 'what's going on?'

I've asked him to join me for a quick drink after work. I have to tell someone, and he'll do. He's got a young son about the same age as the uppity kid. Robert and I work together. I write. He edits. We get along okay.

I dip the tip of a forefinger into my wine. 'You're going to think I'm crazy.'

'Why?'

'Well, it all sounds mad. I went out on a job without the slightest interest in it, preparing for the whole thing to be a big yawn. But it was unbelievable.'

'What, that baby thing?'

'Yes. He was sensational.'

'Didn't you tell Louisa he was a washout?'

I rummage in my bag and pull out a library book. It's given me questions that maybe Robert can answer. 'How old's your Billie?' I ask.

'Oh, fifteen months.'

Good. That means he can remember the twelve-month stage.

'You can tell if your kid's extra smart,' I tell him, tapping my library copy of *The Cleverness Quotient: How Bright Is Your Baby*?

I flip the pages, and start reading out the quiz on one-year-old development. Heaps of detail about awareness and play and sleeping patterns. He looks bored, so I prod him. 'Robert,' I insist, 'this doesn't relate one iota to the child I saw yesterday. He walks and talks. Uses words like "erudite" and "diminutive". And he speaks in perfect, whole, long, beautifully organised sentences! And yet he's just this sprat messing about with building blocks.'

Robert frowns, using a thumb to flick froth off his beer. 'If the kid's so amazing, why were you so half-hearted about him before?'

I take a swig of wine, not looking at him. 'He asked me not to say anything. Said he'd call me later when he was ready for publicity.'

'This baby gave you *instructions*?' Robert's lip is curling.

'And what's more,' I admit, 'he's scary. You don't expect someone so super-young to act so super-old.'

There is a longish pause. He chuckles. 'You've seen too many horror movies.' I can feel my cheeks pinking up. He pushes at the little towel on the bar with the base of his empty glass. 'Maybe the kid's older than you think he is.' Robert rationalises. 'Maybe he's small for his age. Maybe his mother's just one of those pushy types. And anyway, if he's that much of a genius you'll do him no favours by giving him five minutes of fame in our esteemed rag.'

'Never mind,' I say, feeling foolish. 'Go home. It's late. I'll see you tomorrow.'

'Yeah,' he says, easing himself out of his chair. 'Sophie'll be expecting me.' He doesn't like keeping his sister waiting. Since his wife, Kath, ran off with some photographer, leaving Robert to care for little Billie, Sophie has done his daytime child-minding. Such sisterly devotion. Still, Billie is close in age to Sophie's own son, and she's solo too. The arrangement suits them both. He jiggles his car keys, looking at me. Sometimes Robert Finian does that in a funny yearning sort of way. He says I'm the image of Kath with my squarish face and springy brown hair. Her *doppelgänger*. I've seen pictures of her. It's true. We could be sisters. But heck, I can't help that. His gaze clears. 'So what are you going to do about Supersprog?'

'I suppose I've already done it. Nothing. Ignore him. It's all I can do if he won't play ball. It was just weird, that's all.' I shrug, to prove I don't care. 'He's all alone, you know. Mentally, I mean. I'm the first person he's confided in. Sure, his mother knows he's smart. But he holds himself back with her. Doesn't let on.'

Now Robert really looks askance. 'Oh, come on. She's his mother! Why should he pick you to unload all of this stuff on?'

'I don't know!' I'm cross and awkward. 'She's young, you know? Not that switched on. She went off to answer the phone while I was there, and he said he's been aware since his birth. Watching. Evaluating. Deciding

9

what to do. And he's decided his parents can't help him much. The father knocks her around. She struggles to get by. I'm surprised she can even afford the magazine. I dunno. Maybe she picked it up in a waiting room or something. Maybe she wrote to *Maggy* to brighten up her life more than anything else.'

Robert's eyes are sardonic saucers now. 'I'm watching you,' he squeaks, making binoculars of his fingers.

'Knock it off. Go home,' I tell him. 'Billie will be waiting for you.'

'Yeah, well. You're not a social worker, Cyn. No point in dwelling on it.' He pats me on the shoulder as he gets up. He can't keep the smile from his face. 'Just think. It could be you in a year or two being spied on from the cot.'

I shrug off his hand, feeling stupid.

''Nother drink?' asks the barman. You bet, I tell him, as Robert gives me a farewell salute from the door. The next glass slides down easily. An American talk show glows in the corner next to a neon beer sign. On screen the interviewer is hammering at a politician. I've seen the show before and quite like the man's intensity, though he's too quick to cut people off. Too eager to score points. What's his name? Oakes. David Oakes. Robert once told me they worked together for a while in the States. Used to be drinking mates in Roberts' past life as a single travelling man. There was nostalgia and envy in his voice when he said it. But what the hell? Robert's disappointments in life aren't my problem.

It's getting dark as I lock my door and kick off my

shoes. Thirsty after the wine, I get a glass and head for the tap.

A movement in the sink catches my eye. Oh Jesus! A huge spider squats near the plughole. Black. Quivering.

I could smack down the base of my glass and squash it in a second. But I can't. Because that would mean going squish and grind, and then I'd have to wash all the juice and pulp and hairy bits down the plughole. Which would be disgusting.

I reach behind me, groping for a spray can on a shelf. Let him have it.

In a flash the spider has drawn its legs up into a black, knobbly ball. But he's pinned in a torrent of insecticide and he thrashes and jerks until the misty jet forms a thick puddle of foam.

I ease back the pressure. The spider looks much smaller. It lies huddled under white ooze. No movement. Not a tremor.

I want it gone and turn on the tap, gently at first to ease it down the hole and then harder to make sure it's right down the pipe, clear out of the building. The sink shines, wet and empty. And the phone rings. I reach for it with gratitude. Someone to talk to! A friend, I hope. A pal to tell my huge-spider story to. 'Hello!' I cry.

There are faint squeaky sounds, a grippy sort of noise as if someone is readjusting their hold.

The voice is sweet and clear. 'Good evening, Cyn, this is Philip Preston.'

'Philip? How did you get my number?' *How about, also, when did you learn to use the phone? Aren't you supposed to be tucked up in your frigging cot at this time of night?*

'I looked it up in the directory,' he says. 'You're the only C. Moon there.'

Oh, sure. Literacy now, is it? I pace two steps one way, then the other. 'Why are you calling?' Then, snappily, 'Are you aware how you messed up my day? I've just had to deal with the most enormous spider I've ever seen, and now I'm gabbing with a guy who's not even big enough to hold the phone to his ear!'

'You don't have to do that, Cyn.'

'Do what!'

'Kill the spider,' pipes Philip. 'Spiders are quite important to the world.'

I tug at my hair. You are the grown-up here, I tell myself.

'Listen!' he says. *The cheek of him.* 'I don't have much time. I want to talk to you again. It's important. Can you ring my mother tomorrow and ask if you can come back?'

How dare this kid demand my attention? 'No, I can't. Remember, I had to tell her you're ordinary when she thought you were going to be a star? She'll tell me to get lost.'

'No, she won't.' He sounds indignant. 'Not after that tantrum I threw just before you left. She thinks that's why you turned me down. Why don't you tell her you're sorry how things turned out, but you'd like to babysit to give her some time to herself? Spin her a story. Tell her you love babies and never get the chance to be with one.'

My eyes roll. 'But I don't. I think they're squirmy and noisy and smelly.'

The kid is unfazed. 'I have to hang up now. Try, Cyn. Please.'

TWO

'Maybe you need something more gritty to write about than queenish dressmakers and squalling infants,' says Lou Williams the next morning. She hands over some papers. 'People are handing this garbage out on the streets. Someone needs to take the piss out of them.' The top page is centred with a simple drawing of a spiral, bare and thin, like a cartoon rendition of a whirlpool.

She jabs a finger at the first paragraph. 'Just look at this stuff! "As the world nears the end of the millennium, it is time for all its peoples to see and be cognisant of the call of the Signal,"' she booms. '"We must open our minds and touch the thread of wisdom that connects us all. Heed the mind-call of the universe." Ever heard such crap?'

Not often, I think as I leaf through the ravings. I'm not surprised though. With a thousand-year cycle coming to an end, the time is ripe for some mystical hysteria. 'Balls,' says Lou when I try my millennial theory on her. 'The calendar's just a heap of numbers. We made it up. It doesn't *mean* anything.' She's right, of course. This had the makings of a good story. Fanatical zeal. New Age loonies. Appalled parents. I go back to my desk, keen to get stuck in. A pale yellow Post-It flaps on the computer screen. The scrawl says, 'A kid phoned. Said you'd know the number.'

Jesus, he doesn't give up. This pestering's got to stop. He needs to be told. I dial the Prestons. Shirley answers and sounds surprised but quite pleased. Before I've said anything much she starts apologising about the fact that I couldn't make her kid famous. 'Don't feel bad,' she says. 'He *was* awful.'

I tell her it's okay. 'I'm used to tantrums, but usually from people who should know better. You should try dealing with the average celebrity.'

'Really?' Shirley sounds wistful. 'You must meet really interesting people.'

'Oh, sometimes. Often they're a bore. There are lots of times when I think being at home with a baby's a much smarter idea.' I hope I'm not overdoing the empathy. 'Actually, I'd be happy to babysit Philly for a little while, if you like?' I suggest. 'I hardly ever get near a real live toddler. And it would make me feel better for disappointing you.'

'Really?' Hope makes her voice swoop. 'Oh, wow, I was just wondering what I'd do with him on Monday. I badly need a haircut and Jeff – well, he's a truck driver, you see. Long distance. My neighbour was going to help, but she's got this school concert she has to go to. Do you think you could . . .?' And then doubt creeps in. 'You can cope, can't you? I wouldn't want to leave him with you unless you're sure.'

'We'll be just fine,' I say. We agree on 2pm. I don't really have the time but the kid has to be told, once and for all, that I'm not what he needs, What he *really* needs is a friendly professor and a nice university to study in. What the hell do I know about nurturing genius?

I settle down to work on Lou's lead. The Signal Thread outfit sounds much more rewarding than sparring with a toddler. Included in the file is a letter from a mother, an urgent scrawl from a Mrs E. O'Keefe, pleading for help.

She has written to Louisa: '*My son, Evan, has become totally obsessed with this cult. He doesn't do homework. He's given up on sport. I'm afraid for him. He doesn't seem to be interested in anything any more. He's just stuck on the Signal Thread thing.*

'*I don't like the thought of publicity but feel that the media have a responsibility to expose this cruel group to others. I feel you can play a part in alerting other parents to its influence. I am willing to talk to one of your reporters. Please help me.*'

I pick up the phone again. Auntie Cyn at your service.

Shirley's waiting on Monday afternoon, all lipsticked up for her beauty shop trip, a-clank with silver bangles. 'Look who's here! It's Cynthia. You remember her, don't you, darling?'

Philly allows me a grin from a toy-strewn corner, where he's behind the prison rails of a playpen. Shirley hovers anxiously, inspecting him for any signs of woe. 'Now, be a good boy for Cyn.'

'Wave 'bye-bye to Mummy, Philly,' I tell him. His arm pumps obediently. Once she's slammed out of the house, Philip holds out his arms, eager to be picked up.

'Upsy-daisy,' I say.

He looks reproachful. 'Putting up with baby talk is the worst part of being like this.'

'But you're a baby. It goes with the territory.'

'I know,' he sighs. 'Thank you for coming.'

'I almost didn't.'

He looks steadily into my face. Not enjoying the scrutiny, I return him to the floor. He stands, hands clasped, cautious now. I'm not enjoying this, want to get it over. 'Philip, please don't see this as an ongoing friendship. I only came to tell you I can't just drop everything every time you ring me.' My face is hot. God, why do I feel like I'm letting him down? 'You can't keep calling me,' my voice says. 'I know you're very advanced for your age, but I'm not the one to help you. I simply don't know how. I'm not equipped to know what you need.'

He gives me a sober smile. It's a strange expression to see on a baby's face. 'It's up to you to decide,' he says. 'Come.' And he beckons. 'I want you to meet a friend of mine.'

He toddles to his room and kneels by the cot. 'Down here,' he says, pointing under the mattress.

I crouch to see, then recoil. For clinging to a shadowy recess is a huge brown spider, even larger than the one in my kitchen.

My breath rasps while he croons to it in his high small voice: 'Hello, little one. How are you today? I've brought someone to see you. Come on now. Good girl . . .'

And he inches it from under the mattress and holds out his hand, fingers opening like a plump-petalled

daisy. The spider sits quivering, its legs outstretched
to span the moist cushion of Philip's palm.

My guts crawl. 'How can you do that?'

'But why not?' he says, and strokes the spider's back.
'It's not unworthy of affection. Your distaste is really
quite illogical. Look how people love cats, even when
they're cruel. If a cat catches a bird and tears off its
wings and toys with it until it dies, you might be cross
for a little while, but soon you'll be stroking it again.'

'But cats purr.'

'Spiders do too,' says Philip. His eyes are tender. 'In
their own way.'

He holds the creature out to me and it sways. 'Why
don't you hold her? You won't be frightened then.' My
eyes are telling him no, no, no. He scolds me gently.
'Most spiders are quite harmless, you know.'

I find my voice. 'It's all those legs ... the way they
scuttle.'

'Nonsense,' Philip breathes, and brings his cupped
hands up to his face. The spider steps on to his cheek
and clings, its fine legs splayed over the downy curve
of skin. Then it turns, one delicate foot coming to rest
amidst the feathery fringe of Philip's lower lashes, the
other just short of the upcurve of his rosy lips. With one
finger, Philip nudges the foot near his eye to a less tickly
place. 'There. See? They're really very graceful.'

He ignores the disgusted noises I'm making as he
returns it to his lair.

'The aspect I find most fascinating,' he says from
under the cot, 'is that spiders are so like people. Yet,
most humans see spiders only as horrible monsters lying

in wait to paralyse their prey. They see no humour, no tenderness, no bravery – no appealing qualities at all.' He re-emerges and gazes at me, hands on rounded knees. 'You will have been courted by men, yes?'

I can't help smiling. Courtship is not how I'd describe the behaviour exhibited by Gary, my most recent ex. 'That's kind of an old-fashioned kind of concept these days,' I tell him.

'Maybe. But it's basic human behaviour. And a male spider also has to court his lady. A hazardous business it is too, for she's just as likely to attack him as to fall at his feet. I dare say many young men, approaching a woman, feel they're treading an emotional minefield which is just as dangerous as a spider's web, wouldn't you say?'

'Sometimes. But it goes both ways. Men can be real ratbags.'

Philip chuckles. 'Ah. Just like the wolf spider! He takes along his version of a box of chocolates when he goes visiting. He hopes to please his beloved by presenting her with a tasty titbit – a freshly caught insect all wrapped up in a silk parcel of his own making. It's his equivalent of cellophane and a pretty satin bow. But he tricks his lover by spinning his silk around an empty husk. Or else runs off with the present after they have mated.'

I make a wry mouth. 'Sounds familiar.' And then I realise how he's sucking me in. 'Come *on*, Philip. How can you make comparisons with humans? It's instinct you're talking about. Not intelligence or loving or sensuality.'

'But even spiders can be sensual, Cyn. There's one, *Xysticus cristatus*, who even throws a silken veil of thread over his partner so he can caress her before they mate. He's very romantic.'

He cocks his head, fixing me with those big baby greys. 'Could you do some more spider research for me?'

'But why, Philip? What for? You've got your whole life ahead for reading and study and .. and .. just playing and enjoying yourself like a normal kid.'

And he sighs. 'Ah, but that's it, Cyn. I'm not a normal kid.' He looks at me steadily. 'Not normal at all.'

'So . . . who are you, for heaven's sake? Why are you like this?'

He looks away with a tiny, secret smile. 'I think I know. But I'm still trying to understand. I promise I'll tell you . . . when I'm sure.'

His grey gaze comes back at me now, full and shiny, and I'm slain by his hope and youth and eagerness. 'Damn you,' I mutter, and he laughs with gladness.

'You know what I *really* need to know about?' He's quivering with excitement. 'Webs. I'm dreaming about them. They haunt me. I know only this basic material I've gleaned from a *Reader's Digest* my father left on the floor.' My head tries to absorb an image of this infant lying in his cot with a secret copy of the dear old *Digest*, sucking in knowledge. 'But I know nothing about webs,' he's saying. 'There's a specialness about them that I can't put my finger on. I have to know more.'

'What about your pal under the bed? Can looking at its web tell you anything?'

'No, it's the sort of spider that just makes a messy sort of cluster of threads. It's those big round webs I want to know about, the ones that radiate out from the centre.'

I shudder. 'The ones that stick to you when you walk into them?'

'Yes, yes!'

For the next hour he holds forth on the mating and hunting habits of spiders. And about laxatives, cars, whales, face cream, and a thousand other things he's hoovered into his brain from one old issue of a magazine. He asks questions I can't answer, dying for detail on life in the world outside his four walls. Then there are footsteps outside. Shirley. I bundle Philip into his cot, hearing his high pink yawn. 'I could do with a nap,' he says. 'It's so tiring being this young.'

'It's all right for some,' I mutter, thinking of the mountain of work on my desk. I tuck him under a downy blanket.

He reaches for a teddy and hugs it to his chest. His thumb slides into his mouth, just like any baby's, and his waxy lids flutter. Then suddenly he adds, 'Spiders have amazing sexual organs, did you know that?'

'No,' I say grimly, straightening his pillow.

'They can mate only with exactly the same sort of spider. Their sex organs are very, very complicated – all knobs and curves and dips in a certain pattern – and it's only if the spiders are literally made for each other that mating can happen. It's like a very complex lock – the key has to fit precisely. I'm looking for the key, Cyn

– the one that'll help me understand what's happened to me. Why I'm here.'

'Hello!' calls Shirley. Her eager face slides round the door, framed by flaming hair. 'I had a colour,' she announces. 'Like it?'

'Mm. Great,' I lie.

Shirley bends over her baby. 'Hello, my precious.'

Philip waves his teddy. 'Mum, mum, mum,' he says. 'Dat Cyn. Cyn nice.'

'Of course she is, poppet. Would Mummy leave you with anyone nasty? No, we wouldn't do that, would we?' Shirley coos. She glances up. 'You're welcome to come back and see him any time. You like to see people, don't you, Philly?' she says, her hand caressing his curls. 'Oh, you are my special boy, aren't you? Don't you think he's special?' she asks me, her thin face proud and radiant.

I drive home. It's late in the day, too late for returning to the office. And I feel tired. Don't know why.

I close the door behind me, dump bag and keys and mooch about. Open the fridge. Close it. Snap on the TV and stretch out on my white and yellow couch. And soon am asleep.

I dream.

I am standing on a long curved surface, similar to a huge pipe. All around, it is black and limitless and vast. A great dark emptiness, except for a sprinkling of faint, glimmering stars. I am . . . standing in space . . . that's what it is, atop this long silvery-grey tube, like a great air-conditioning duct suspended in the middle of nowhere.

How far behind me it extends, I cannot tell. I do not want to turn and find out. This surface upon which I stand is sealed off ahead of me, the metallic stuff curving out of sight. It is as if I'm standing upon the finger-end of a giant glove.

One of the reasons why I'm too scared to turn around is that my pipe is not made of something solid like concrete or steel. It is wrought of immensely strong mesh – fine, metallic-looking stuff, woven from millions of very, very fine glistening threads. It has resilience. Whenever I move, it sways and bounces a little, just enough to make me queasy.

There is another reason for staying still. I have to listen. Something is about to happen. So I wait. Then the tube ripples under my feet.

And I open my mouth to scream, one of those silent bad-dream screams in which you pour out anguish and terror and make no sound at all, and right in front of me a slashing knife rips through the surface upon which I stand, and steely pincers grab my leg, tugging me down. I grab at the edge of the torn springy stuff, but the ragged strands slide through my grip and I fall – oh, such a bruising thud! – down into the pipe.

And the rest is a blur of hurting and scratching as I feel myself turned and bundled and bound. In seconds my arms and legs are strapped straitjacket-tight. I have a blurred impression of black pistons and joints and snapping, robotic claws, and there is an acrid stench – like ants, yes! – that nose-wrinkling insecty smell.

The thing steps back and I can see all its legs and its great, dark abdomen and its monstrous head as it moves back to the gaping tent in the ceiling. There is a soft sound like the hiss of clingwrap unrolling from a cardboard tube, and a silken stream pours forth from the body and the legs stretch the silk and weave it – oh, the marvellous, awful dexterity of it! – and, snick-snack, the jagged hole is closed and I am locked inside the grey tube. Then the spider turns towards me . . .

I scream again. This time, really scream. I wake with a painful jerk and find myself huddled on the floor.

'Aah,' I gasp. 'Oh, Jesus.' I kneel up, slow as an old woman, on my hands and knees. The television is still blatting away. The American talkshow guy, David Oakes, is arguing, stabbing the air with his fist. 'Speak sense!' he's shouting at someone whose face is stiff with dislike. 'The American people deserve to hear good sense!'

Good sense? What's that? I reach for the remote and flash him into oblivion.

At *Maggy's* staff meeting the next morning, Lou is impatient for a progress report. 'Found a Signal Threader yet who'll let you get close?'

'Fingers crossed,' I tell her. 'A counsellor I know mentioned a run-in with a guy called Martin Vortex. I spoke to him last night . . .'

Louisa's lip lifts. 'Vortex?'

'He says he's a hairdresser, but is devoting more and more of his time to the "spiral experience", as he puts it.' There are snorts and giggles around the table. 'The trouble is, he's away for a few days. But I've spied another story idea I can do fast.' I hand her an American magazine.

Louisa squints at a big picture of a lab technician cuddling a very large rat. The headline reads: FLESH-CREEPERS. Then there is a splash of bold type: **'Sure, you love animals. Everyone does. Especially when they're furry and appealing. But those aren't the right words for rats or snakes or spiders. We meet three people who can't understand why the rest of us go cold at the thought of cuddling up to something scaly.'**

There are more photographs – one of a small child playing in a nest formed by the coils of a huge pet python, and a grinning teenage boy with a tarantula on his shoulder. 'Yuk,' says the art director, peering sideways at the layout.

I pour on persuasion. 'Sort of turns your stomach at the same time as it turns on your pay-attention switch, huh? Good photos would be the thing. I could start with spiders. Minimal words. I could wrap it up fast in between interviews for the Signal Thread story.'

Louisa eyes the snake picture. Shudders. And agrees.

Luke Beebie, entomologist, is thrilled to be inter-viewed about why he loves spiders.

When I arrive at his research lab the next morning, on a day that dawns damp and misty, he bustles out to reception to greet me.

'Hello,' he cries. 'I must say it's a pleasure to meet you. Most people who call aren't really interested in my field – they're just convinced they have a killer in the bath and want to know how to destroy it.' He sidetracks me into a kitchen area. 'Tea or coffee? Plastic, I'm afraid. We don't run to good china around here. Cost-cutting affects us, one and all.'

He twinkles at me as he dumps brown powder into cups and sloshes in water, a small man with a mass of wiry grey chin-length curls. 'I know!' he crows suddenly. 'Let's go outside. It's a perfect day to show you something wonderful!'

I follow him out. The building is surrounded by a garden filled with sizable dew-dripping trees.

He peers around. 'Ah, there!' he says, slopping coffee as he points. 'Isn't that beautiful?'

A round spider's web hangs between two trees. Dinner-plate-sized, it is limned with bright beads of moisture. A breeze makes it ripple like river weed shifting in a deep stream.

Beebie gazes at it with a beatific smile. 'Immaculately conceived and precision built. See this?' He points out the topmost horizontal strand strung between two twigs. 'That's the spider's bridging thread, her starting point.' Beebie is up on his toes like a kid admiring a shiny new Christmas bike. 'Then she spins a loose line of silk, anchors it at each end of the bridge, and scampers back to the centre – so that she's weighing it down, like a child in a rope swing, you understand.' His hands wave to and fro to illustrate. 'And then she attaches a vertical drop line and takes it down to a third anchor point so that she's formed a taut Y shape. See, here?'

'Yes.' I take notes industriously.

'The Y – special name, you understand, the first fork – is the foundation for everything. Next come the rest of the spokes of the wheel, and the sticky spirals come last. It's amazing, isn't it?' he gushes. 'Round and round she goes, working from the centre out and then in again, knowing exactly when to stop the sticky silk when she gets back to the hub. That leaves her a safe circle, you see, called the free zone – a place where she can sit and wait.'

He laughs, a scoffing noise. 'We humans think we're so clever with our data networks. But this little creature doesn't need a laptop. She's had this device for hundreds of millions of years.' He peers closer, points to a single strand which stretches from the hub out beyond the web's perimeter to a dark crack within a twig. The spider's lair. 'The second she feels the thrumming of the signal thread, she knows what she's got, precisely where it is, and how to handle it.'

'You say "she" all the time?'

'Oh, yes, web-builders are always female.'

He chats on as we stroll back. Such is his passion that there's no stopping him. 'There are many different types of web. Absolutely ingenious, some of them. *Therididae*, for instance – they make a very interesting type, like a three-dimensional trellis. And the purse-web spider, *Atypus*. Marvellous creature! Lives its whole life in a home-made silk tube about nine inches long. Hangs about all day in there waiting to detect something tippy-toeing over its roof. And then, wham! Out with its chelicerae . . .'

I stumble, chilled by a fleeting memory of my horrid nightmare. 'What?'

'Oh, a fang, like a sharp sword. It slashes a hole in the tube, grabs the insect, yanks it inside, wraps it up to have for dinner later on, and then repairs the cut in the roof, ready for next time. I say, are you all right?'

'Yes. Just reminds me of a dream I had.'

'Hollywood,' he scoffs. 'Forever making movies about spiders big as houses. So stupid. Giant spiders are a biological impossibility. They have a hard exoskeleton and have to keep on shedding it as they grow. That takes a lot of energy. There's no way they could consume enough food to fuel the effort necessary to keep on moulting.'

I'm pleased about that. Idly, I ask, 'Did you know that there's some new mystical cult called the Signal Thread? They seem to think they're in touch with some web of universal energy.'

He giggles. 'Good lord, really? Amazing, isn't it, how men are always trying to ape nature? Trouble is, it's always smarter than we are.'

Later that day I go to meet Liz O'Keefe. She talks. On and on. I listen, drive soberly back to the office and begin to push out the story, amber characters marching in rushes across my screen, knowing I won't want to listen to the tape again.

Evan O'Keefe used to be an ordinary sort of boy. A gangly sort of kid and a bit clumsy, says his mum, but with a giant appetite for life. He was curious, friendly, and, underneath the teenage joshing, a bit of a softy. He cared about the world.

Like many boys his age, he was a whizz at computer games. And could he run! A bookshelf in the house is loaded with polished cups, won at club and school activities.

But Evan is not in the mood to run anywhere now. Instead, he sits on his bed and gazes at the walls, or sways, eyes closed, in a trance. His PC hasn't been turned on for weeks. He won't go to school.

Evan, says his mother, is like this because of an obsession. He's the latest victim of a cult which church leaders, psychologists and school counsellors are condemning as sinister and dangerous.

Evan has become a Signaller – a member of a rapidly growing international group calling itself the Signal Thread.

Evan's mother, Liz, contacted Maggy begging us to write a story on the cult she believes is ruining her son's life. She invited us to her home so we could see the problem for ourselves.

Evan is her only son. Until now, he has been the joy of her life.

'I thought he might grow up to be a computer engineer or something technical . . . he's clever like that,' she says. Her coffee cup rattles in its saucer. She's tired and nervy, she explains.

'Evan hardly ever sleeps now.'

Liz has taken him to doctors, but believes it is pointless to ask for more professional help. 'Evan behaves so well for them and they give me that sort of look, you know, where you can tell they're wondering whether I'm the one who's going crazy.'

Liz says her son's obsession with the Signal Thread began when someone gave him a pamphlet outside the school.

He came home and went into his room. He often did

that to work on his computer. But that night he was terribly quiet, and when I went in he was just sitting there, staring.'

He'd used a spray can of black paint to daub a huge spiral on his bedroom wall.

She takes me to see him. His room is gloomy, curtains drawn against the sunlight outside. Evan is sitting in a chair, gazing at the wall.

The whole room is now a maze of spirals. There is even a ceiling spiral that looks down on him as he sleeps, like a giant eye.

The room is otherwise tidy. His mother says he has cleared it of all the things that used to give him pleasure – old toys, tools, sports gear. He spent a weekend stowing them in the basement. 'I'm cleaning out my life,' he told Liz.

He looks thin and pale. Liz tells him I'm interested in the spirals.

'Why?' he asks abruptly.

I tell him it's hard for her understand. And she is concerned because she hears that many other young people are focused on the spiral symbol.

'Yes,' he says. A smile burns in his face. 'That's good.'

But it doesn't seem good, I argue, because he has changed.

'That is not important,' he says. 'The Signal is the only thing of importance.' Then he asks us to leave. He takes no notice as his mother closes the door and asks me, 'What is to become of him?'

It seems to be a question many more parents like her

*will face if the Signal Thread continues to lure young
disciples . . .*

'It's a weird thing, Cyn,' says Ron Stevenson. He's a
psychologist I've got advice from before. 'I've seen a
few of these kids. They can talk sensibly: they're not
raving. But when it comes to this Signal Thread stuff,
they're absolutely immovable.'

'Is there any common ground between them?'

He grunts in a depressed sort of way. 'Only the fact
that they used to be bright and friendly and promising
– above average, if anything. The sort you'd look at and
feel, hey, that one's going to go a long way. Their parents
describe them as sensitive children, and yet when you
meet them . . . hell, they're the coldest teens I've ever
dealt with.'

'So what's the future for them?'

'I hate to think.' Then he adds, 'I did get one odd
phone call. It was a guy I counselled a few weeks back.
His son, Joe, is the star fullback of his football team. He
gave it all up for this Signal Thread stuff.

'Joe took out the family car and drove it into a
tree. He told the ambulance guys he was following
the spiral. The spiral led him there, he kept saying.
Then he lapsed into a coma. As a last resort the family
got some sort of psychic up to the hospital. He . . . '
and Ron clears his throat with a believe-it-or-not sort of
noise, '. . . went into some kind of a trance and chanted
by Joe's bedside. And in five minutes, Joe came to. He's
fine now.'

'So . . . can you understand that?'

'Hell, no,' says Ron. 'But if it works, it works. Who the hell am I to say it's a load of mumbo-jumbo?'

'You couldn't give me his name, could you?'

'Sure. Joe's dad wanted to give it to me. "You have other parents in trouble, you tell them about this," he said. I take that with a humungous grain of salt, Cyn. Still, his name's Jimmy Lightbody.' He gives me a number.

Lightbody, I'm groaning as I dial. I've met his sort before. Not content with Brown or Smith they get bitten by the New Age glow-bug and before you know it they're John Dreamweaver or Mary Happyheart or some other silly-ass label. The man takes rather longer than the speed of light to answer his phone. His speech is slow, not grudging exactly, but cool. I tell him I'm researching the new cult. 'Someone told me you were called in to help . . .' There is silence. 'Could I come and see you?'

He still doesn't speak, but I hear him breathing. 'Mr Lightbody? Can you help me?'

His voice is cautious. 'Possibly.' I ask for an appointment. Tomorrow does not suit, he says. 'Perhaps the next day?' I push. 'I have a deadline. I'd like to see you sooner rather than later.'

He does not speak for some time. Or is he whispering? Sibilance seems to flutter against my eardrums like tiny birds' wings. 'Come at ten,' he says. He gives me the address and then, abruptly, he is gone.

THREE

I'm about to leave the office when a call comes from
Martin Vortex's salon, Spiral. He is back in town, can
see me tonight at nine.

The salon is svelte and grey, subtly sheened here and
there with touches of chrome. Soft grey leather sofas
form a luxurious U-shaped waiting area. There is a low
glass table with a bowl of orange lilies and the usual pile
of magazines. I'm amused to spot a fresh copy of *Maggy*
knocked into place atop the reading stack. Vortex knows
his PR.

The lilies' musky scent wrestles with the odours of
bleach and perming lotion. I sip tired coffee and
watch late-leaving customers, sharply groomed, pay
their bills.

'Cynthia!' Martin Vortex, scissors in hand, greets me
as if we're friends who haven't met for ages.

His forehead is broad, the cheekbones high and
prominent, the face then narrowing to a strong jaw.
The mouth is mobile, pleasingly curved as he falls into
the couch opposite me. Eyes brown and interested. His
skin is honey gold and the dark hair . . . oh, such hair . . .
is straight and silky and long – longer than I've seen on

any man – falling silkily down his back to his waist. He has carefully trimmed his sideburns to a sharp, sleek, diagonal point high on each cheek.

I find myself smiling back at his beauty. 'You have amazing hair,' I tell him.

He preens a little. 'It's good for business.' He considers me, head on one side. 'Hair is my business, of course. I can never resist improving people. Your fringe, for instance. Too heavy. I'd have edged into it just a bit more to make it more feathery. D'you mind?' he says, and in one crook-legged stride is on his knees before me, scissors raised. 'I promise I won't ruin you.'

I surrender. He is so close I can hardly say no. He is wearing a sharp, headswimmy fragrance. His sharp blades make a fine rasping noise as he snips and snicks, tugging at the front strands. 'There, look.' There is a smoky-mirrored wall alongside. He's right. My eyes looked wider, my broad face better balanced.

'Can't leave anyone alone,' he says with a rueful smile, arranging my brown clippings on the table in a neat little heap. He settles back. 'So, what are you expecting from me?'

'I want to talk to you about the Signal Thread and the impact it's having on people. How it began, what it involves, what its appeal is.'

He sits straighter, alert again, and his scissors rap a delicate tattoo on the table's edge. 'We're all looking for a better life, aren't we? And finding it – well, that has to have some appeal.'

'Have you found a better life then?'

'Oh, yes,' he says. His dark eyes are direct and

compelling. For a moment I see a glimmer of something like glee or ecstasy, but then the instant is gone and he looks simply warm and interested.

'How did you get involved?'

'I went to California on holiday and stayed with a friend I hadn't seen for a couple of years. I was struck by how mellow he'd become. He'd always been prickly, kind of strung-out, you know? But this time, he was different. The world didn't rub him up the wrong way any more. I asked him how come, and he told me he'd started meditating on a daily basis. Twenty minutes. Half an hour. And it had changed his life.

'The thing is,' and he's staring at me, 'this isn't just any old meditation. You go on an inner journey of exploration. And with some practice, you can reach and stretch . . .'

Vortex closes his eyes, whispering now. 'But you don't reach out. You reach *down*, striving for the current that connects every one of us.' His lids flick open and he gives me an almost tender smile.

Music suddenly stops - a wash of violins that has been so unobtrusive I only notice it when it's gone. The last customer has left and the receptionist bustles past toting bag and sweater. 'Night, Marie,' Vortex says, eyes still on me. The door swings closed and it is very quiet. An orange petal falls from one of the blazing lilies on the low table, scattering about itself a minute explosion of yellow pollen.

I pick it up and whisk the glass clean of the golden blush. The petal is satin-slick in my fingers. I clear my throat to fill the sudden emptiness with sound. 'So, what can happen, then, when you're "in touch"?'

'Oh, it's like being tapped into the life force itself.' Vortex's face is alight. 'And you can feel the other minds tapped into the flow. Not just feel. *Talk* to them.'

'Talk?' It's hard to quell the derisive edge that's sharpening my voice. 'Like on the phone?'

'Oh, yes,' he says airily. 'Worldwide if you wish. We all have a mental finger on the Signal Thread, you see. We're like spiders, one finger on the strand that leads from the great global web to the private space we call our minds.'

The petal suddenly feels oily and seductive. I put it down. 'Is it difficult to learn how to do this?'

'No, of course not. That's why so many people are taking it up. You just find a quiet space, breathe deeply, relax, and think about the spiral. Imagine it in your head. Around it goes. And you follow it – an easy slide into that other dimension. I do it twice a day – seven a.m., seven p.m. – for an hour. Keeps me humming all day.'

He impales me with a long look. 'You must try it, Cyn. You can't write a story about something without experiencing it yourself, can you? Do it tonight,' he urges. 'Just draw a simple spiral on a piece of paper and gaze at it awhile. It's easy. Round and round you go, just like curving into a whirlpool.'

I tear my eyes away. Sit with straight back. Assume stern look. 'The trouble is, there seem to be adverse sides to it all,' I say. And I tell him about Evan O'Keefe.

Vortex is unperturbed. 'And how many of these . . . adverse . . . cases have you heard of?'

'Four or five, I suppose.'

He smiles. 'Well, then. I can introduce you to hundreds of people whose experience is one hundred per cent positive. We can't be responsible for everybody in the world. People have to be in charge of themselves, wouldn't you agree?' He is back on the edge of his seat, the scissors rat-a-tat-tat on the glass table. The hair from my fringe shivers with the vibration.

'But what happens to people like Evan in the end?' I want to know. 'Can they find their way back to normal life?'

'What's normal?' asks Vortex. His eyes are stony. 'Doing a lousy job on some assembly line in a dirty factory? Standing in line to collect the dole? Feeding the mind on televised crap?'

I ease back. 'I just think that some of the people I've met are justified in being worried about family members who now seem . . . removed . . . from them.'

Vortex shrugs. 'But that's foolish. They just need time. The Signal is healing them, correcting their imbalances. Left alone, without being hassled, they'll find their way back.'

'But will they be the same as before?'

Vortex looks amused. 'Better. They're enhanced by that time deep in the spiral. They'll work well at surface level because they have so much energy – I mean look at me, my business is booming – but they'll also form strong strands of the Signal Thread.'

'That could cause great friction between family members.'

'So what? Telling one of us to ignore the Signal is like

telling us to throw away the Merc and go back to a Model T. This is big, Cyn. It's important. And if families want to stay together, they'd better be Signallers together. It's as simple as that. Have a glass of wine.'

'What?' His sudden switch startles me.

'Sauvignon,' he says as he gets up and strides around a corner into the salon proper. I hear the muted 'thwock' of a cork's release. He is back quickly, with stemmed glasses and a pale golden bottle. 'You must work hours that are almost as bad as mine,' he says, pouring. 'Do you have an early start?'

'Depends on what you call early. Six-thirtyish if I feel like a run before breakfast. Later if I'm feeling lazy.'

He takes a long, considered sip and raises his glass. 'Here's to your story.'

The wine is crisp and burnished. Nice. 'Have you always been called Vortex?' I ask.

'Hell, no.' He is relaxed now, one arm stretched along the back of the sofa. 'Changed it. It was boring as hell in my previous life. Vortex is much more romantic. And . . .' he waves a reminding finger, '. . . it's damn good for business. People remember me and it reminds them of the salon.' He stands in a quick, lithe rush. 'Come. I'll show you something.'

I feel a niggle of apprehension, check my watch, and invent a let-out clause. 'I have to meet a friend in a few minutes . . .'

'It'll only take a moment.' His smile is knowing. 'I'm quite harmless.'

He beckons and I follow him around the corner into the centre of the salon. Our shadowy double image bounces back from all the mirrors around the room. A tap drips. I can smell the grey-brown aroma of salon coffee left on the heat for too long. Hair dryers hang on racks, air nozzles like the beaks of predatory birds.

'There,' says Vortex, long hair swinging free in a shiny ripple as he looks at the ceiling.

I glance up and lurch. It's like vertigo. But that's all wrong. I'm looking up, not down. Up at a huge sinuous spiral, painted on the ceiling in a rush of glossy midnight black on grey. Its outer perimeter begins at the far reaches of the big room and circles in upon itself, whirling steeper and whip-thin as it careers into the centre, trailing off into a line so fine, that I can't see where it ends, no matter .. how hard . . .

Suddenly he's holding me at shoulder and waist, his voice sharp. 'Are you all right?' And I'm clutching at him (how embarrassing!), knees loose and mushy.

I stagger and pull away. 'Okay. Yes. Fine.' I seem unable to collect the single words into a sentence. 'Sorry. I haven't eaten today. Must be the wine. Silly. I really do have to go.'

He steps back with an inoffensive touch on my arm. He is being kind and innocuous but all at once I feel anxious to be home, with a comforting bowl of soup and toast with butter, and the mindless chirping of the television to shut out the world.

'Think about what just happened, Cyn,' he says as I gather my things. 'I think you may have an extraordinary affinity with the spiral. You were halfway there. Perhaps it's calling. The Signal emits a very strong homing beacon for people like you.'

I don't want to look at him. He holds open the door with great politeness. 'I expect to hear from you again quite soon.'

There are too many people expecting things of me lately. I wish they'd leave me alone.

I just want to do my job, see my friends, go to the movies, eat out and have a laugh or two. But here's pint-sized Philip with his pleas for help. Martin Vortex placing me on the brink of a cliff I'm damned if I want to step off. Liz O'Keefe with her brimming eyes, yearning for me to rescue her son. Lou Williams demanding the stories which will sell her magazine. No buts, no excuses. I decide, as I plod up my stairs, that life has become too complicated.

Bed beckons. A quick drift into sleep.

Just before morning, in that half-drifting state on the cusp of consciousness, I dream (yet another crazy dream) of standing high on the edge of a precipice. The mountainside drops dizzily away beneath my toes. Clouds boil overhead. The cliff-face upon which I teeter is scored with deep grooves. There are knobbly spines of wet, dark rock running way down to flat land which spreads to a distant sea. It is as if a giant has taken a mountain range between his hands and, using them like mighty bookends, has squeezed until the earth has buckled and folded upon itself. The vertical ramparts look like a giant accordion slumped in grotesque pleats across the surface of the earth.

The mountains moan, organ-like, as a warm wind

hurls itself against the cliffs. It buffets at me, but I'm not afraid.

My hair whips about me and I see it is even longer than my outstretched fingertips. It is a strange, silver-grey colour. Not the grey seawrack of old age, but shiny like silken strands of mercury. Gauzy robes ripple and flap as the gale flattens them against my body and streams the fabric out behind.

This is fun! I fling out my arms and stand on tippy-toe and a giant gust of wind whisks me off my feet and I'm floating free with the clouds. I feel myself dissolving, at one with the vapour, and I drift, weightless, leaving the sharp mountain ridge behind. The drifting is such bliss, far from worries, away from the phone. The phone. The phone is ringing. Next to my head.

I grope. My 'Hello' comes out in a croak. There is a furry silence, the prickly sensation that speaks of awareness at the other end. And then there is a quiet click. 'Up yours,' I mutter, dropping the receiver.

It rings again. This time I'm good and snarly. 'Yes!'

'Good morning, Cynthia. This is Martin Vortex. I'm sorry to wake you.'

'So you should be. Was that you just then?'

'Guilty. I wanted to make sure you were awake.'

'What?'

'I felt sure you would be having a dream. Most people do after their first encounter with the spiral. You were dreaming, weren't you?'

'I don't know. Maybe. I never remember dreams for long. Especially when they've been shattered by dawn phone calls.' I'm pointing my toes under the sheets, stiff and knotty with tension. Angry. Scared, too.

'It's a very special dream. It has a purpose. It comes to give you a taste of the experience that can be yours when you decide to open yourself to the Signal.'

I have to sit up, can't get mad lying down. 'How the hell do you know what I'm dreaming?'

'A vivid dream of flying always happens to initiates right at the end of their next sleeping period. It's not the same dream of course – everyone's different and your subconscious conjures up something that's right for you. But it's very strong, isn't it? That's so you'll remember it. I thought you might appreciate knowing that the dream is no coincidence. It's a token. A blessing if you like. A hint of what's to come.'

'I am not an initiate,' I snap. 'Stop pushing me into things.'

'I'm not pushing, Cyn. Your awareness has awakened of its own volition. What happens next is up to you. You can keep on existing only in the world of the obvious. That's fine. But be aware that it will be impossible for you to write well about the Signal Thread unless you open yourself to it. Enjoy your day.' And he hangs up.

I throw myself back on the pillows, pound the bed with my fists, open my mouth and make a very satisfying screeching noise.

All that day, Philip's pleadings keep nagging at me. I'm irked by the realisation that I won't be able to shrug him off until I've delivered what information I've been able to glean about cobwebs. And then, *finito*. When I phone Shirley, feeling for some excuse for yet another visit, she drops an invitation in my lap.

'It's Philly's birthday,' she says fondly. 'He's one today. Do come, even if you can only make it for a minute or two.'

And so that afternoon I deliver a present, gaudily wrapped in blue paper splashed with trucks being driven by manic-looking bunnies.

Perhaps it's a fortuitous choice, because Jeffery Preston's truck is parked outside. But he's less than gracious when I knock at the door. A wiry man with eyes that jitter, he mutters about having 250 kilometres to drive today with a cargo of spa pools, concrete pipes and fence posts.

The present-giving is perfunctory while Jeff whinges to Shirley about how she hasn't told him I was coming and growls about the news media and how he doesn't go for publicity and what a good thing it was that the magazine turned them down over that crazy Superbaby idea.

As the talk ricochets between them, I tap at the base of the box which holds the toy crane I've brought, hoping Philip will notice. For taped inside its base are my web notes.

After a few minutes I make excuses and go, relieved to be able to walk away, but sad for Philip that he can't. He's stuck here, poor kid, with his timorous mum and dour dad. How on earth did those two produce such a luminous child? *Enough, Cyn. Not your problem.*

So I slink back to the office, suppressing the memory of my last glance at his face all abrim with equal parts of hurt and hope. I'm eager to bury myself in more urgent things. Things I can actually *do* something about. In the clear light of day Martin Vortex seems less intimidating. I feel like a challenge.

So I grab a few minutes with Lou. I want to run a test, I tell her – the aim is to disprove Vortex's claim that he can connect with other Signal Threaders telepathically. I'll find another devotee and say, okay, I'd like you to prove something. Tune into your mind-net and broadcast a description of me. There's someone out there I want to receive a picture of me. I'll wear something special that makes me distinctive, something Vortex will recognise.

Lou frowns. 'What if you can't find anyone to play ball?'

'I will. They have to play if they want to be taken seriously.'

She purses her bright lips. 'And how are you going to test if Vortex has got the message?'

'I think someone else should do it. Not me. Someone he doesn't know, maybe you can ring him up. As soon as the session's over, I'll let you know. And you can check him out.'

She pulls at a fleshy ear lobe. 'I suppose there is the faintest of possibilities that he'll say. "Well, gee, Ms Williams, I just had a vision in my head of that writer of yours."' There's a small silence. 'What would you do then?'

I spread my hands. 'Announce the dawning of Homo Telepathicus.'

'Balls,' says Louisa. 'Do it fast. Your deadline's only a few days away.'

I breeze back to my desk. Robert grins. 'You look as if you're about to hit the yellow brick road.'

'First things first,' I reply. 'Got a wicked witch to knock off first.'

'Pardon?'

'Well, sort of. Some whacko psychic called Lightbody.'

I head for home thinking it hasn't been a bad day, all up, and I'm chopping tomatoes for a salad when the phone goes. I wedge it between chin and shoulder, still slicing, but a high shriek down the line stills my knife.

'It makes sense now, Cyn. Thank you.'

'What?'

'All your information about web-making. I've been focused on the spiral strands but it's the Y-shape that is important, Cyn, the first fork! And the free zone! It's too complicated to explain over the phone. I have to see you again.'

My eyes roll. 'I told you before, Philip, I can't drop everything for you. I've got something on in the morning. And Shirley will think I'm nuts if I turn up again tomorrow.'

'But it's important. It's *crucial*. You'll have to come and get me. Please? I need to be somewhere where I can think for a while, be myself, stop acting like a baby.'

I slap down the knife. 'Oh, come on! Where could I take you?'

'To your place,' he announces. 'Just for an hour or two.'

'No, I couldn't! What would Shirley say?'

'She wouldn't have to know. You could come and get me at night and return me before they wake up.'

'Grow up, Philip!' I can almost feel the shrivel of his disappointment. 'It's too risky. Skulking around with someone else's baby in the dark . . . it's crazy.'

He sounds bewildered. 'I don't see why it's so difficult.' Then, 'I have to go now,' he whispers. 'I hear Shirley. You *must* help me. Please.'

'I can't help you!' But I'm moaning at dead air.

FOUR

Mr Lightbody lives near the beach in a small, slope-roofed house that was once a weekend cottage but is now drowned by suburbia.

His garden is lush and loosely arranged, like the hair of sensuous woman, bright with impudent flowers. A front hedge stands up bushy and eager. Hibiscus bushes blaze each side of the peeling blue front door.

A thin old man opens it, wearing a white shirt and droopy brown trousers. He does not look welcoming but there is no hostility either. There's a sort of separateness about him, as if I am making no difference to his day one way or the other. He inclines his head. 'Miss Moon. Come in, please.'

The front door opens into his small living room. An untidy kitchen space occupies an L-shaped corner. A blue bowl of spilling wild ginger perfumes the whole space. There's a faded star chart pinned above the fireplace, a high cabinet filled with small bottles of unnamed liquids. I don't look too closely. The furniture is worn and old, draped with rugs. There is evidence of children – a doll abandoned on a chair, toys heaped from a basket.

'My grandchildren,' he says, 'Rob and Becky.' And shows me a framed photo of a leggy girl and grinning boy. I make the approving noises that seem mandatory at photo-showing moments. He asks if I'd like tea.

'Please.'

He goes to the kitchen with slow grace. His movements are fluid for such a thin and angular old man. It's hard to tell how old he is. White thinning hair. Brown face deeply lined. Seventy-something.

'A biscuit, Miss Moon?'

'Thank you. Call me Cyn. Miss Moon sounds so formal.'

'Ah, but I like that,' says Lightbody as he brings my tea, complete with shortbread on a floral plate, and eases himself into an old rocking chair. 'There is so little formality left in the world. It's good to stand back and get to know people slowly. Their character emerges then in small increments, not in a torrent. One can appreciate them better, learn their nuances.'

I sip, knees pressed primly, feet together. There's a stillness about this man that makes me want to get up and stride around. Jiggle or something. If I still smoked, I'd be itching for a ciggie. Instead, I sit stiff and straight. Wary. He reads my mind, smiles into his tea. 'You must have been wondering what to expect on your way here today.'

'Well, yes. People like you aren't . . . common.'

'People like what?'

'Psychics. Healers. Actually, I'm not exactly sure what it is that you do.'

His eyes crinkle. 'I merely listen to my voices. Follow my heart. Do what is expected.'

'Your voices?' My own voicebox has got the squeakies. I mean, *really*.

'Ever since I was a small boy,' he says evenly, 'I have been aware of other presences around me. My grandmother was Maori. An extraordinary woman, though I didn't know how special she was when I was small. She taught me to respect my voices and it wasn't until much later that I realised other people couldn't hear them too. Just he and me . . .' His voice fades for a moment before he continues. 'Anyway, I live my life according to their advice. They come from the Source.' It seems like he says it with a capital S. 'Some might say they are God-given,' he goes on. 'Some call them guides. They are special beings. I'm just a man. No one special. But I was born with this odd ability to be aware of them. And it means that sometimes they can help me to help others. Not,' and suddenly his eyes are sharp, 'that I'm likely to reveal any of this for the amusement of readers of glossy magazines.'

'Glossy doesn't necessarily mean gassy, Mr Lightbody,' I nip back.

'I should apologise,' he says, though he seems not at all repentant. 'I didn't mean to imply that your publication is more flatulent than most. I must admit I've never read it. But you have to admit that as a genre women's magazines aren't renowned for their depth of wisdom.'

My cup hits the saucer with a smack. 'As you haven't read *Maggy*, isn't that a little presumptuous of you?'

He holds back his chair with the tips of his unshone brown shoes, enjoying his little joke, watching me simmer. I don't know why I'm bothering with this. The man's obviously in outer space. I've come about the boy, I explain. Joe. I want to know what was wrong with the boy he fixed.

His sparse eyebrows go up. 'Who told you I fixed him?'

'The boy's father mentioned you to a psychologist I know.'

Lightbody rises from his chair, picks up my empty cup and takes it to the sink, distant and disapproving. 'I am not happy he did that. It is private business.'

'But . . . if you can explain somehow what the problem was, mightn't it help other people?'

He folds his arms. 'It's hard to throw light on something so dark. I do not like talking about it. Even to speak of it is to give it power.'

'But I think it's my duty as a journalist to examine it.' It sounds pompous even as it comes out, but I keep on pushing. 'You don't agree?'

'We live in different worlds, Miss Moon. In mine, one works quietly to help those who ask for advice on a close, personal basis. Things happen in their own good time. And I do not "fix" people – I am merely a conduit through which higher powers can do their work. My role is not to make a great noise about it. Such a clamour would be offensive.'

'This is one magazine article. Hardly a clamour, I would have thought.'

'Enough of one to add strength to a force which I

have no desire to encourage.' His eyes are flinty. 'An evil miasma had settled upon the boy.'

I struggle to keep my face straight. He can tell.

'Do not doubt it,' he snaps, fiercely. 'Such sorcery may be old but it is still very powerful. It comes from the ancient gods of darkness.' He actually shakes his fist at me. 'Do not print any of that in your magazine. You do not have my permission.'

'But you have already told me what happened. Why did you do that? You should tell me in advance if something is off the record.'

He lifts his palms. 'What rules are these? I don't recall establishing ground rules. I have my own rules. And mine forbid you to write of these things.'

I'm angry now. I do my best to be patient with the foolish and the obstinate, but this is too much. I grab my things. 'There's no point in carrying on then, is there?'

'Wait, Miss Moon, I haven't finished. You should not think like that.' He steps past me to the door, barring the way. 'I agreed to see you today out of concern for your welfare. You should not write this article.'

There is heat building inside my skull. 'Why? You don't know anything about me, you don't know what motivates me . . .'

'Ah, but I do. Time pressures. Deadlines. The need to sell magazines. The need to please your boss. The importance of "moving product" – isn't that what they call it? All of these things are urgent imperatives for you, I realise that.'

'Then don't waste my time!' I push past him and stride down the path. Silly old geezer. He's right about one thing. We do live in totally different worlds. Make that two things. There's no way I'll be printing his ramblings. I'd look a complete fool if I laid a load of stuff about sorcery and ancient gods on Lou's desk.

He calls out, follows me, plucks at my sleeve. 'I mean what I say. Please listen to me. You should leave this subject alone.'

I shake him off. 'I make my own decisions about my work. And anyway, you act as if there's some way I could be affected by this stuff.' And I laugh. It comes out as a snigger, more brittle than I mean it to sound. 'I don't believe in it, Mr Lightbody. I can't be touched by something that's not real.'

He twitches. I expect offence to register but it's a touch of sorrow that rumples his bony face. His hands drop to his side. 'Come back again if you wish,' is all he says.

I can't think of a single reason why I should want to return.

That night I eat at home, clean up the kitchen, watch some television. The news is awful, as usual. A bloody new war in Africa. Mass dolphin deaths in the Mediterranean. A food poisoning scare in the States. An inexplicable rise in foetal abnormalities in Western Europe.

I jab at the remote control, too jumpy to watch any more, aware of an indefinable itch. I keep thinking of Vortex. 'It will be impossible for you to write well about the Signal Thread unless you open yourself to the experience,' he had said.

Now or never, I decide. I slip on a loose robe, switch off most of the lights. Now what? I opt for a comfortable chair. Lying prone seems kind of silly and I don't have the legs for the lotus position.

So I sit, wriggling to get comfortable, let my hands curl in my lap. I close my eyes and self-consciously breathe deeply a few times.

And begin.

It's hard to think about nothing. Any empty mental space is soon filled. There are idle thoughts. Faces, too. Like Jimmy Lightbody's. Such a strange, imploring expression in his eyes. I let him drift on through, paying him no heed. Itchy nose. I scratch. The lungs pump on, soft and slow. A sort of lassitude descends. My face is slack. I feel loose and open and dozy and aware, all at the same time.

Vortex said something about whirlpools. I go for a flower instead. It looks more benign. Start on the outside and curl in towards the centre. I try for a rose. Ah, there. Pink, it is. My mind drifts towards it, a curving slow-motion skim. I sink into the enfolding outer petals, banking into the tightly folded centre. The pink deepens to cerise, then violet. Deepest indigo finally glooms to black. I'm not fond of the dark, but there is nothing savage lurking here, just a timelessness. I wait. For a long time. And just as I'm about to give up, a shape begins to paint on my ebony mental canvas.

I want to reach out and touch. Tendrils explode from a central burst of light. It's like a sea anemone – the small green ones whose arms reach up in rock pools to enfold your probing fingertip, sucking away, hoping that you're food. It is cloudy-white in colour and at the end of each arm is a gleaming red star. I feel neither fear nor elation. It is simply there.

Awareness returns. My feet are tingling, crossed under my chair for too long. Slowly, I stretch, grimacing at the blood-rush. My face feels stiff. I'm surprised to find that twenty minutes have gone by. The space around me seems clear and still. That's it then. What's the big deal?

I go to bed. Sleep comes easily. In the morning I scoop my morning paper from the doorstep and slop into the kitchen for cold orange juice. Idly sipping, I spread out the paper, scan the headlines, turn to page three. And there it is. I can't believe it. I peer closer. It's the shape I saw in my mind last night, the very one – that odd, irregular outline. A brooch! Pinned to the lapel of a suit worn by an angular model in a fashion ad, a woman who's all eyes and hair.

'Aaah,' I breathe. For the starburst isn't an anemone but a silver spider, a mass of legs springing from the rounded body. It has a big chuckly grin. And each of the legs is tipped with a tiny jewel.

'Animal Crackers!' shout the words under the picture. 'Hans Jensen, master silversmith, has created a collection of offbeat animal shapes you'll adore! Pin on a spider, sparked with rubies. Clasp a scarf with a croc. Let a terrier light the lapel of your favourite suit. Pure silver jewellery, set with semi-precious stones. Only at Mr Whitby's.'

An hour later, I'm standing before the jeweller's brilliantly lit display case. A menagerie of silver animals capers on black velvet. The whimsical spider is missing. An assistant smiles when I ask for it. 'You're about the third person to ask for it already.'

'You mean it's gone?' I feel half hopeful, half relieved.

'No, it's out the back. Just a moment . . .'

He's back fast, sensing a sale. 'Here it is. I was just getting someone in the workshop to blunt the pin a little. It was too sharp.' The pin tapers to a fine glittery point which he tests on his finger. 'That's better. Wouldn't want you bleeding to death.' He chuckles and passes the brooch over. 'Would you believe the first two people pricked themselves with it? But it's fine now. Perhaps you're meant to have it.'

My heart is beating fast as I cradle the silver shape in my hand. The spider's splayed, garnet-tipped legs spread almost across my palm. 'It has a very enigmatic smile,' I say lightly to disguise the *inevitability* I feel.

'Hans has done a beautiful job,' prattles the salesman. 'It's his favourite piece.'

I step to a mirror and try the brooch at my shoulder. 'It suits you,' he urges.

My credit card comes out. God, up to the limit again. And as I leave the shop, I realise I'm just a few minutes' walk from Spiral. Saturday morning. A good time to drop in on Martin Vortex. I can tell him I'm sorry I was so short-fused when he phoned me the other morning. And I can wear the brooch. It's so bold that an artistic guy like him can't fail to notice it. And it can be the distinctive item I need to put him to the test later on.

Feeling cheered, I pluck the spider from its suede box and pin it to my lapel. I'm wearing jeans, white T-shirt and a loose black linen jacket. I can see from a shop window reflection that it looks just fine.

At Spiral the grey couches are laden with a complement of waiting clients. Hair dryers roar. Water sloshes. There are bubbles of laughter, snickers of gossip. A junior with a broom sweeps a matted pile of hair clippings from around the cutters' stations. Martin Vortex is making money.

He comes bounding to me, long hair flying. His face is smooth and pleasant, eyes alight with interest. He spreads his hands, indicating the chaos behind him. 'This is a terrible time.' And before I can open my mouth he adds, 'How about dinner tonight? Are you busy?' His invitation is tossed with such quick confidence that when I reach for an excuse I can find none that sounds convincing. I can't say, 'sorry, but you're too weird.' And anyway, plenty of people are weird but interesting with it.

'No. Okay. Thanks,' I hear myself say. He flicks my lapel. '*Nice*. You should wear it tonight.'

It takes a while to get ready. A short-skirted deep red silk suit seems about right. The curvy jacket's broad, wide-set collar wraps about my shoulders, showing off my neck and collarbones. My bones aren't bad. I'd like a little less flesh on them, but tonight, in my silk plus spider, with my thick hair full and feathery, I think I look okay.

He tells me I look delicious and takes me to a friendly

waterfront restaurant where we dine with enthusiasm and drink rather fast. Away from his salon, Vortex seems wound down a notch, more willing to listen rather than talk. We blab about music and favourite places and childhood pets and politics and movies. He wears a cream linen jacket, his sensational hair slicked back into a pony tail. He looks at me a lot. I like the feeling. I enjoy living alone and being independent, but I like this too. And when, on the way back into the city, he asks me to his place so we can talk some more about the Signal Thread, I hesitate for a very short time before saying yes. Of course it's fine, I tell myself. You are working tonight. Well, sort of. And you do need more material for your story.

His apartment is above his salon, in a converted suite of offices. Inside, he switches on a few soft uplighters that cast cloudy pools of light. The living area is spare and open, the walls painted deepest blue. Lamps and accessories shine with the dull gleam of burnished steel. The space is saved from sterility by big potted trees.

He drops his keys with a clatter on a low glass table with curved steely legs. 'I make very special coffees,' he suggests.

'What's in them?'

'Aah. If I told anyone it wouldn't be special any more. But they're good.'

'Okay. Surprise me.'

He heads for a compact kitchen. I hear snicking sounds made by well-fitted cupboard doors, chinking of spoons and china.

'Coffee won't be long,' he says as he comes back.

And he sits and gazes at me across the shiny expanse of table. 'You know, you're very different from the woman I met the other night. You were very . . . restrained, then. Cautious. It was like there was an invisible wall around you.'

I shrug. 'I was nervous. I thought you might be kind of weird.'

'Am I?'

I have to laugh. 'Slightly. But I don't think you're about to lean out your window and bay at the moon.'

His mouth quirks with amusement.

'Hey,' I protest, 'it's not easy for a cynical media chick like me to cotton on to metaphysical stuff.'

'Don't do that.'

'What?'

'Put yourself down. You're not a "chick". You're a beautiful and intelligent woman. Wait,' he says. 'I'll get the coffee'.

He lays the cup before me almost reverently, dropping to one knee. He has loosened his hair. I sip at the brew through a froth of cream. It's very rich and mellow and underlaid with a solid foundation of a liqueur I can't name. Sweet and fiery and flavoured with . . . aniseed? Rum? No, it's almost herbal, but it has a sneaky sort of nip to it that soars straight to my brain, makes me fizz. 'Whoo! That's wonderful. What is it?'

He watches with a small smile as I down some more. 'Not telling,' he says.

He is sitting alongside me now, but still a distance away, elbow on the back of the sofa. He leans his head on his fisted hand, his black hair streaming over his knuckles and falling in a silken coil over his arm.

I'm feeling very strange, super-aware. I can hear the cream settling in my cup, feel my pantihose slide minutely over my kneecap. My eyelashes descend and bounce against my lower lid . . . *doïng* . . . like a gong, as I blink. 'Oh,' I say in a small voice.

'Are you okay?' he asks.

'Fine.' My voice booms in the bony cavity that is my skull. I'm smiling, I think, lips slithering over teeth.

'So,' he says, sipping his own coffee. 'Have you tried meditating yet?'

'Yes, just last night. You were right, I had to try it. Mind you, I did get warned off as well.'

'Oh? Who else have you been talking to?'

It seems outlandish, sitting here in this metallic, modern space, to speak of Jimmy Lightbody. 'Just a contact. A man who hears voices.' I shrug.

Martin looks startled. 'What on earth led you to him?'

I mumble that I'd heard about him, thought he might be useful for my story. Martin swishes back his hair with a sharp flick of his hand.

'You have to be careful with silly old codgers like that. He sounds totally irrelevant.' Lightbody slips away, pale and feeble.

'What happened in your meditation?' Martin asks.

'I conjured up this shape, a very definite shape in my head. And then this morning, when I opened the paper, there it was. Weird, huh?' I lift my collar with its cheeky silver beast. 'It's exactly what I'd envisaged, right down to the red tips on the legs.'

Martins'eyes are alight. 'It was meant for you, yes?' He slips off his jacket. His glossy mane makes a satiny band across the brown skin of his arms. The black T-shirt reveals muscle and tendon. Velvet and steel.

Almost involuntarily, I reach to stroke a strand of his hair. 'Do women like this?'

His voice goes husky. 'I don't know. I don't have it for women. I like it for myself.'

He reaches out a hand to touch mine, and then enfolds it in his. My empty cup is still in my lap. He shifts it to the floor and tugs me towards him. Not a rash, passionate jerk, an inexorable pull. His eyes burn. His other hand is behind my head and he kisses me. It is a slow, soft kiss. He does not open his mouth. The kiss might be called chaste, except that tiny muscles around his mouth are trembling, fluttering beneath his skin.

A clear but tiny voice in my head says, 'What are you doing?' But I'm not listening. There is only the hardness of muscle and the velvet delight of skin and the midnight hair that drapes about us as we roll off the sofa and grapple, laughing, with buttons, zips and cloth.

FIVE

Awake in the morning in my own bed, I squint at the ceiling. My eyes unglue reluctantly. An ache is banging away in my skull. *Stupid tart.* Foolish. More than foolish.

I roll over, put feet on the carpet, try the eye-opening again and totter to my mirror. Tangled hair, blotched cheeks. Just as well I taxied home. Falling in lust with Vortex is one thing. Waking up next to him in the morning, toothbrushless, is another. I hadn't wanted that. And when I told him I was going, he hadn't demurred. He probably likes his own space, too. After all, we hardly know each other.

'You have to come back,' he told me softly when I left. 'You haven't finished your interview. Your mouth,' he said, nibbling at me, 'has been far too occupied.' So tonight I'm going to his place. He's going to cook. And we're going to try meditation together. I have to admit that I'm curious, want to know more. The man is so *together.* How can this Signal Thread stuff be so bad when it's doing him no harm?

I shower, haul on some clothes. My Sunday mornings have their own routine – a walk to the shops for weekend papers, fresh bread from the Vietnamese bakery, then breakfast. It'll be an effort this morning. A faint aftertaste of Martin's strange coffee still lingers in my mouth.

Outside, there's alternating glare and gloom as bulging cumulus clouds trundle in from the west. It's still and heavy, smells like rain. I do my shopping and scan the headlines as I head for home.

'Miss Moon,' someone says. 'What a surprise.'

I look up, startled. I hadn't noticed the old man at the bus stop. A shaft of watery sun makes his silver hair flare. His hands are folded atop a gnarled walking stick. Alongside him on the seat, sneakered feet swinging, are two solemn children. Their names pop into my head. Rob and Becky.

'Mr Lightbody. You're a long way from home.'

'Ah, well, they make good bread here.'

'And cakes,' pipes the girl.

'We came to get some,' says Lightbody. 'And now,' he waves his hand at a garish pink Plymouth so old it has tail fins, 'the car won't start.'

I look bleakly at the three of them. 'You'll wait a long time for a bus. There aren't many on Sundays.'

'So we have discovered.'

'I'm bored,' says Rob.

'How much longer is it going to be, Grandpa? whines Becky.

He pats her knee. 'Soon. We just have to be patient.'

I hear a splat, see a wet, button-sized circle on my newspaper. A few more raindrops punch large holes in the dust at my feet.

'Oh dear,' says the old man.

Damn. 'I live just along the road,' I say weakly. 'Do you want to come and phone for a taxi?'

A smile gleams. 'That's most kind of you, Miss Moon,' He gets up, quick and nimble. 'Come, children, before the heavens open.'

The clouds unzip when we're fifty yards short of the front door. The children shriek as we all huddle under the splashing awning. I fumble with my key. 'In, in!' I cry and they spill into my living room, wet and giggling.

I dump soggy bread and papers on the bench. 'Ours is dry,' says Lightbody, holding up his plastic shopping bag. 'Please take it. It's the least we can do.'

'No.' I feel invaded, reluctant. 'You need it for the children.'

Then we'll share it,' he announces, opening the bag and laying his fragrant offerings on the table with an air of finality. 'Children, help Miss Moon,' he instructs. So I pass them plates and cutlery and offer drinks. Lightbody makes his call and comes back to the table looking apologetic. 'The taxis are at full stretch. They said there'll be some delay.'

The kids eat. Fast. And in minutes are restive. Rob's heel bumps against the leg of his chair. Thump. Thump. Thump. My headache begins to gallop in unison with the beat. 'Would you like to watch cartoons?' I suggest hopefully. 'There's a television in the bedroom.'

Instant yes-please noises. I remember now that I didn't see a TV at Lightbody's house. God, I'll never get rid of them now. I install them on my unmade bed.

As I shut the door they are squabbling over who is going to have the remote.

'How is your research proceeding?' Lightbody wants to know.

'Fine thanks.'

'I think I was unkind to you the other day,' he admits.

A small shrug is all I'll give him. 'You said what you thought was right. We're just coming from different places.'

He inclines his head in acceptance but stays silent. Small talk is obviously not one of his things.

'Why did you choose your name?' I blurt.

He frowns, puzzled.

'Your name,' I blunder on. 'I assume you changed it to be in keeping with your . . . work.'

He humours me with a smile. 'It's the name I was born with, Miss Moon. No need to change it, is there?'

'No, of course not. Sorry. I've just met a few people lately, you see, who have.'

'You should never change yours,' he says.

Now I'm the puzzled one. Does he think I'm getting married? 'I don't intend to. Women often keep their own names these days.'

He shakes his head. 'That's not what I mean. This name of yours, that you've had all your life. It makes you very special.'

'Pardon?'

'Well, Cynthia is just another form of Sina. She was the mythical moon goddess for peoples who lived all over the Pacific. Go back even further to Babylonia and you find a moon goddess called Sin. In ancient Egypt, the moon goddess is also the boss of maternity and the art of weaving, as in Sina in the Pacific.

'So, there you are. A great web of coincidence stretching back through the millennia – all the threads culminating in the person of you, Miss Cynthia Moon. You would appear, with those two names to be doubly bathed in lunar essence.' He is leaning back, eyes almost closed but watching me.

This is too much for a Sunday morning. Especially in my state of health. I laugh, high and awkward. 'Oh, come on. It's just a name. But it's a nice fairy story. I'll tell it to my grandchildren.'

'You may well do that, Miss Moon.'

The rain is unrelenting. Through the wall the Road Runner goes beep-beep. Still the wise eyes watch. Uncomfortable, I get up to clear away the dishes.

'Miss Moon, will you laugh at an old man if I tell you a story?'

I screw the lid on the honey jar. 'Probably. It depends on the story. It's a you-and-me sort of story, right? Not for publication.'

He smiles. 'Right. It touches on young Joe but it's broader than that. I'd like you to listen. Sit down, if you would.' I leave the dishes reluctantly.

'When we met, I was somewhat critical of the way you are enmeshed in your world.' He looks amused all over again. 'You and your faxes and your cellphones and your TV in the bedroom.' I open my mouth for a retort but he holds up his hand. 'I know. You can't help being the way you are any more than I can help being a man of my times. And I know how hard it is for people to believe in magic in an age when pragmatism rules.' He leans forward, fixes me with his brown and burning eye. 'But there *is* magic,' he hisses. And he says, 'My old ones speak to me.'

I stare at him *What, now?*

'My spirit guides,' he explains. 'I told you before. We all have them. It's just that some of us hear them better than others.'

The hairs go up on my arms. 'So what have they been telling you?'

Lightbody pauses. 'That a goddess of the moon would soon come to my home.'

Spare me.

'I was shown a picture in my mind,' he insists. 'You'll be pleased to know you don't really look like her. She had long silvery hair and wore gauzy robes. She was standing on a mountaintop with a shining man, sun-blessed to balance her lunar energy. Their arms were upraised and each of them held a sacred stone. It was the beginning of a great moment.'

Lightbody falls silent. He looks grey in the thunderous gloom.

'Do you mean you had a dream?'

'No, much more powerful. I would call it a vision rather than a dream.' I let slip a giggle, a bubble of incredulity. 'And are you . . . suggesting . . . that I'm the goddess of your vision? Why would your voices tell you this? And why would it be me? *Come on . . .*' I hear the scathing tone in my voice.

He takes no notice. 'Next I saw an old, old woman

standing on a lonely beach. The sand was pale gold and it stretched not only along the beach but high up over the hills behind as well, rolling mountains of sand, as far as the eye could see.' He falls silent, remembering. 'You know the place of which I speak.'

'Do I?' And I do too, dammit. The Hokianga harbour, a narrow, sand-rimmed place where I'd spent one magical summer as a child. The golden hills had fascinated me when I was ten. But I'm not about to tell him.

Still, I'm curious. 'So who was this, in your dream?'

'The wisest of my wise ones. No stranger to me. She had visited me often ever since I was a young fellow.' He grins at the look on my face. 'Don't be frightened. Spirits aren't the dour creatures of fiction, you know. We laugh a great deal. I used to call her Old One so she said, "Better call me Oh Two for short."' He giggles, a creaky old man's wheeze. I don't find it funny.

'Our communication had always been verbal,' He goes on. 'This was the first time she'd shown herself. It was quite a moment for me.' He nods to himself, remembering. 'I stood on the beach and she beckoned me closer. She told me that there is work for you to do.'

I'm a rabbit in his headlights. I feel hot, then cold. 'For God's sake,' I laugh. Brittle, edgy. 'This is *nothing* to do with me.'

He looks at me sadly. 'You're such a child of the modern world. You believe in the six o'clock news, the space shuttle and microwaved popcorn – not in visions. But,' and he pauses, 'are you sure you've had none of your own lately? No odd dreams? Sometimes, in the rush of daily life, one forgets or takes no notice.'

I close my eyes and the jagged cliffs and the mercury hair and floating robes wash through my mind. 'I did dream. Something.' I rub by cheeks, confused. 'But he said everybody had that dream.'

'Who said what?'

'Martin Vortex, a man I went to see about the Signal Thread. He rang the next morning and told me that strange dreams happened to everyone who is beginning to get in touch with the Signal.'

'Phyaw!' scoffs Lightbody. 'He is a conjuror. He trifles with you. Your dream is important but not because of that Signal Thread trash.'

'But I can't believe you any more than I believe him!'

Lightbody's still chittering on. 'There is one thing about Oh Two's visit that I didn't tell you. She was not alone. There was a tiny child with her, little more than a baby, but standing upright and with an adult demeanour. A boy, I think. He could speak as well as you or I. It was very odd. But you know how it is in a dream – the most peculiar things seem commonplace.

'The child fixed me with a brilliant smile, a blaze of a smile it was, as if we were sharing a joke. And then he said to me – and his speech was most surprising for he was a child too young for talking – "the moon lady may not believe your story. So in order to convince her, you must do as I did the first time we met."'

And Lightbody gives me a great wink with one wrinkled, drooping lid – a grotesque echo of the one from Philip's baby eye on the day we met.

'Does this have meaning for you?' Lightbody asks.

I'm stunned.

From the room next door comes a long whistling sound followed by a crash as the coyote suffers another defeat in the cartoon canyon.

'No,' I say.

Lightbody's voice is quiet and low. 'I believe it does.'

I stand up fast and swing around the counter into my kitchen, start crashing about with the dishes. The rain seems to be easing. Lightbody brings his cup and saucer. 'Are you keeping yourself safe?' he asks. I squirt a fierce gout of detergent liquid into the sink. 'You would do well,' he says, 'to be asking for protection. Every day you should be saying a prayer. The standard Lord's Prayer is a good one, very powerful. It's like building a little spiritual wall around yourself.'

I'm fizzing with outrage. 'I *told* you. All this stuff isn't real for me.'

But I can't knock his serenity. 'Just be aware that not all the entities in other dimensions are benevolent. There are tricksters, too, just as there are here on earth.'

Rob appears in the doorway. 'Grandpa, there's a taxi tooting.'

'Take your sister out. I'll be there in a minute,' says Lightbody. I'm scrubbing a plate. He takes the dish from my hand and turns me to face him, then touches my forehead, feather light. I feel an odd surge of sweetness. 'God bless you, Miss Moon.'

I watch him go, a slight old man with a battered plastic shopping bag.

I crash the next plate into the sink and jab the ON button of my windowsill radio. Some rap-crap thumps at me, but it sounds fine. Normal. I swish knives and spoons in the sudsy water. The track ends. A car dealer croons do-I-have-a-deal-for-you. Another voice says that Lila's fantastic annual jeans sale is on.

'What's ya favourite radio station?' screeches the DJ. 'You said it! 84FM, the *big* noise in town!' Yeah. Give me noise. Give me the real world.

Nothing for it on a bad day like this but to clean out the wardrobe. As I sort and discard things, my mind's full of jump and jitter. Martin. *Ah.* No other man ever had me eating out of his hand so fast. And Philip. I already know (don't I?) that I'm not willing to let him be my problem. But that wink? Jimmy Lightbody's wink? How the hell to explain it? And his spirit friends . . . *right* out of sight.

I consider my old burgundy sweater. Might as well keep it. The spider brooch might look good on it. Damn thing. Why did I dream it up? How did I know I'd see it the next day? Coincidence, for crying out loud. *Stop spooking yourself.*

I discover, later, that Martin cooks well. We eat Thai with just the right balance of spicy and fiery. Then, in accord, we clear the table and stack the dishwasher. Sometimes our hands brush and my skin tingles. At last he takes me by the shoulders. 'Are you ready?'

I nod and he dims the lights and then leads me to the centre of his living space. He seats himself cross-legged on the floor. I follow suit, wriggling to get prepared for a long sit. He tells me to pull a cushion from the couch. 'It's important that you're comfortable,' he says. 'We want no distractions.'

Ah. Better. We sit close, facing each other. He's looking at me. 'Now,' he whispers. 'We're going to journey together, round and round, down the spiral, so that we can tap into the Thread. You mustn't be frightened. I'm in control. When you're with me, you can't be harmed.'

'How harmed?' I ask, feeling a niggle of fear. 'What do you mean?'

'Shh! It's not important.'

'How will I know when I'm there?' I persist.

Irritation knots his eyebrows for a moment. 'Don't talk. Just listen. You'll know.'

His eyes close and his face goes curiously blank, all emotion rinsed from his features. 'Close your eyes,' he instructs me, as if through his closed lids he can still see my inspection. I do as I'm told.

'We're cruising in space, Cyn,' he murmurs. 'All around us is darkest blue, immensely restful, such peace, such expansiveness – we feel huge and powerful in this space. Nothing can conquer us. We are the masters.'

He pulls me outside myself into an endless indigo sky. After a while, reality fades. I no longer hear the dripping tap in his kitchen. There's no traffic noise. Just the sensation of effortless flight in the dark vastness.

'Your heartbeat is slowing, Cyn,' says his voice from a space far away. 'You're easing into a state of extreme sensitivity. You're the eagle, cruising with deadly beauty, wings spread, eye acutely focused. Feel it, Cyn. Feel the breeze over your feathers, the faintest whisper of wind sliding by the tips as you soar and wheel.

'And now look down through the blue, Cyn. Way down below, there's a glow.' Yes, I can. *I can see it. In the dark. A golden ribbon of light.* 'There's something burning. It's beautiful, isn't it? Don't you want to be part of it?'

Oh, yes.

And down we rush, in a spiralling dive. I see him swoop ahead and we're rushing headlong, closer and closer to the curving thread that unreels as far ahead as the eye can see. I can see now that it's pulsing with life, indistinct shapes roiling and tumbling in the flow. It's a living tube with a translucent skin and energy bubbling in its core. *I want to touch it.* I see Vortex reach the thread and his face turns to me with a wild cry of glee and the skin opens up to receive him. In a second he's inside, a dark shape arrowing through the unearthly cable. And, oh God, I'm inside it too.

The noise! I'm shocked by the roar of voices, a tumult of humanity. Babble! Crying and laughing and arguing and screaming. A rage of sound. I'm alone in a rubber raft, hurtling down a river filled with a tumbling mass of minds, a torrent of consciousness. Speed. Buffeting. Breathlessness. *Stop! Let me out!*

'Cyn.' Vortex is tapping at my face, making my eyes open, forcing me to focus. 'Come on, come back, you're okay. You're just fine.'

Awake now, trembling, I stare at his face. He looks exultant. A car goes by in the street below, pulsating with the closed-window drumming of a stereo wound up to the max. A door slams somewhere in the building. I blink, hands to my face. My palms are hot and dry.

'You were fantastic,' he says.

'Was I?'

'Oh, yeah. You made it right inside, first time. Most people don't get close.'

'Shit.' My heart is a hammer. 'What *was* that?'

'That's the Thread. You were joined into the Thread.'

'And the voices?'

'Other Signal Threaders. All tapped into the network. It's there, available, all the time.'

I stare at him. 'But it's chaos.'

He smiles. 'Only at first. As you progress you'll learn to dampen the static. It's like tuning in to the right station on a bank where every frequency is jam-packed. In a while, individual voices become clear.'

He takes my hand. 'How do you feel?'

'I don't know.' I need to stand, to stretch cramped legs. He helps me to my feet. I'm light-headed, fizzing inside, jumping. Suddenly, I want to laugh. He grins, reaches out both arms and slaps my shoulders, like a coach congratulating the winner. 'Hey,' he crows. 'Welcome to the Signal Thread.'

There is no sex tonight. He sends me home to absorb what I've learned. Says he wants me to keep the experience pure and clear, unmuddied by other sensations. And, in truth, I'm drenched with sensation. Wired. Electric.

I can't sleep, listen to music all night. It's beautiful. I feel every note. And I muse on what connections there might be between Philip's fascination with spiders' webs and the incredible sensation of being tapped into Martin's Signal Thread. Perhaps Philip, with peculiar intuition, is somehow seeking for the Thread. I must tell him about it. *No, you won't. You've done with him.*

SIX

Monday is a breeze. Fresh despite my lack of sleep, I attack the day, supercharged, fingers flying over the keys as I work up more notes on the Signal Thread. I re-read my stuff on Evan O'Keefe. Wonder at how depressed he made me feel. Can't believe, now, how he got himself in that state. I feel so *good*.

Surely Martin's right? Evan must be an aberration. Too young, maybe. Not quite ready for the power. Or in need of a good teacher to help him gain control. On the spur of the moment, I ring his mother.

She sounds even more down than before. 'But you mustn't worry,' I soothe her. 'I've been delving into this with an expert – and I just wanted to tell you I'm sure Evan will be fine. He's just a little off balance. The Signal Thread's powerful. I know, I've had a taste of it myself now. But it can be very empowering.'

'I beg your pardon?' she says. All chilly-sounding. 'I thought you were going to help me with this.'

'I'm trying to . . .'

'Doesn't sound like it to me.' she retorts. 'You're talking like one of *them*.'

Hurt, I hang up. Hell, I was only trying to make her

feel better. I notice that Robert's giving me doubtful looks now.

'Are you on something?' he asks. 'You don't seem like you today.'

'Nope,' I grin. 'On *to* something, more like it.'

The office looks grey and boring. Robert hunched over his keyboard. The art department beavering away. Lou in her office, wrestling with budgets. Tired faces. Clockwork brains. And *none* of them tuned in to each other. All that potential wasted.

I'm deep in my WP when the phone rings. The voice I hear is high and hopeful. My hear sinks. 'It's me,' Philip says. 'I've only got a minute. Can you come to see me tonight? I have to talk with you. Please? I can climb up on my toybox and open the window. I've been practising. It's easy.' His tone is wheedling. 'If you come to get me at twelve we could spend a couple of hours together and then you can return me. It would be so simple.'

'No, it wouldn't,' I mutter, aware of Robert pretending not to listen.

'Tonight!' pleads Philip.

'But . . .' There is a clatter, and he's gone.

I hang up too. Robert's curious as hell but I can do without his pennyworth. I give him a vague look and start typing again, thinking at full revs. *Why can't this child leave me alone?* Of course, I could simply fail to turn up. End of story. But, damn him and his big hopeful eyes.. I know how he'll fret if I don't show.

So. All right, all right, I'll do it. But just for a moment. We can have a quick whisper at his window and then I'll shove him right back inside. I can explain about my career, my full and busy life in which I simply have no room for him, no *capability*. I'll tell him he's got parents, that I can't be a stand-in. If he's got things he wants to do he'll just have to wait and grow up a bit. Time passes, for God's sake. One day he'll be bigger than two foot tall and can do things for himself. Not rely on me or some other patsy. Yes, I'll tell him. And I can give him a quick rundown on the Signal Thread, so he's got something new to muse on. Maybe that's what he needs. Hey, after last night, I know nothing can go wrong . . .

But despite my confidence, I'm jittery as I wait through the crawl of the evening hours. I can't bear television, go out for a run, take a long shower, down too much coffee and raid the fridge for comfort food. Dark chocolate. Guilt-inducing. Good.

Finally, it's time. Okay. Running shoes. Baggy pants with matching sweatshirt. Dark enough for camouflage but athletic enough for (God forbid) rapid flight. At 11.30, I'm on the road. The night is still and humid, the streets greased with moisture. Low cloud. Fuzzy haloes round the streetlights.

I park half a block away, beneath an overhanging tree where the shadows are deep, get out and nudge the door closed. Turn the key in the lock. A dog, not too close, woofs once. Leaves rustle in a whiffle of breeze.

I breathe deeply a few times, chest tight, and pad off down the street, slowing as I near the Preston home.

Damn and blast. A massive truck-and-trailer rig squats fatly on the road outside. Jeff Preston must be at home. A complication. Is he up and alert, about to leave on a night haul? Or will he be leaving in the morning? Surely he wouldn't shatter the surburban quiet by starting up all that horsepower after midnight. I relax a little. The man's asleep. Probably.

My pulse thuds, *g-boom, g-boom*. I creep along to a point where I can see the house. A big transformer sits at the pavement's edge. I peer around its humming bulk, checking for lights or signs of life. Under the streetlights, the unkempt garden is black and ochre, like a snap from an old photo album. Windows seem shut tight. No lights showing.

I cross the road. Ridged soles squidge-squeak on the asphalt.

Now I'm at the gate. If someone looks outside, they'll see me. Can't stop now. Tip-toe over the grass to the corner of the house, hard up under the windows. I creep past the living room and the kitchen. A narrow strip of tangled herbs takes me by surprise. A foot tangles in the knee-high plants and I reach out for balance. My knuckles rap, once, against the wall. *Shit*. Freeze, heart hammering. Wait. Thirty seconds. Sixty.

I'm perspiring. Sharp mint scent rises from bruised leaves.

I squat, thigh muscles quivering, and peer along the rear wall. The humid night has cooled and is turning misty. It's harder to see sharp detail. But there it is, ten feet away. A pale movement. Small hand signalling.

Philip's window is higher than I thought. He's strad-dled across the windowsill in a stretchy sleep suit, bottom thickly padded for the night. With a grin of delight, he clutches at me. I have to grab to stop him falling and he thuds against my chest, warm and chubby.

He hugs, pressing a velvety, silent, intense kiss against my cheek.

And then – *Christ!* A light snaps on, just feet away, and I hear a cupboard door open and the clatter of someone rummaging amongst bottles and packets.

'Shirl?' Jeff Preston calls. 'Have we got Panadol or anything? I've got a bitch of a headache.'

A muffled reply. Panicky, I try to push Philip back up inside but he's *heavy* and he clings, fights me, won't let go. His lips are pressed close to my ear. 'Go!' he urges. 'Please!'

And against all reason (*why don't I just drop him and run?*) I bend and creep, crabbing past the bathroom window. Another harsh square of light suddenly sprawls out upon the lawn over our heads. Clearing the end of the house now. Straightening up to pound over the shaggy grass and into the empty street, around the behemoth truck and over the road towards the safety of the car.

Pelting around the corner, Philip bumping against me, I spare a second to look back. The truck is outlined against a hazy glare. *God help me.* Now I'm absolutely over the wire.

There's the car now, under the gloomy tree. I jam Philip under one arm, scrabble in my pocket for the keys. Can't find the lock in the dark. There! I wrench open the door, toss him across into the passenger seat, hear him go 'Ouch!' as he hits something on the way. As I scramble in after him, I somehow flick the keys into the space between the seats. Fumbling for them with one hand, I haul the door closed with the other.

Oh God, what's that noise? A bellow in the night –
Jeff Preston's truck being kicked into life, revving,
crunching into gear.

I panic. 'Philip, I can't find the keys!'

'It's okay,' he says. 'Calm down,' He's crouching on
the floor now and reaches easily into the narrow space.
He passes the jingling bunch up to me. 'Don't worry.
It'll be all right.' He gives my shin a comforting pat. I
shake him off, furious. This is all *his* fault.

I tear away from the kerb, lights off, dreading to see
the Kenworth looming from behind. No sign of it. 'Cyn,
put the lights on,' comes the small, quiet voice from the
floor. 'And slow down.'

I have to do as I'm told. There's a stop sign ahead.
Major intersection. As I brake there, a police car races
by, its roof ablaze with red and blue spark-and-flash.
The two men in the front do not glance at me as they
howl past.

I'm trembling, pull away from the corner slowly,
realising at last the need to drive sedately, do nothing
to attract attention.

The dark cave of my garage has never looked more
welcoming. Once in the house, cautious, I close all the
blinds and drapes before switching on the lights. I drop
him at one end of my couch. He looks smug, which
doesn't help my sense of humour.

'Why didn't I *leave* you there?' I mutter. 'Just drop
you outside your window, instead of this, this ...
kidnapping stunt.'

'But you haven't kidnapped me,' he says 'I wanted
you to take me.'

'They don't know that.' My hands flap in frustration. 'You can't stay here.'

'Why not? The more you simply carry on as usual, the less likelihood there is of anything going amiss. Go to work tomorrow like you always do. I'll be fine here.'

I knead my forehead. 'Don't be silly. I can't leave you on your own.'

'I wouldn't mind.'

'But you're only little! You can't reach things. You can't get to the taps to wash or get a drink. What will you do for food? And . . . the toilet.' I have to laugh. 'You might fall in and drown.'

'You worry too much,' he tells me. 'We should go to bed. You have to look normal in the morning.'

'Normal!' It's a despairing sort of splutter. 'Philip, this is a disaster, and you're talking normal! What am I going to do with you? Not just in the morning but after that? You've got to go back.'

'No,' he says. 'Not possible. I have too much to do.'

'*What*, for crying out loud?'

'You're too overwrought to hear it now. We should sleep. The next few days will be testing.' And then he has the nerve to yawn.

He's *tired*? When I'm still afizz with adrenaline? How can he sleep? But he's droopy-eyed, like a puppy suddenly tuckered out. I surrender.

I give him a drink of milk and an old T-shirt that swamps him but is at least fresh and clean. His own clothes are dirty from the floor of my car. No, he doesn't need nappies, he says haughtily (just as well, as it's hardly the sort of item I keep handy), so I pile

some books next to the lavatory so he can pee in private.
Soon he's cuddled into me like a warm teddybear. We
have to share. I don't have another bed.

'Goodnight, Cyn,' says his small voice in the dark.
'Thank you for coming to get me. It's all going to be
all right, you know.'

'I suppose,' I answer. And as I stare, sleepless, into the
gloom and listen to his quiet even breath, I know that
he is the comforter and that I, the big grown-up one,
am the one who takes most solace from the soothing.

The alarm-radio blares. I jerk out of sleep as the
morning's news spews out.

'There is shock and grieving in an Auckland home this
morning as police investigate the overnight snatching of
a baby boy from his bedroom.' I shrivel inside as the
newsreader gallops through the details. Describes the
shock of the parents, the puzzlement of the police. An
interview rolls. 'This is a most distressing case,' says a
cop. 'We are very anxious for any information that can
help – anything at all.'

'How is Mrs Preston?'

'She's under sedation.'

'Do you think the person who did this could be
mentally ill?'

'I'd prefer not to comment.'

'Are you expecting a ransom to be asked for Philip's
return?'

'It would be surprising. The Prestons are just an
average family. In any case, we've had no contact
at all . . .'

I jab at the OFF switch.

'It's not your fault,' says Philip.

But it is.

'I tried to reach Shirley in my dreams but she's not sleeping. I can't get through,' Philip is saying. *In his dreams? What is he on about?* He looks woeful. 'But I can't turn back now. I can't go back. It would put you at risk, after all. We just have to be resolute. I'll contact them when I can.' He squares his small shoulders.

Dread curdles my guts. I have to be normal today. I have to be me. I have to be at work. I chant my intentions in my head like a mantra.

'May I use the bathroom?' Philip turns on to his stomach and levers himself off the bed. The T-shirt rucks up, showing his bottom.

I resist the temptation to smile. 'Do you need any help?'

'No,' he says with dignity as he walks from the room, berobed in my shirt, holding the hem off the floor.

'All you need is a pair of wings and you'd look like an angel,' I tease.

He says over his shoulder, 'That's not altogether out of the question.'

I sit staring at the space he's just vacated. The phone snaps me to attention. My attempt at an unbothered hello seems to come out all right.

Lou's barking with excitement. 'That baby. The one you saw. Someone's kidnapped him! Snatched him right out of his cot.'

'Snatched him?' I don't have to pretend. Louisa's gabble makes me shiver.

'Why? Does anyone know why?'

'No.' Her voice drops. 'It's a great story, Cyn. Best chance you've had for months. See if you can get it for us exclusively, huh?'

My free hand is gripping at the fabric of my night-gown, knuckles bony, screwing the cotton tight. 'But, Louisa, it's a today story, not our sort of thing. We're a monthly. By the time we can print anything, it'll be history.'

'But you can get the story nobody else can get close to. You *know* this woman. She'll trust you. She'll need to talk to someone. You're halfway there! You can be there, day by day, as the search progresses. Chart the hope and despair, the full bit.'

'I'm supposed to be finishing the Signal Thread story.'

'It can wait. This is much better.'

Philip, standing in the doorway, sees me smash down the phone.

'It's impossible,' I moan. 'I'm going to have to ask cops whether they've found you yet. And I'll have to hug Shirley as she weeps over her lost boy.'

'You can do it,' he says.

And the damn phone rings again.

'There's a missing child,' says Lightbody. 'He's the one, isn't he?'

'What *one?*'

'Miss Moon,' he says. 'Do not obscure reality in this way.'

Anger sharpens my voice. 'Do you think I meant this to happen? I was only trying to say goodbye and now

86

I'm stuck with him!' I happen to glance up and see the flash of hurt on Philip's face. I look away.

Jimmy is talking. 'It's not such an imposition. I'll look after the child. Rob and Becky have gone home. No one will seek him here.'

I begin to protest that he can't, that he's an old man, it's too much trouble. But then relief begins to flood in. *Let him do it, yes, yes.*

'Thank you,' I tell him, throat tight.

'I can't wait to hear how you two met,' he says. 'Oh Two will be pleased.' My insides squirm at that but as I put down the phone, I'm feeling marginally better.

'I think we're going to be okay, Philip. Someone else is going to mind you, someone you can trust. Don't have time to tell you now, my boss is baying for me.' Breakfast next, I announce. He trots behind as I make for the kitchen, asks for a glass of milk.

'I'll buy you some more clothes later,' I promise as I pour from the carton. 'What on earth do kids your age wear, anyway?'

He takes a glass of milk from me. 'I don't care. Make it the bare minimum, so you don't look obvious. And please, no nappies. Shirley did persist. I can't tell you how good it is not to have a plastic-wrapped posterior any more.'

I grin. 'And what do you want to eat during the day? I can leave yogurt and fruit down low. Can you open the fridge?'

'Of course,' he says, bracing a small foot against a cupboard and heaving at the rubber-sealed edge of the door. It sucks open. 'There! Don't worry. As long as there's a chair or something for me to climb on, I can reach most things. I've got the radio. I've got your books. I shall be most content.'

Robert bustles into the office as I punch out the Prestons' number. 'Isn't it appalling about that kid?' he mouths. I nod, waiting, as he raves, 'Jesus, there are some sick people in the world . . .'

In my other ear a cool female voice says, 'Preston residence.' *Uh-huh.* Police.

'Good morning,' I say shakily. Maybe it doesn't matter. No harm in sounding a little upset. 'I'm a friend of Shirley Preston's. I'm just ringing to see how she is.'

'Can I have your name?'

I tell her and there is a rustling silence. And then I'm startled to hear Shirley's voice. 'Cynthia?' It's thready, little more than a whisper.

'Yes.' *I don't know what to say.* 'I hope I'm not intruding . . . I just wanted to tell you, I'm so sorry.'

'Oh, Cynthia,' she wheezes. 'He's gone. My baby's gone.'

Jesus, this is hard. 'I thought I might come round this morning. The time must be passing so slowly for you, waiting for news.'

Shirley sounds grateful. 'Would you? You might be able to think of something. I told the police about you last night. I've told them about everyone who knew . . . knows . . . Philip. Maybe you saw someone. Who could have done such a thing?' The voice wobbles.

Robert's watching. My face is stiff with effort. *Be cool. Be natural.*

'Try not to worry too much, Shirley, I'll be there soon.'

I hang up and gather pad and pencil. There's a camera in the bottom drawer of my desk. I slide that into my bag too.

'How does she sound?' Robert asks.

'Terrible. I feel terrible, too. Louisa's expecting an exclusive.'

'Well, sure. It's a great story.'

'I dunno. I just feel too close to it somehow.'

'Hell, Cyn, it's been dropped in your lap. How tough can it be? Kind of spooky, though,' he muses, 'that you should meet them just before this happened.'

I snatch up my car keys. 'You make me sound like some sort of omen.'

His eyebrows lift. 'Hey, lighten up. Coincidence. That's all.'

There's a crowd outside the house. Police cars, TV cameras, reporters, curious tourists. I park down the road and work my way through to the fluttering plastic ribbon that cordons off the rubberneckers. A policeman holds them at bay. I give him my name and hear a jealous grumble ('How come she's allowed in?') as he lets me duck under the tape.

The lawn is marked off with string into small squares. People are head-down, searching for clues. I hope fervently that I've left none.

There's a murmuring huddle of cops in the living room. Heads swivel as I walk in. One of them indicates that the Prestons are in the kitchen. He adds, 'I would like to talk to you before you go.' My stomach turns to lead.

The Prestons are sitting at the kitchen table. A crunched beer can lies curled upon it like an aluminium foetus. Jeff holds another in his fist. He is smoking, head down. Shirley rises, hands clasped in front of her. It's as if she might fly apart if she lets them go. I give her an awkward hug. 'What am I going to do?' she whimpers. We cling together and rock, each suffering a separate pain.

Jeff drags on his cigarette. 'I see you didn't waste any time getting here.'

'I asked her to come!' protests Shirley.

'Why? We don't need her sort.'

'I need a friend, Jeff.'

His lip curls. 'Come on, Shirl, she barely knows us. She's been here, what, two ... three times? You ask her why she's really come. You ask if she's just come to hold your hand or whether she's got something else in mind.'

Shirley disengages herself. She looks hunted. 'What does he mean?'

He's seething, thank God. All the easier to make them loathe me. I have to force some distance between us, make it impossible for me to come back to this house. 'I really do want to help if I can,' I say. Jeff sneers as I struggle for words. 'It might help if you make an appeal to the kidnapper. I work with words all the time. It's easy for me. I could help you write down what you want to say.'

'We don't need any nosy reporter putting words into

our mouths.' Jeff's eyes are slits. 'We're not thick, y'know. And anyway, what would you want in return for all this help of yours?'

'I'd like to write your story.' Heat blooms on my cheeks. 'Look, I'm just a reporter, all right? I happen to know people who happen to be at the centre of a big news event. I'd be lying if I said my editor wasn't interested. It probably sounds very hard-hearted . . .'

'My oath!' says Jeff.

'. . . but it's pure coincidence that we've got to know each other.'

Jeff's mouth turns down. 'See, Shirl, I told you.' He turns on me. 'You can bloody well get out. Now.'

'Stop it!' Shirley wails. 'Stop it, Jeff. We've had enough upset without you getting all angry again.' She lets out a harsh croak. 'He thinks it's my fault, you see. Philip's window was open. I left it open to air the room for a little while, but I'm sure I closed it when I put him to bed. I did. I know I did!' She shakes with despair. 'But I can't have, can I, because there's been no one else in the house. It's all my fault!'

Her head goes down on her arms on the table. Oh Jesus. *Do it now.* I grab my bag, pull out the camera, and point it at her. It's on motor drive. It clacks and hums above the sound of Shirley's sobs.

Jeff leaps at me, snatches it. 'Bitch!' He tears the back open, rips out the film and slams the camera on the table.

The door flies open, a firm hand grasps my shoulder. 'Out,' says the policewoman.

I pick up my battered camera, can't look at Shirley. Jeff spits on the floor as I leave the room.

And still it isn't over. A plain-clothes sits me down in the living room, emanating stony disapproval. Woods, he says his name is. My stomach is quivering and I fold my arms over it, trying to still the fear. His fellow officers have gone outside and are studying the grass. 'Surely you didn't think you could get away with it?' he says.

I almost die on the spot. *He knows*. But I wake up in time. Just. He's only talking about my ratbag reporter act. 'It was worth a try. Mr Preston was about to eject me anyway. He doesn't like the media.'

'With good reason, I'd say,' he drawls. 'I thought you were a friend of theirs?'

'We've met a few times. Their son's cute. And I felt a bit sorry for Shirley. She doesn't get out much. I babysat Philip once when she wanted to have her hair done. And I called in on his birthday last week.'

'You don't seem the sort of young woman who'd volunteer for child-minding.'

Creep. I do have some feminine traits. Shirley seems quieter now. I feel stronger without the sobbing noise from the next room

'Look, I'm under a lot of pressure,' I blather. 'My editor wants an exclusive. But Jeff was hostile right from the start. It wasn't on, I could see that.' Carefully, I relax my arms, mindful of how he might read defensive body language. 'I thought maybe a photo might mollify the boss.' The cop looks scathing. 'It's a big story. I have to earn a living.'

Woods shrugs. He moves on to my association with

Philip. How long had I been here? Had I noticed anyone hanging about? And then, 'Where were you last night, Miss Moon?'

It is as if he's slapped me. An alibi. I haven't thought of an alibi. My voice sounds brittle, even to me. 'What time?' I ask.

He hedges. 'You just tell me about your evening.'

'I was tired. Went home around five, the usual time, and just stayed home. Oh, I went for a run around seven, I think.'

'What was on television?'

'Don't know. Don't watch it much. I read, played some music, went to bed around eleven.'

'Can anyone corroborate that?'

'No, I live alone.'

The kitchen door opens a crack. Jeff eyes me sourly and then slams it.

'I think you've outworn what little welcome you had, Miss Moon.' The policeman seems to derive a certain enjoyment out of adding, 'I hope your editor manages to find something else to fill the space.'

SEVEN

Philip's lying on the floor listening to Mozart when I struggle in the door at five o'clock with a clutch of supermarket bags. He springs to his feet.

'Don't ask,' I warn, heaving the bags on to the bench. 'Shirley was a mess, Jeff was furious, my boss was pissed off that I'd blown it. Have you managed okay?'

He smiles. 'Bliss. You've no idea how good it is to have space. And time. None of that relentless infant routine. Nap, food, play, gurgle. Wearying in the extreme.'

Lucky him. I haul milk, fruit, bread and cheese from the bags. While he eats, I run him a bath. Soon as I close the door, he's sliding into the water with an old man's sigh of satisfaction. His grubby suit needs washing too so I poke it down out of sight amongst a pile of my stuff in the machine, measure out powder and push buttons.

Just after seven there's a knock at the door. 'Under the couch,' I whisper. Philip needs no urging. He's already wriggling out of sight.

But it's only Jimmy at the door, an airline bag in hand.

As he comes in, Philip squirms out from his lair,

rolls easily to his feet and dips his head. 'It's good to meet you.'

Jimmy sinks into the nearest chair, eyes bright with curiosity, and the old man and the infant beam at each other. I clear my throat, feeling the odd one out.

'I suggest that Philip begins,' says Jimmy. 'I'd like to hear his story.'

Philip crosses his feet, hesitating.

'Is there a problem?' I ask.

He looks a tad embarrassed. 'Not really. I'm just not sure whether you'll believe me. Jimmy will. But for you, it will sound, what's the expression . . . over the top?'

Humph. 'Try me.'

'The thing is, Cyn, I shouldn't be here.'

'I know,' I say tartly. 'You should be at home, in your cot, with your parents.'

'I don't mean that. I mean, I shouldn't be here, period. In the world. Not now, anyway. I was born . . . by mistake. You see, I'm what you might loosely call a guardian. An angel, maybe. One of many souls whose job it is to watch over the Earth and observe its state of balance.'

'You're saying you're some sort of *alien?*'

He considers. 'Hardly. Just from a different dimension. There are many of us around the planet all the time. You just can't see us . . . well, not unless we inadvertently become flesh, as I have. And we're worried about this planet. Once it was beautifully balanced, but now it's overworked. Its energy web is being squeezed and pulled and pushed, bulbous here, frail there. It's not in good order, I'm afraid.'

I'm staring at his babyface. Hearing his words. Absorbing very few of them.

'Tell me about the web,' says the old man.

Philip ignores my open mouth and basks in Jimmy's warmth. 'Oh, glorious, shimmering. An intricate mesh, all interconnected.' He thinks for a moment. 'It surrounds the globe like a giant string balloon – the most beautiful, interdimensional spider's web you could ever imagine.'

He points to a shelf where I keep an old globe. 'It's rather like those latitude and longitude lines, but much more complex. Where many threads join, they form vortices of spiritual power. Primitive peoples knew these places. Stonehenge, the Pyramids, Mayan temples, medieval cathedrals, were carefully sited atop such conjunctions. The web is as necessary for earth's survival as the air you breathe.'

Blithely, he says there are whole teams of spiritual guardians out there trying to keep the web's integrity intact. *Angels on patrol?* Yes, he explains, that's what he was doing when he noticed the child being born and the malevolent soul about to invade it.

'I tried to fend it off and slipped somehow – and suddenly I was howling in the delivery room, lodged inside the baby I was trying to help.' He's laughing. 'I couldn't believe it. Back in human form again! Still, I have only myself to blame. I broke the first angelic rule. Thou shalt not interfere.'

I've kidnapped a kid who thinks he's an *angel?* And here I am conspiring with some barmy old psychic who's seen him in a dream?

And then someone hammers on the front door.

I find this morning's grim policeman, Woods, on my doorstep. I should have known. Chilly air seeps in, or so it seems. I have to fight the tremors I feel coming on.

'You're working late, Inspector.'

He takes a small but purposeful step, forcing me to inch back. 'Regular hours don't exist in police work, Miss Moon. A little like your job at times, I expect. May we come in?' A younger man with heavy shoulders and a rash of acne is just a step behind him.

In the living room, Jimmy has adopted an affable position leaning against the mantelpiece. I do the introductions and ask them to sit, taking care to plant myself on the couch over the spot where I'm hoping like hell Philip is hiding again.

'I wonder if you'd mind if Constable Fleming takes a quick look around?' says the Inspector. 'You're entitled to say no. We don't have a warrant – but it would be a quick way of covering the ground . . .'

I wave my hand in acquiescence.

Woods says, 'You'll appreciate that we have to follow up all possible leads. And you're one of the few people who expressed an interest in the Preston baby.'

Some incredulity wouldn't hurt now. 'You have *me* on your suspect list? I'm at work all day. Where on earth would I find time to fit in baby-care – even assuming that I wanted a baby, and someone's else's at that?'

Woods is unperturbed. I can hear Fleming opening and shutting cupboard doors. My ear strains for the faint squeak of the washing machine lid.

Jimmy eases the tension. 'How are you getting on with the hunt? Do you have anything to go on?'

'Very little, I'm afraid.'

'It's a tragic business.' Jimmy is suitably sombre. 'How are the parents tonight?'

'As you'd expect. Miserable. He is very angry. She blames herself. Oh, well.' He slaps his knees and stands up. 'We're doing all we can. A baby can't disappear into thin air. We'll find him.' Fleming re-enters the room. His face blank.

'We're off then,' says Woods. 'Thanks for your co-operation.'

I want to slam the door behind him but am careful to let it simply click into place, knuckles white with control. I lean in relief against the cool slab of wood. It's not a thick door. I can hear them clearly as they go.

'No sign?' says Woods.

'Nope. Hey, she's a bit of an intellectual though,' sniggers Fleming. 'There's a stack of books a foot high in the lavatory.'

I race to the laundry and fling open the washing machine. The spin cycle has wrung the clothes into a coiled rope of damp cloth within which a small blue piece of towelling fabric is just visible. It seems undisturbed. I go back, limp with relief, to the living room, where Jimmy's helping Philip out of his hiding place. 'I thought you'd be safe here,' I wheeze. 'Didn't occur to me they'd come and search.'

'It was more a polite inspection,' says Jimmy. 'A cursory look was all they needed to find a live baby.'

Live? Jesus. If they get to thinking it's a body they're after, they could well come back.

Jimmy pushes with his toe at the airline bag. 'I'll take Philip to my neighbour's house. She's away – I'm looking after the place. Not due back for weeks yet.'

Philip's eyes are shining. 'That sounds perfect.' He turns to me. 'You wouldn't have a little celebratory port, would you? Old monks like me are partial to a little spot from time to time. Did you know I was a monk last time around?'

Is this a reasonable thing to expect? I pour him a thimbleful. Jimmy says no. I slosh out a hefty dollop for me and, despite my antagonism to this turn my life has taken and because I'm curious, I ask, 'Can you actually remember being a newborn?'

'Oh, yes. Most distressing. A normal child starts with a clean slate, of course. But because I was wrenched so fast from one plane of existence to the other, I had a headful of experience. I had no way to communicate at first. I could do little but lie there. All I could think of was that I had this task to perform – to do with webs, though I couldn't say why.' He pauses to explain to Jimmy how we met, how he cajoled me into seeking out information for him. Jimmy smiles at me, a bit smug. 'Cyn did the trick. When I saw her notes, it all came to me in a flash.' Philip takes a lip-smacking sip of his port and salutes me with the glass. 'This is very good.'

I'm impatient. 'What flash?'

'The connection between webs and the energy net that sustains the earth. Both are made the same way, of spokes and spirals. Both are important as symbols for us. And it's easy to be seduced by the glittering spiral, to feel the tug of its power. But the really great mystery lies within the first fork – the Y-shape.'

Philip holds his chubby arms high and wide. 'The Y lures us, though we've forgotten why. It's just another letter. But it stirs your soul! Think of the moment when a whale dives and heaves up its tail. For a split-second moment it hangs there – and we gaze, awe-struck. Tall trees inspire us, too, because they're a collection of Y-shapes – branches raised to the sky.'

'People make Y shapes too,' offers Jimmy. 'In ecstasy or despair, up go the arms.'

'Of course,' Philip agrees.

Even I'm intrigued now. 'How about the soppy-movie shot – the lovers running to meet each other, arms open wide? That's one of your Ys too?'

'Of course. So is the baby raising his arms to his mother, making himself irresistible. And then, of course, there's the most famous Y-shape of all. Jesus upon the cross. That shape, along with his message of love, is his most enduring legacy – the ultimate sign.'

'Of what?' I ask.

'Balance. Perfect balance. A huge tree moves us because it is perfectly balanced, close to immortal, roots anchored deep within the earth. It's utterly centred. We recognise its sublime nature without being able to put it into words. It's about the profound line from the Bible: "Be still and know that I am God."'

The child smiles at me. 'There's more.' He lifts his arms. 'The central point of the Y, the spider's web's "free zone", has its counterpart in your own body.

LINDSEY DAWSON

Where your heart lies.' He taps at his chest. 'Not your physical heart, but that deep-down, crunch-point, innermost place where your free will lies.'

He leans forward, rocking. 'The Y is a sign that says that sometime, we as people will have to choose what sort of world we want to live in. And that time is soon. You see, the web that cradles the earth is fragile now – so burdened by the chaos we've created that it's close to collapse. You can hear it creaking all over the universe,' and he raises a finger, 'if you have ears to listen. That's why so many angels are here, me and many more. My friends are on constant patrol, soothing stresses where we can.'

'And so . . .?' I prod.

'The Earth's people are teetering in the centre, in the free zone, waiting, as the spider does, for something to happen, to feel that tug upon the signal thread.'

'Philip . . .' I start, bursting to tell him about Vortex, but he hushes me.

'What's going to happen is that the web will soon make one last effort for stability. It will make itself known to us all. It needs our help, you see, if it's to be restored to full strength. I can't wait!' He grabs his toes in delight, face beaming.

'What if we don't respond?' asks Jimmy.

'Not a pleasant scenario, I'm afraid. The planet would have to take steps to clean things up, give itself some breathing space. In a way, you'd be lucky to witness it. It doesn't happen often. Of course, the world will endure.' Philip rocks contentedly. 'It always has. Everything would simply be returned to the unspoiled way it was before, and the survivors would begin the journey all over again.'

I blink at the chill word, 'survivors', but Jimmy seems unperturbed.

'So, when this time arrives, what should we do?'

'You say yes.'

'Yes?'

'Simple as that. Yes to love. Yes to courage. Yes to hope.'

He says this with such complete conviction that it withers my urge to sneer at the outrageousness of it all. Jimmy's nodding in his corner. Apparently it all makes perfect sense to him.

The baby turns to me. 'I must start warning people that the decision time is approaching. That's why I've kept pestering you. You know how to get publicity. If I'm going to have any impact in the short time that's left, I need to get exposure.'

'God almighty. You want to say all this on television?'

'Well, I think so. It'll cause a stir, no doubt.'

I stare at him. 'People won't believe you,' I tell him flatly.

Jimmy snorts. 'When Philip's saying it? A mere infant? Of course people will listen.'

'But there are nutcases out there who'll think he's Jesus re-born. He'll be mobbed. How can I protect him from that sort of hysteria? Oh, and there is a small matter of my . . . no, our . . . complicity in what everyone thinks is a kidnapping. We could find ourselves in jail while he's out there tap-dancing. And when the networks have finished with him, what then? Where will he go? How will he live?'

'My future is not a concern,' says Philip. 'Bless you for bringing me here.' He smiles. 'You don't know how much I appreciate it. And thank you for listening to me without scoffing. Well, not much scoffing. I know it's a lot to absorb. I think we should go, Mr Lightbody,' he adds. 'Cyn looks tired.'

'But what about your parents, Philip?' I insist. 'We can't just leave them . . . *dangling* . . . like this?'

'My parents are my responsibility,' he soothes. 'Not yours. Come and see us tomorrow and we'll make some plans. You mustn't worry.'

I gather Philip's new clothes and his damp suit and he eases himself into Jimmy's overnight bag for the trip to his safehouse. He gives me one last look from between the zippered edges.

'I shall pray for you,' is all he says. Which doesn't help. You pray for people who are on life-support. Not for people like me. I'm okay. A bit frazzled, but basically fine. Not in need of God-bothering.

After they've gone, I keep on worrying. Can't get Shirley out of my head. Woods was right. The least I can do is say sorry. Not, 'Sorry I snatched your baby.' I'm not crazy enough (yet) to admit that. Just, 'Sorry I was so awful this morning.' *Quick. Do it now! Before you chicken out.*

She answers. I force out my apology.

'It's okay. It's a terrible time for all of us,' she whispers, soft and slow.

I swallow, amazed at her grace. 'I hope Jeff's looking after you.'

She makes a sad, accepting sort of sigh. 'Well. You know. He's a hard man – kind of runs on rage. It's how he copes. He's out just now. Needed to get some air, he said.'

Just as I'm about to stumble through a goodbye, she speaks again. 'He came to me today,' she says. 'Philip.'

I feel my jaw drop. 'What?'

'I managed to get some sleep,' she sighs. 'And I *saw* him right here with me. Felt him even. It was more real than a dream. I felt his weight in my arms. Smelt his smell. He's coming back, you know. We don't have to worry any more. I feel so strongly that he's just gone away for a while.'

That's really nice, I tell her, and hang up very fast. Very nervous.

Next morning I listen anxiously to the news but there's nothing fresh being reported. Anguished Shirley and Jeff stare at me from my newspaper's front page, hollow-eyed and stricken. I cram the paper into a rubbish sack and call in sick, for I can't face the thought of the office's idle-chat machine. Tummy bug, I tell Lou. 'Christ, Cyn, you're not much use to me these days,' she grizzles. I tell her I'll make up for the kidnap story débâcle by giving her a really good piece on the Signal Thread.

'It'd better be,' she grumbles as she hangs up.

It's not hard to keep at it. For one thing, it gives me a chance to see Martin again. I can't stay away –

and now that Philip has talked about signal threads too, I'm feeling more at ease about continuing with Martin's tuition. (Hell, if *angels* go for this stuff, why should I stand back?) And I'm determined to get some proof for any doubters that Martin's claims have some substance. What's more, if I keep busy I might be able to avoid thinking about when the cops might come back. I'm still not out of that particular swamp. *Come and see us,* Philip said. Not if I can help it. Not until I've had time to think.

Over the last few days I've collected plenty of clippings about Signallers. I flip through my sheaf of stories. Lightweight and breathless, mostly. Like this one . . .

"Hello . . . Are You There?' says the headline from a weekend paper. The text goes on, *'When you want to call a friend you pick up the phone, right? Not this woman. Miranda Lewis claims she can talk long-distance with the power of her mind.*

"Lewis says she's not alone. Many other members of her loose-knit group, who call themselves Signal Threaders, are also developing telepathic skills.

"The former fashion buyer says she spends at least two hours a day in meditation, immersing herself in what she calls the "universal power of the spiral". And she and her friends "talk" to each other this way.

"You too can get started. It's one way to cut down the phone bills! Lewis is willing to demonstrate her skill to anyone who is interested. The story ends with her phone number.

I call her. She's home. And she has a cancellation late tomorrow.

I scribble 7pm in my diary. The second I hang up, the phone rings again. Jimmy.

'Morning,' he greets me, all breezy. 'When are you coming over? We've done the video.'

My guts roll. 'What video?'

'We've decided,' he announces. 'Philip makes a tape. You take it to the world. It's the best way. Philip stays secluded while you get things organised. Then, when he's ready, he emerges. Everyone will be used to the idea then. His mum and dad. The police. We'll let it all calm down before he comes out. We've told them, by the way.'

I make a little moaning noise. 'Who?'

'The Prestons. Not fair to let them suffer. We went to a phone box early this morning, *miles* away.' He lets out his old-man's tee-hee. 'Did the job and came back with no one the wiser. It was rather fun.'

I picture them rolling through the streets in Jimmy's ludicrous pink car, terribly pleased with themselves.

'It was stupid, Jimmy. You need a car seat. It's illegal to carry a baby not strapped in. You could have been pulled over.' I shake my head, seething. 'Why did you *do* that? The cops will be on your doorstep in five minutes.'

He stays calm. 'But why should they? Why would anyone suspect a harmless old geezer like me? I didn't speak to the parents. Only Philip did.'

'But what did he say? What did they say?'

'They weren't happy,' Jimmy concedes. 'Shocked, too, of course. They hadn't really heard him *talk* like that before. But he told them he had work to do. That he couldn't stay at home in his cot. That he loved them but had to go away for a while.'

'Did he mention how he got away?'

'Of course not, Miss Moon. Don't worry, you're not implicated in any way.'

Yet. 'My God, Jimmy. I don't feel good about any of this. Did they want to see him?'

'Philip kept it short, so the question didn't arise really. He just wanted to reassure them that he was fine. You will help, won't you?' For the first time it seems to be occurring to him that I might just walk away from this shambles. 'You'll find the best outlet for the video? I simply wouldn't know where to start.'

I'm silent.

'Miss Moon? The world needs you . . .'

It doesn't help at all to realise that the old lunatic means it. I heave a sigh and tell him I want to look at the tape before I decide anything. I refuse to go to his house though. And I don't want his conspicuous pink heap turning up again at my place. We compromise. He'll ask a boy who lives nearby to deliver the parcel to me. The kid often runs errands for him. He won't think anything of this one, Jimmy assures me.

And later that day, after school, a gangly lad knocks on the door and gives me a brown-paper parcel. An old-fashioned package, with knotted string. I wrestle with it, grumbling, pull out the video and sit down to watch.

When it's over I pick up the phone. I've had enough of coping with this on my own. I need to show it to someone I trust. Someone who's calm and sensible.

'I thought you had some lurg or other,' Robert says.

'I'm okay. There are absolutely no germs about my person that you could catch. Really,' I assure him. But I do need some advice. Please?'

Robert grumbles, but I can tell he's curious. He gives in. And after work, he arrives at my door. I install him in an armchair, put a beer in his hand.

'The Preston baby,' I say, picking up my remote. 'Remember?'

'Of course,' he says, eyeing me.

I press play.

There are streaks and blips and then there appears on-screen a large old-fashioned stuffed armchair. Philip sits on its broad seat. He wears one of the little jumpers I bought him the day before. An embroidered red fire-engine chugs across his tummy.

He looks very solemn. The image wobbles, then steadies.

'Are you ready?' Philip asks in his high piping voice.

'Yes, you can start now.' Jimmy's voice booms loud, off-screen, nearer to the camera.

'What is this? Who's that?' demands Robert. I hush him up, wanting him to hear.

The tiny boy is chuckling. 'I'm sorry about these preliminary fumblings. My friend's too old and I'm too young for all this modern technology. We've spent twenty minutes trying to establish what white balance means.' He chortles.

Philip waves. 'Hello. I assume that because this tape is being played, somebody there is sufficiently interested in me to allow this audition to take place.'

He takes a deep breath and declares, 'I would like to appear on a top television show.' He flashes one of his cherubic smiles. 'As you can see, I'm a singularly unusual child. I wish to make myself known to a large audience, not because I have a desire for fame – on the contrary, fame and all of its trappings have little allure – but because it is necessary that as many people as possible are quickly acquainted with some truths about themselves and their world.

'I'm not eager to expose myself to popular gaze. But I find myself in a situation which makes this course of action necessary. I will elucidate when we meet face to face.'

Robert's eyebrows swoop up. '*Elucidate?*'

'It's difficult for people to accept me at first,' Philip is saying, 'I am such a precocious child that it will be easier for some to deny my existence than to accept the truths which I bring. But accept them they must if humankind is to take the next step towards becoming more perfectly evolved beings.

'I think, now, I have said enough. I send you greetings. And to my parents I send love and gratitude, and my sorrow that I cannot be with them at this time.'

The image lurches once and then dissolves into snow.

Robert's face swivels to me, open-mouthed. 'My God, Cyn,' he says finally.

I twist one foot behind the other. 'It was an accident. I just went there to talk to him. It went wrong. I got stuck with him.'

His head swivels as he scans my living room, eyes wide. 'So where is he now?'

'With a friend – the other voice you heard on the tape.'

He gawps at the empty screen again, then at me.

'But it's kidnapping, Cyn. You'll have to go to the police.'

I squirm. 'Philip argues that it isn't. He wanted me to take him. It wasn't against his will so how can you call it kidnapping?'

'But he's a baby, not responsible for himself. You took him from his parents who were undoubtedly very bloody unhappy about it.'

'Not responsible? Try telling *him* that.'

Robert looks at me steadily. 'It's a thin argument, Cyn. I wouldn't like to have to test it in court.' And as my mouth turns down he adds, 'You realise it'll probably come to that?'

'Of course,' I snap. 'D'you think I don't know the trouble I'm in?'

'So am I now you've told me about it,' he says and swigs at his beer.

I feel my cheeks warming. 'Sorry. Didn't think of that.'

'Oh, well,' he says. 'You'd better spill it all.'

And so I do. Well, the Philip part. Not the playtime-with-Martin part.

At the end he wants to see the tape again. Now that the shock's worn off he watches more closely. 'Jesus,' he says, as it comes to an end. 'He's something else.' He screws up his nose. 'But this angel stuff, and the evolved-beings crap . . . I mean he's amazing, but you don't *believe* it all, do you?'

I make a hand-whiffling gesture. 'I don't know what I think any more.'

'And of course you realise that none of this is going to endear you to Lou,' he reminds me. I look at him blankly. 'Well, the Prestons, having heard from their little prodigy, aren't likely to keep it quiet, are they? And when people start saying, "But how did the kid phone them, he can't talk yet, can he?" then his budding genius is going to be revealed and Lou's going to want to know why you refused to do your story about him in the first place . . .' And he stops to draw breath.

'And then I'll tell her what I told you – that he asked me not to.'

'The kid doesn't pay your wages. Lou does.'

'Oh, Lord,' I sigh.

'Forget the legalities, Cyn, 'cos you're in the shit no matter what,' he decides. 'And the case is so weird you just might get off. I'd play along with the kid. See what happens. You're his friend. He needs you. And he'll be great copy. "Angel baby kidnapper tells all",' he writes in the air with his finger and I shudder. 'Oh, stop being so damn prissy. Go for it.'

As he leaves he waggles his elbows. 'Watch out for falling angels,' he chortles. I poke out my tongue.

EIGHT

Later, at Martin's place, his kiss says he's glad to see me. He draws me inside and plies me with cheerful banter and another of those coffees he makes so well.

I drink it quickly, eager to start. I'm keen to tell him about Philip, too, but it can wait until later. I want to put all the clutter out of my mind first. Immerse myself in his world.

There's a different air about him tonight. The teacher has gone and our intimacy is back. He wastes no time. My eyes close as he begins to slip open the buttons of my silk shirt. I hear the tiny whispers as each disc slips through each satiny opening. And although I didn't mean this to happen again so soon (*oh, no?*) I'm instantly on fire. Silk lies around my feet.

'You seem intent on giving me carpet burn again,' I murmur. His earlobe taste delicious, flavoured by the pungent brew that still lingers on my tongue. I lick and suck and feel him shiver.

'There's a better place than this,' he whispers. 'Come.' He walks away. Not once does he turn his head to see if I follow. He knows I will. His hair swings about his slender waist with each stride, accentuating the dimples atop the curve of each taut buttock. I'm aching with desire as I stumble in his wake.

He ignores the bed in his room and opens another door. I step into its darkness. The space seems empty. 'There's no furniture,' I giggle. 'Did you run out of money?'

'Money has no power in this place,' he says. 'Only the mind.'

'And the body, I hope.' I take a few unsteady steps in the gloom. There are scratchy match-lighting noises and he's touching a tiny flame to the tops of candles atop four ornate gilt candlesticks that stand head high. 'Oooh, that's so-o-o-o pretty,' I breathe. I feel like a three-year-old all aglow in the light of a birthday cake. The tall candleholders are set equidistant from each other, marking out a square.

Martin stands at its centre. The shadows cast by the flickering candles make his face seem hawklike.

'Here,' he commands. The floor is soft and spongy. It is like walking on padded satin. 'Wow, Martin, this is crazy,' I say. The huge cushion I'm standing on is patterned with curving stripes, black and white. I tilt my head and stumble. He reaches out to steady me.

'Don't you see how special this surface is?' he asks. 'It's a spiral, Cyn, a centring place. An entering place. When we make love here, at the spiral's very core, it is love like you've never known before. Deeper, fuller, more profound.'

'I bet you say that to all the girls,' I smirk.

'Cynthia.' His voice seems very distant. 'Stop it. This is a sacred place.'

I shake my head. He is hard to see. I can't understand why I'm having trouble focusing on his face.

He gestures. 'Come on, sit. It's very comfortable.'

Gently, as if he's helping to lower an old lady, he supports me as I wobble to the floor, knees erratic. It is cool and resilient. Like a cat, I lie down and stretch.

'Be still,' says Martin, his voice husky. 'I'll be right back.' I close my eyes for a time and then I hear him. Swish. Rustle. He looms over me in a long hooded cloak, a grandiose sweep of heavy grey silk.

'A dress-up game!' I cry.

His shadowed face is grave. 'I told you before, this is not a game. I want to honour you with a very special experience.'

Mirth slipsides inside my mind. *Go for it, Marty. Woo-hoo!* He kneels, holding something – ribbons and a box. 'I am going to prepare you,' he says and picks up one of the ribbons – a slim, lustrous stream of grey satin. He pulls it, slithering between the pads of his fingers. 'Give me your wrist.'

I watch, entirely without alarm, as he ties the ribbon around my wrist, fixing it in a big shiny bow, one long end trailing. He picks up the second ribbon, waits. Obediently I stretch out my other arm. I feel feeble. 'This is starting to look decidedly kinky, Martin.'

He concentrates on his task. 'You're not nervous, are you?' He's holding my shoulders now. I shake my head. He ties first one wrist, then the other, to the base of two of the tall candlesticks. I am pinioned by the soft strands, arms outspread. I feel no fear. The cowl of his robe slips forward, leaving his face in deep shadow.

Then, without touching me (*oh, please touch me*), he settles himself cross-legged beside me. 'We're going to meditate together now, Cyn,' he says. 'Looking again for the path that leads to the Signal Thread.'

'Like the other night?' My lips feel thick and the words roll in my mouth.

'Yes,' he says. 'Are you comfortable?'

'Hmm.' A hum is all I'm capable of.

'Relax then. Relax.' He breathes the word out softly so that the 'a' became a sigh and the 'x' sounds like a kiss.

'Breathe slowly and deeply. Feel your feet, your lower legs, your knees, your thighs, relax. Loosen all the muscles at your hips and waist, feel the warmth creep up through your stomach into your chest. Relax your back . . . and shoulders . . . let your arms lie back as if they weigh no more than a bird's feather. Feel all the tension drain out of your face and scalp and neck. Yes . . . that's right. You're doing wonderfully.'

I'm almost numb, eyelids lead-weighted. Sinking into a sea of warm oil. Fleeting panic. Where's the deep blue skyspace from last time? This is different. *I might drown.* But then I'm rocking in the long slippery swells. 'Now we're off.' His voice is shimmying at me from miles away.

'Join me, Cyn, take your mind into the spiral,' he whispers. I feel like a human arrow now, long and lithe and supple. My arms above my head are joined and pointed and I roll around a black slippery curve, gathering speed.

Once or twice I've ridden one of those curly plastic

slides at a swimming pool, riding the rushing water through endless tubular curves, borne in a gleeful headlong rush to the big blue pool below. This is similar, but much slower, more greasy. Inexorable. No way to stop. And no friendly, clear-blue chlorinated splash lies at the bottom. Nothing but darkness.

The tube is a downward spiral, slowly pulling tighter and tighter in a velvety squeeze. I am a snake, snug within its sinuous skin. I am inside the stamen of a dark, exotic flower, in a silk-lined vein that caresses every inch of me as I slip deeper into the bloom towards its black, fragrant heart.

And there's the crowd again. I can't see them this time but I know they're there with me. Cacophonous, as before. A roar of approval. Muted though. They're crooning. *They like me.* And they're *touching* me. Other fingers stroke and pat.

I thrum with sensation. Far off, Martin is making a monotonous, rhythmic sound. Then he falls silent. And he is standing at my feet unfolding something grey and gauzy. His hands flip wide, as if he is floating a big square cloth over a table, and a mist of grey tulle descends to settle itself over and around me. *Like a web.* I can feel it over my face. Its tiny holes fracture the candlelight into galaxies of minute stars.

Martin lifts the edge of the gauzy coverlet, crawls underneath and pulls it back over us both. He is naked now and we are marooned together under the silvery transparent cloud. Now he smoothes and nips and caresses. I am open to him, but he holds back. Oh, it is strange, very strange, but I'm gone far, far within myself, conscious now of nothing but wanting. 'Oh, yes!' I moan.

Now my head is spinning. No, *he* is spinning, constantly changing position as he devotes himself to me. He is moving about me in a crouching embrace, the tulle membrane that forms the roof of our gauzy tent sliding over his back as he turns round and round.

I protest muzzily. 'What are you doing?' I can't tell what part of him is where as he slips about me, round and round, his fingers and tongue tipping and stroking and probing. Oh, wild. Hot. Molten. And the voices are louder now, roaring, sniggering, laughing, *jeering. They're watching!*

And suddenly, for some reason, Jimmy Lightbody's face, forbidding, shimmers for a moment in my head. And an echo of a baby's voice, whispering in my ear. *There's one spider who throws a silken veil of thread over his partner before they mate. He's very romantic . . .*

Nausea now. Leaden in my gut. No more wild joy. I am naked and exposed. My arms and shoulders, held for so long in one position, start to hurt.

'Martin,' I whisper. It is still hard to speak. My tongue lolls.

I try to raise my head to peer at him through the tickly sheet. I blow at it ineffectually. He whips it away, tossing it aside into a scratchy grey heap. The room, Martin, the candles, now loom in cold clarity. His face is remote as he kneels between my legs. My knees are spread. I want to close them now and turn away, hiding myself. But I can't move!

He is holding the box. His eyes are closed and he is

murmuring again, on and on, as he slowly raises it high as if making an offering to some god.

He lowers it and his eyelids click open. He smiles, opens the box's lid and reaches inside. When his hand comes out the fingertips are curved downwards, tips just touching as if holding something precious. He reaches out to a point just above my breasts and opens his fingers. A large spider plops into the pale valley.

Oh, Jesus. My flesh crawls and I open my mouth to scream. 'Be still!' Martin growls.

I suck in breath, a rasp of terror, as the spider sways, brown and plump. It turns slowly and I feel tiny prickling sensations as its feet seek purchase. It takes one step and then another to the edge of my ribcage and on down over my stomach. Vortex is crouched between my thighs, eyes glistening as the arachnid lurches towards him.

The tiny scratch of a spider foot slipping on the rim of my navel shocks me out of paralysis. 'Get it off me!' I scream. I wrench and kick, my heel smacking Vortex in the face as I heave to get rid of the small, loathsome weight.

The tall candlesticks wobble. One tips and falls as I convulse. Vortex is sprawled on the floor. The spider scuttles under the pile of grey gauze. I yank at the ribbons, snapping at a trailing end with my teeth. One hand comes free and I'm on my feet, fumbling at the other wrist.

I stagger to the door, flailing at the handle. My clothes are crumpled on the living room floor. I haul on pants and top, buttons awry, jamming underclothes into my bag. I feel sick, stupid and ashamed.

There is a rustle and I whirl, backing away. Vortex stands by the bedroom door, hands clasped to his breast. The dark tips of many legs protrude from between his fingers.

'Don't come near me,' I quaver, stamping feet into my sandals.

He has pulled on his wrinkled robe. His hair is tangled and ropelike. I snort with disgust.

'Don't you snigger at me,' he warns. 'No one laughs at me. And nobody desecrates the sacred ceremony the way you have done.'

'Sacred? What the hell were you trying to prove?'

Vortex opens his hands to let the spider stand on his palm. 'She's a symbol. Weaver of the Signal Thread. The one with her foot on the strand, the one who feels each and every vibration. We honour her. You must too if you want to partake of the Signal's strength.'

'You're ill. You need to see somebody.'

'Don't cross me, Cyn,' Vortex calls after me. 'I'm powerful.'

I slam the door and stumble down to the street. My insides churn. I try to walk a straight line along the pavement, fingers trailing along shop windows to keep my balance. A gap appears between buildings, a mini-park filled with shrubs and flowers, and I lean over and vomit into a bed of pretty flowers. A couple pass by, their footsteps quickening, the woman trailing disdain.

Shakily, I wipe the drool away. There's a women's lavatory over the road. No one else inside. I fill a basin with water, strip off and scrub at the skin where the spider has trodden. Then I dab myself dryish with paper towels and dress properly, replacing all the garments I didn't have time for before. It feels better to be encased in the normalcy of cotton and elastic and silk. Myself again.

In the smeared mirror above the basins I look wild and wretched. I wipe at the streaked face and dab on more colour, straighten the sweaty tangles of my hair with wet fingers. That'll do. I find an idle cab at the corner and fall into its back seat.

The driver's one of those talkers. 'Had a good evening? Me, I've had a shit of a night. The moon must be full or somethin'. All sorts of drunks and crazies out tonight.'

'Yes,' I say. 'I know.'

At home I lock my door, make sure the windows are shut tight, and crawl into bed. Very early the next morning, I'm dragged out of heavy sleep by the phone. It rings and rings. I lie in the half-light, mouth full of gall, comforting quilt up to my chin. And listen.

I'm tottery at get-up time. A week ago, life was rational. Now, the landscape I used to trust is beginning to shift and distort. I bare toothpaste-foamy teeth in the mirror, sneering at myself. I was a fool even to dip a toe into Martin's domain. And with a dark red rush I'm remembering the tube and its awful *suckiness*, the way I slipped inside ... and all at once I'm giddy again. I bend to put my head down and find myself on the floor, the blouse I planned to wear crushed beneath me. *What's happening?* Shit, what if it keeps *on* happening?

I sit up and lean against the bathroom wall, elbows on my knees to stop them trembling. It's Thursday. I should be at work. But I need to talk to someone. I've already unloaded enough on to Robert. And I don't want to tell him about this. It's too embarrassing. So who? Lightbody, damn it, is the only person I can think of.

I phone the office to say I won't be in ('I still feel like death'), and then I'm in the car on the way to Lightbody's house.

The hibiscus blooms are huge and sheened with morning dew as I knock on the door. The old man appears, dishtowel in hand. His lean face crinkles with welcome. 'Ah, good morning, Miss Moon.'

He ushers me in, and pulls out a chair at the table. 'Have you had breakfast?' I wrinkle my nose. 'But you must,' he insists.

He puts a small plate of fruit and a knife before me. I demolish an orange and then he brings hot, golden toast and butter and honey and good coffee. The mug warms my hands. 'Thank you. I feel about a hundred per cent better.'

He spins a chair to straddle it, arms folded. His voice is soft. 'You're not well?'

I look into my coffee. 'Philip,' I start and then I look up. 'Where is he?'

Lightbody waves a don't-worry hand. 'Hidden away at my neighbour's house. It's empty there. Quiet. He likes being alone.'

'That tape you made . . . I still can't decide what to do with it. I can't be responsible for him. I'm almost thinking it would be better to go to some government office or welfare agency, where they can decide what's best for him.'

Lightbody shudders, disapproving. 'You must not hand him over to anyone in authority. He brings his own.'

I hunch up, not wanting to hear this. 'I don't understand,' I complain. 'Not any of it.'

'You will.'

I pull a face. 'You're always so damn sure about everything.' And I'm just about to launch into what happened last night when he gets up and kicks the chair into place with a clatter. 'What you need is a beach trip. I'll get Philip. We'll all go.' He pauses. 'Should you be at work?'

'Not now. I called in sick. But I've got an appointment at seven tonight.'

He promises to get me back in time and tells me to make some sandwiches while he goes to get Philip. I'm happy to take orders. Content to put off my confession. And I don't want to be at home by myself.

Philip bestows a kiss on my cheek when we meet in Jimmy's garage. He has the grace not to ask why I'm here as I help him into the back seat. 'You'll have to keep your head down,' I warn him. 'In case you're seen. And anyway, babies are supposed to be strapped in.'

'I know,' he says. 'A very good idea it is too. Mankind is improving matters in some respects.'

Lightbody's car glows rosily, all hot-breath shine and

chrome fenders. I ask him if it's running okay now. For a curious moment he looks shamefaced. It makes me wonder whether Sunday's mechanical glitch was real. But in a second he's merely proud and pleased and dusts the windscreen with his sleeve. 'Yep. Just a little battery trouble. Thirty years young, is Geraldine. Fleet as a gazelle.' He slaps her pink flank. 'Let us away, Miss Moon.'

'Everyone else I know calls me Cyn,' I protest as he swings behind the wheel.

'I prefer Miss Moon,' he says firmly. 'It's a matter of respect. Now me, I'm different, just an ordinary old geezer. Jimmy's right for me, not Mr Lightbody.' He pats the worn vinyl of my seat. 'Relax now. Sleep. There's a pillow under the seat.'

He drives on. Geraldine burbles, her speed more flaccid than fleet. Jimmy turns on to the main route north. Philip sings to himself in the back. I wedge the pillow against the window and drift off.

Awake suddenly. Metal chips ping and rattle underneath the car. Where are we? Geraldine is bumping along a gravel road in a green, unfamiliar valley. A narrow creek coils through paddocks, its banks fringed with white arum lilies. Brown and white cows chomp at shaggy pasture.

'I thought it was time we went to Hokianga,' the old man is saying. 'I want to show you that the realms you're beginning to explore can be productive. That what I told you the other day is truth, not trickery.'

'Oh, Jimmy.' I'm dismayed. I was expecting a picnic and paddling. 'Why didn't you ask me first?'

'Don't worry,' he says. 'You don't have to do anything. Nothing will harm you. Just wait and watch and see.'

'Wait for what?' I'm grumpy now.'

'No idea,' he grins.

And whistling between his teeth, he swings down a narrow track, steers the pink Plymouth around the side of a hill and pulls up outside a sprawling weatherboard farmhouse. It hasn't seen paint for years. A wide verandah flossied with wooden lacework runs along the front of the house. It stands on a knoll overlooking a sheltered jade-green bay.

Alice is a tall rangy woman in a cotton print dress, her long greying hair in braids wrapped about her head. Norm ('We went to school together,' Jimmy explains) wears dungarees strained over a generous paunch. They accept me with easy warmth and hug Philip. No questions are asked. There's an assumption that he's mine.

We sit on the front steps. Bees nuzzle at the throats of blowsy pink roses. There is talk of the price of milkfat and last week's neighbourhood wedding and how the fishing is this year. Alice slaps her knees and declares she'll rustle up some lunch.

'No need,' says Jimmy. 'We brought our own.'

'Get away with you,' says Alice and spreads a table with cold lamb and just-picked tomatoes and thick-sawn bread. I add the food we've brought and we tuck in. I'm ravenous now . . .

'Long way for a day trip,' says Norm.

'Well,' says Jimmy, 'Miss Moon and I just felt like it. She turned up at my place this morning looking a bit peaky and we just decided to take off, didn't we?' He looks at me, bright-eyed.

'You hijacked me,' I grumble.

'One place Miss Moon's never been to is the northern side of the harbour. She's got this hankering to see the sandhills up close. Any chance of borrowing your boat, Norm?'

I squirm out of my chair, alarmed. 'I didn't say that,' I protest, stacking dirty plates. 'And it's late.'

'Aw, go on. What's a few more hours?' cajoles Norm. 'You can't come all this way and just turn around again. I'll take you over myself. You coming, girl?' he asks Alice.

'No, I've got things to do. And leave those dishes now.'

Tide is buffeting against wind as we thump towards the vast golden sandhills across the harbour in Norm's study fishing boat. We gaze up at humpy ochre ridges as we near the northern shore. Fine grains streamer from the tops of the sand-swamped dunes. Norm eases back on the throttle and his old Evinrude burps. The boat drifts into the beach in the sudden quiet.

'Shall we walk?' Jimmy suggests when we're all on shore. There's nothing else to do on the bare strand. I jam my hands in my pockets and stride off in the direction of the harbour mouth where the shifting sandbars are marked by white lines ruled upon the blue of the open sea. 'Many ships have come to grief out there,' says Jimmy. 'One full of corpses. A hundred years ago Chinese miners working the gold down south saved up to send back home the remains of men who died in the mines. But the ship hit the sandbar out there,' Jimmy nods at the distant surf, 'and the ship went down with eighty-odd coffins. And the crew.'

We trudge on. 'And it's special for Maori people,' Jimmy adds. 'The great explorers who crossed the Pacific a thousand years ago . . . they drew their canoes up here too.'

Broken shells crunch underfoot on the hard sand below high-water mark. The sea shifts restlessly. After a while I turn to look back. The air is very still, shimmering with heat. Norm is just a dark blob, hunkered down on the beach. Philip toddles in the shallows well behind us.

I'm thirsty. 'Isn't this all a bit pointless, Jimmy? There's nothing here.'

'Very well,' he says without rancour, turning on his heel. 'Let's go back.'

As we near the boat, Philip approaches, face glowing, trotting as fast as he can but awkwardly because he's holding something in both hands.

His small chest is heaving as he comes straight to me. 'Look,' he breathes. His chubby fingers are wrapped around a circular pearly white stone. In its centre is a smoothly worked hole. Carved grooves radiate out from the hole to the perimeter and there are transverse lines too, spiralling in . . . A spider's web stone. It is no more than an inch through but as wide as my hand, weathered almost smooth, the edges of the grooves worn down by time and sand.

'It was calling,' he says. 'Not for me. For you.'

Unwillingly, my hand goes out. The baby drops the

rock into my cupped flesh, then backs away. I stand still, anchored by the stone while the old man and the baby watch my face. Grit in my palm. The tide surges, a ripple sneaking up the beach to lap about my feet before receding with a sigh.

'Well?' says Jimmy.

I am stunned because I swear it just throbbed, inside, like the beat of a heart. Just once. 'It's only a rock,' I say but there's a tremor in my voice. I turn the drab thing over.

'Not that one,' says Jimmy. 'It's not just a rock. Never was. Never will be. May I?'

He takes it carefully. Heaves a deep, ragged breath. His eyes tear. 'It has waited here for you. You must keep it.'

I'm quivering inside. 'I don't want it.' But he hands it back to me, slaps his skinny thighs and calls across the barren sand: 'Norm! Time to go . . .' And he picks up Philip and strides off, leaving me to follow with my burden while the angel's eyes watch me, bright and wide, over Jimmy's bony shoulder.

Norm is quite fascinated by the stone. 'Will you look at that?' he mutters. 'Lots of old artifacts wash up here. Maori stuff and white man's junk too.' He rumbles with laughter. 'Some high falutin' joker built a mansion on this beach back in the early days. The sand came and covered it up, grand piano, chandeliers and all. So you find the odd silver spoon in the sand. But,' and he hefts the stone, 'never seen anything like this before.

'Know what it reminds me of? Local tribe had a wise

old man here a few years back. Used to yarn with me for hours, full of Maori folklore. He was into spirals. You seen 'em on Maori canoe prows?' Norm holds up a flat, brown thumb. 'He reckoned they mirrored man's uniqueness - just like your fingerprint, eh?

'And he thought God made spiders' webs to help us muse on the notion, too. *Wharepungawerewere.* Spiders' webs. How's that for a mouthful?' he chortles as he pushes the boat off the sand.

We speak little on the drive back to Auckland. I tuck the stone into my bag next to my feet. It seems to lean against my ankle and I keep shoving it away. Back at Jimmy's, I get out of the car and watch as he checks that no one's there before he helps Philip out. 'Aren't you lonely by yourself?' I ask before Jimmy takes him to his hiding place in the house next door.

'Never,' he assures me. And gives me his usual swift, sweet kiss.

Jimmy is back within minutes. 'Are you happy to drive home?'

His paternalism grates – I'm sort of grateful for his concern, but irritated too. And I'm being dismissed. If I don't tell him about Vortex now, I never will. 'Can I come in for a minute?' I suggest and he ushers me inside.

I sit and wait in his living room, while he potters in the kitchen, making a hot drink. The sun casts a low, soft glow through the window. Jimmy's quiet clatters and shuffles make me homesick for the warmth and safety of childhood. I wish he'd stay there quietly so I can just sit and soak up the comfort. But now, here he is. One of his knees clicks as he sits down. He rubs it absently, intent upon me.

I can't return his gaze so I look at my tight-locked hands in my lap instead. 'I came here this morning to talk to you,' I start. 'Something bad happened to me last night. The Signal Thread . . .'

I hear a tight noise in his throat, feel the chill of his disapproval. And then I'm appalled to find my mouth contracting. 'Oh, damn,' I wail. 'I hate crying. I go all snotty.'

Jimmy gets up to find a box of tissues. He sits down to listen without speaking. It's hard to voice it all. When I've finished, I wipe my nose childishly with the back of my hand. 'What really gets to me,' I snuffle, 'is that after having seen someone like Evan O'Keefe, and after what you said, I still got sucked in. I was ready to do anything he asked. I *did* do anything he asked. It was only when he brought out the spider that I snapped out of it.'

I make myself check Jimmy's face. He seems almost stricken.

He springs up and paces the floor, hands waving. 'It's so dangerous, you could have . . .' His voice tails away. 'You are under his dominion now.'

Fear churns inside me. 'That sounds so old-fashioned.'

'Old words work best,' he grumbles. 'You are in thrall to him. It's an old-fashioned thing. That brew of his was probably full of sorcerer's herbs to make you more biddable.' *Oh, come on, Jimmy . . . sorcery?* Then he demands, 'What else are you planning?'

I tell him about the test I'm setting up this evening with Miranda Lewis.

'Don't,' he says.

'I have to.' My voice rises. 'My job's on the line here.' Silence. 'Oh, Jimmy,' I sigh. 'I didn't come here to be growled at. I thought you might help me make sense of it.'

He pulls at an ear. 'I doubt that I can. Except to say that Vortex and his ilk seem to have learned how to tap into the great web of energy that surrounds the world. They're sucking at its lifeforce instead of working to nourish it. They're on quite the wrong track. The web has the power to enrich humanity, not debase it.'

'But Philip blabs away about webs and spiders too, just like Martin does,' I say in despair. 'And he's not evil.'

For the first time, Jimmy gives me a small smile. 'See. You know that already.'

He sends me away then. Says I must do some thinking. Tells me I can't walk in the darkness and the light at the same time. Whatever that means. That I should have nothing else to do with the Signal Threaders. I try to offload the spiral stone on him, but he won't allow it. I need it, he says. And he repeats his admonition of the day before – that I must give myself spiritual protection. *Hah.* Imagine telling Lou that I have to ditch this story because I'm vulnerable to spooks. I know what she'd say. Get bloody real.

All the same, on the way to Miranda Lewis's, I try to remember the Lord's Prayer. It comes out garbled. It's a long time since Sunday School. 'Oh, hell,' I mutter. 'Just look after me, please.'

NINE

Miranda Lewis's apartment building is on the coast and looks like the sort of house a child builds from plastic blocks – all odd angles and sharp colours. The weathered wooden deck outside the door looks out upon the steely Pacific.

I press the buzzer. When the door opens, it's a struggle to keep my hello-smile steady. The woman who stands there has a pantomime face. She's been heavy-handed with the blusher. It's meant to make her pretty. But her skin has been so stretched by some surgeon's needlework that there's no life left. When she smiles, her mouth slides into a crooked lurch. Thin blue veins lie in a frozen squirm beneath the skin at her temples.

She tucks a long strand of platinum hair behind an ear whose lobe is dragged low by an ornate silver hoop. My $65, the agreed fee, slips into the pocket of her green silk robe.

'It's good of you to see me at such short notice,' I say as I follow her frail figure up polished wooden stairs.

The thin shoulders shrug. 'The time was available.'

We climb to a round turret room that looks out over

the beach and suburban sprawl. The room is furnished
with red carpet and plump floor cushions in shades of
red and white.

Lewis seats herself cross-legged on one of the cushions.
Even in the low light of dusk there's a nasty discordance
going between her green silk dress and the scarlet floor.
I see without surprise, a swirling spiral painted on an
open window. Out on the beach a tractor is raking
up litter. We talk for half an hour. I've heard all
the spiral-babble before, from Martin, but I work at
sounding keen, asking lots of questions. 'Tell me,'
I urge, 'is it really true that Signal Threaders can
communicate from a distance by tuning in with their
minds? I met someone recently who told me he can
do that.'

Lewis sits very still, calm but cautious. 'Yes, it's
possible.'

'Could you attempt it for me now, so I can get a
feeling for it?'

Lewis gazes at the darkening sky. 'Oh, I don't know,'
she says slowly.

I keep pushing. 'I know he's probably meditating
right now. This time in the evening is when he's tuned
in. It'd be really remarkable if you could contact him.'

Lewis rubs her knees. Her nails are fibreglass talons.
The only ornamentation is a silver spiral painted upon
the horny curve of a thumb nail. 'Will you write about
it in your article if I succeed?'

'Yes, of course. It would prove to doubters how real
the whole experience can be.'

Her crooked smile is cold. 'And if nothing happens?

What if you receive no proof of contact? Will you then get out your sharp little pen and write nastily about a crazy lady who talks a lot of baloney?'

I opt for nonchalance. 'If it doesn't work, it doesn't work. He might not be listening right now. But it's just such a wonderful opportunity. I mean, I know he's adept. I believe you are, too.' The flattery falls softly and is accepted.

Lewis shifts on her haunches. 'Very well, I'll try. Do you have a message, or do you want to ask him something?'

'I suppose ... I'd just like to let him know that I'm here and still working on the story. And instead of using my name, how about just trying to describe me?' I touch my shoulder. 'This brooch I'm wearing. I think he'll recall it.'

Lewis looks sceptical. 'Maybe. Let me hold it.' I unpin the spider and pass it over. 'Do you have anything which belongs to the man you want to reach?'

I find the magazine clipping I've brought. It shows Martin at a fashion parade, champagne glass in hand. His smile blazes. The black hair shines. 'Will this do?' I'm hoping she doesn't know him. There's no sign of recognition as she studies the scrap of glossy paper. She holds the brooch and the picture on her knees, one under each palm. She begins to breathe, deep and slow, gazing at the spiral upon her window. Then the eyes droop and her head dips, the pale hair draping slowly down until it hides the awful young-old face.

I sit still, staring. My bottom aches from sitting too

LINDSEY DAWSON

long. The turret creaks as its roof contracts in the cooling air.

Minutes pass. Then Miranda Lewis shudders. Her right foot jerks. Her whole body convulses and her mouth gapes, the eyes staring, cords rigid in the aging neck. She drools a little. 'Aaaaarh,' she howls.

I scrabble in shock, pushing away from her. She quivers on the floor. Green on red. Leaves on blood. Then, as suddenly as it began, the spasm ends. Her mouth snaps shut. There's a tiny thud as the silver spider tumbles to the carpet. She hugs herself, eyes closed tight, the smeary cherry mouth compressed.

I'm up now, back against the wall. My voice wobbles, 'Are you okay?'

Lewis's eyes are streaming, the mascara forming grey bowls of murk that spill over to dribble down fragile cheeks. She looks as if she's been slapped. 'Oh, such power,' she keens.

Then, at last, her eyes clear. She pulls a tissue from her sleeve and blows her nose copiously. 'Help me.' She reaches out a hand and I feel the bones beneath the sweaty skin as I haul her upright. 'That man,' she croaks. 'He's frightened of you.'

I'm stunned.

'He's like a lighthouse broadcasting out there. I was the moth. Sucked in. Bam!' She smacks a fist into an open palm and begins pacing the small room. 'And then, I started projecting an image of you and that silver spider . . . and, he went wild. What happened between you two?'

She points a craggy finger. 'You rejected him. Nobody's

done it to him before. That's why he's fearful. Somewhere deep inside you is some powerful magic. He doesn't like that.' Lewis is looking stronger now. 'And I don't think I like it either.' She moves closer. Her breath is sour. 'Did you come here trying to catch me out?'

I hiccup, tense and nauseous. 'I was looking for information.'

'Don't give me that crap, Ms Moon!' She's on the attack now, hands on her hips. 'You don't even believe in the power, you stupid bitch! You don't know what you're capable of!'

I explode. 'At least I know the whole damn thing's sick, okay? You're all crazy, you know that? Sick and crazy! I'm going!'

'You're damn right you are! I want you out of my house. Right now!' She hustles me down the stairs, pushes me out and slams the door. There's a ghostly tinkle as the vibration shakes a windsong hanging on strings under the eaves.

I almost run to the car, lock myself in and switch on the engine, jabbing at the air-conditioning controls. I need to sit for a while, face thrust into the frigid artificial breeze before I'm steady enough to drive. And then (it's *all* I need) I see the tank's almost empty, so I stop for petrol. And as I wait, fingers drumming, at the counter for the guy to zip-zap my card, I hear a news update on the radio he has prattling in the corner. 'The police search for kidnapped baby Philip Preston intensified today . . .' I hear as I shakily scrawl my name on the credit-card slip. 'Have a nice evening,' says the Shell man as I scuttle out, face burning.

My phone is ringing as I unlock my door. It's Lou, working late at the office, all aquiver. 'Vortex! He just rang me. He wanted to know what the hell you're up to. I started to huff and puff and he tells me you're interfering. Says you're playing games with another Signal Threader. And he mentioned your brooch! It's incredible, Cyn. He really *can* tune in.'

Lou sounds very excited. It gives me a bad feeling. 'So it works. It doesn't mean it's a good thing.'

'But perhaps it could be? The fact that people can do this doesn't mean they're evil. If we leap to that conclusion, we're no better than witch-hunters.'

'Did he say that?'

'Well, yes, but it's a good point.'

'But Lou . . .' Okay. Time to say it. 'I think it's evil. It destroys people.'

She snorts. 'Get off the grass, Cyn. Evil's in fairy stories. What brought this on?'

Good question, Lou. Nothing. Everything. *The stuff you don't know about.* I rattle, 'The woman went into a trance and had convulsions and then threw me out. It was very unpleasant.'

'Was she aware of contacting Vortex?'

'Yes.'

'Really?' Lou's fascinated. 'What words did she use?'

'Why?'

'So we can compare what *he* said with what *she* said.' Louisa's tone is the sort you use to an obtuse child.

'She didn't use any actual words. She just . . . fell apart.'

'Oh, come on. You never get upset like this.'

138

I grit my teeth. 'I'm not upset, I'm bloody terrified. The more I get into this story, the more it gives me the creeps. I'm not going to whitewash it, Lou.'

'Jesus,' says Lou in disbelief. 'And I thought you had your head screwed on. For God's sake, go get a stiff drink and finish the story off. One more thing,' she is saying. 'Martin said he had something to tell you. He said, "Tell her I have her here in my hand."'

'What the hell does that mean?'

'He said you'd know.'

I roll my eyes. 'I've got work to do, Louisa.'

'Yes, you have. And don't go all sanctimonious on me. People love this sort of stuff, Cyn. Telepathy works! No wonder it's blowing people's minds. Write about it.'

We hang up on each other. I crash on to my bed. What a flip-flop she's done. Hey, Lou, didn't this all start with wanting to expose the Signal Thread as a con-job? Mind you, I have to admit to myself, that's how I thought too until I got the idea that it was the best thing since LSD. Not now. Flip-flops all over. Everything has changed. Lou just wants a story. I want my life back.

Jeff and Shirley are starring on page one again the next morning. 'Who could be so cruel?' shrieks the headline over their picture. Shirley's woeful. Jeff's snarling.

'*Pranksters are making Jeff and Shirley's Preston's life a misery.*' reads the story. '*Yesterday they received a phone call from a young child claiming to be their son and saying he had to leave home because he had a job to do.*'

'*"It's garbage," says the furious father. "The really sickening thing is that someone has persuaded a kid to make that call.*

They might have thought it was one hell of a joke but we're not laughing.' Meanwhile, the phones are ringing at police headquarters as the public call in with information. And unconfirmed reports say that the kidnapper left clear footprints at the back of the house outside baby Philip Preston's window . . .'

Filled with dread, I take a detour on my way to work, driving miles off my usual route to a supermarket car park where I remember seeing a charity collection bin for old clothes. Into it goes a heap of the stuff I sorted out last Sunday and the running shoes I wore on Monday night. I keep remembering the damp night, the smell of mint, the soft ground. And I'm really scared. So I dump the shoes. But I can't dump all my shoes. Can't cut my damn feet off. Who knows what telltale signs you leave behind in the way you wear down your footwear? Haven't I read somewhere that they can tell height and weight and even what sex you are from your footprints? And what if there was something on the soles of my shoes, trapped in the tread, that might come off, might give me away? Gravel from my driveway, fluff from my carpet. Anything.

I feel hollow and anxious as I sit at my desk. Robert's radiating suppressed excitement. He might as well have a sticker on his chest that reads, 'I've got a secret.'

He wheels himself close, trundling from his desk to mine, still seated in his chair.

'What're you going to do?' he says. And without waiting for an answer, he whispers, 'I've got an idea.'

'For God's sake, Robert,' I say, shuffling papers, trying to look nonchalant. 'Relax. You look as if you're trying to pass me state secrets.' All sorts of weird stuff goes on in open-plan offices. Whispered conversations. Bursts of giggling. But air conditioning and the hum of electronics keep things private unless you're shouting. I glance around. No one seems to be taking notice of our little huddle.

'Take this,' Robert's saying, sliding two small dark blue books in front of me. 'They're Kath's and Billie's,' he mutters.

I stare at them. 'I can't take your wife's passport,' I hiss.

'She won't know. There's all sorts of stuff she still hasn't come back for yet. If she asks for it I'll tell her I haven't seen it.' He flips the cover with his finger. 'Look. It's you. I've always thought you could be twins.'

Well, close enough to fool a busy passport desk officer. Hair's shorter and fairer, the mouth somehow different. She wears scarlet lipstick I wouldn't be seen dead in. But it's passably me. 'And Billie,' he's saying. 'D'you remember I took him to see my mother in Sydney a few months back? I had to get him a passport. He was the same age then as your friend is now. Go on.' And he nudges me with it.

I open the cover. A baby face stares out. Robert's baby, but any baby really. Pudgy. A pale blob. Wispy hair, like Philip's. Too young yet for much of a personality to have marked itself upon the features.

I look at Robert. 'Take him away,' he urges. 'He wants the big time. Give it to him. And make a name for yourself at the same time. Go see Dave Oakes in LA.'

I look at him blankly. 'You know,' he says irritably, 'Dave. With the big talk show. Huge ratings. I knew him years ago. Your kid wants exposure. Dave can give him that.' I say nothing, thinking. Robert moves closer. 'I've got a friend close to the investigation, Cyn. He tells me someone in the Prestons' street was up that night. Looking out. Now they're looking for a blue or green car. And did you hear about the footprints?'

I stare at him. 'Well then,' he says, and slides back to his own workspace. I get up and go to the window which looks out on to the staff car park. My Honda sits down there. I've always liked its pearlised aqua colour. Not quite blue. Not green either. I turn to look into Lou's office. Her door is open. Desk empty. Oh, yeah. Friday sales meeting.

'I'll be in touch,' I tell Robert.

And I pick up bag and car-keys and am gone, telling the front-desk woman that I'm heading for home, feeling ill (which is not in fact far from the truth). 'Have you still got that bug?' she sympathises. 'Hope you're better on Monday.'

I hope everything will be better on Monday.

Next stop, a bank. I draw all the money out of my cheque account and nearly everything from savings as well. The transaction will be noted later, of course, but I intend to be long gone by then.

Then, at the local travel shop, Kath Finian buys tickets to LA for herself and kid, leaving tonight. Family crisis, I explain to the reservations guy, who couldn't care less.

I need hair that looks more like the crop in Kath's passport photo. I glance up and down the street. There's an unpretentious salon just a few doors along, its front window shiny black in the sunshine. As I look, some trick of the light makes the glass seem to shimmer and suck. For just a second my head swims. I shove the muzziness away. Calm down, Cyn, it's just stress. Move yourself. The salon seems almost empty as I push through the door.

A delicate boy seats me at a basin, tucks the towel around my neck, drapes me with a plastic cape, and pulls a lever on the seat to tip me back, neck on the basin lip. The phone rings. He mutters an apology, trips off to answer it. I wait, uncomfortably.

Fingers rake back my hair. The brisk, professional preparation for shampooing. But there's something intimate about this touch. Too slow and lingering.

'Why Cyn,' says Martin Vortex, leaning over me. 'There you are. Isn't it odd? I was just thinking about you. And you seemed so close it was as if I could reach out and touch you.' I gape upwards, eyes rolling with shock as he smiles his sharp smile and turns on taps. 'It's all right,' he calls to the boy. 'I'll take this client.'

His hand presses on my forehead from behind, holding me down. Hot water torrents over my scalp. Supine in the chair, feet off the ground, I'm helpless under his sluicing. I can't *believe* this.

'I've just bought this place,' he says conversationally. 'It was time I opened a second salon. Horrid little set-up, isn't it? Ghastly decor. But it's got good potential. I'll tart it up, get the staff jumping. It'll start pumping cash flow. Signallers can't stand still, you know, Cyn. Ever expanding, ever growing!'

The towel around my neck is too tight. He chats on in lilting tones. 'Feeling better, are you? You were in a state when you left the other night. Been busy since then, too, haven't you? Messing about with that crazy Miranda bat. Really, you could have found someone smarter than her to play your silly games with.'

I hear the glutinous squirt of shampoo squeezing from a nozzle. Vortex begins lathering. His fingers slide and scrub. 'Still, the message got through despite it all. It was interesting talking with your boss afterwards. She sounds most amenable, I must say.'

Push, push, he goes with the foam. Around and around the thin-skinned dome of my skull.

Hot water squirts down my face, making me gasp. '*Terribly* sorry,' he smarms, making solicitous dabs with a towel.

'Louisa doesn't seem very impressed with your, um, professional judgement on the Signal Thread,' he goes on. The water's too hot. I struggle to sit up, but he presses my head back, squirts more shampoo, reworks the foam. 'We're meeting tonight actually,' he says. 'She seems quite fascinated by the Signal Thread. We might even try meditating together. She could even prove to be better at it than you, Cyn.'

I lie there, seething, as he rinses off and then attacks me with conditioner, kneading at my scalp now, his fingers hard and painful. 'You're hurting me,' I cry at last. The slim boy is only a few feet away, attending to a pensioner's perm. He turns his head, curious.

Vortex eases off. 'Are we tender today?' he asks, all solicitude.

'No. We are not,' I snap. 'You are pressing too hard.'

'Just the usual, Cyn,' he says airily. 'Just the usual. You have to be firm to do any good.'

He starts up the water flow once more and, ever so gently, rinses my hair for the last time. It squeaks beneath his stroking fingers.

'It's really very pleasing that you should come in here today, Cyn.' he whispers as he leans close to press a towel over my head, soaking up the wetness. 'You were in my mind all morning. And every time I thought I was getting through, some old geezer kept on getting in the way. I couldn't scare him off at all. Who is he, Cyn? Some old fool who's got the hots for you?'

I tear off the towel, heaving myself out of the tilted chair. Martin's laughing and the slim boy goggles as I make for the door with sodden hair, ripping off the plastic cape.

And then I'm in my car, scuttling home. I phone Robert and ask him to do what he can to jack things up with David Oakes before we arrive. My bag gets packed, helter-skelter. I have no idea whether I'm throwing in any clothes that match. And just as I'm snapping it shut, my shoulder twitches. It's as if someone's tapped me there. The itch persists. I scratch, wriggling to reach over to my shoulder blade, and as my chin turns with the movement I spot my beach stone on my bookshelf. The spider's web stone. I put it there when I got home and haven't touched it since. *It wants to go too,* is the weird thought that flares in my head. *What?* But in two strides I've snatched it up and thrown it in with my jumbled mess of gear.

I phone Jimmy and tell him my plan, then spend ten

minutes practising Kath's squiggly signature. The next job is to prop her passport up on my mirror and cut my own hair, scissoring awkwardly until it looks more like her photo. It's rough, but it'll do. I remember, as an afterthought, to throw in my real passport too. Just in case.

There's one last task. Louisa wants the Signal Thread story finished so I'll damn well do it. I sit down at my laptop and type. I make it serious and strong. I know Louisa wants a breezy hey-listen-to-this tone, but I can't be upbeat about this. My encounter with Miranda Lewis was too chilling for that. I write it as it happened, giving Vortex a false name (why give the bastard publicity?) and avoiding any mention of the fact that I was for a short time obsessed with the man. I don't ever want anyone to know about that.

I conclude: *The Signal Thread followers of the '90s are on a trip that is as dangerous as any experienced by LSD trippers in the '70s. But this trip promises to be more seductive, more mind-blowing than any drug can ever be. For getting in touch with the Signal Thread requires no kick-starts from a bottle or a pill – just the willingness to mentally descend down a spiral path into the secret recesses of the mind. And its followers get hooked. When they're plugged in, the rest of the world can go to hell. And that makes the world, for all the rest of us, a more perilous and hostile place in which to live.*

That's it. Done. I push it through my fax to *Maggy*, seeing it in my mind's eye squeezing out of the slit in the office machine. I feel a huge sense of relief.

At Jimmy's, I find he's conjured up a baby buggy from somewhere and packed a bag with the sort of stuff a normal kid would need. Disposables. Bibs. A cuddly toy. 'This is a good idea, Miss Moon. Best to go somewhere less oppressive.'

I don't want to succumb to that idea. 'It's more that LA's better for what Philip wants,' I say as I pick the baby up. 'Are you ready?' I ask him.

'Oh, yes,' he says. 'It'll be most amusing to ride in a 747.'

'Huh. You might be from outer space,' I grump at him, 'but you're still a small boy.'

And later that evening Mrs Finian and her son Billie fly out of New Zealand. There are no questions, no suspicious looks.

The baby is really good on the eleven-hour flight. 'My, aren't you an angel,' gushes a flight attendant as she brings a warmed bottle for him. He gives her back a smile that you could describe as gorgeous or smug, depending entirely on your point of view.

TEN

A bloated sun is wallowing in curry-coloured smog as the plane thuds on to the runway at Los Angeles International Airport. It's dark by the time we're out of Customs. I pick a hotel from the array of pictures on the wall in Arrivals and make a quick reservation. Then we're outside in the kerosene-tainted breeze. Roaring buses and glittery limos and brightly daubed hotel shuttles elbow their way past the terminal.

Our shuttle driver has a small loop of silk flowers and a gilt crucifix dangling from his rear-vision mirror. And as he drives out of the airport on to Sepulveda Boulevard the tiny Y-shape upon the cross swings back and forth, silhouetted against the lights of oncoming cars. Philip looks up from his perch on my knee and gives me a nudge.

Our hotel is a pile of pink-beige concrete scalloped with turquoise balconies. 'Hi, little fella,' beams the desk clerk. Philip goos back at him. 'D'you want a cot sent up, Ms Finian?' For a moment I'm blank. *Wake up, Cyn. That's you.* Don't worry, I tell him. We'll share.

Our room is frosty grey-blue. There is a vast bed. Delighted, Philip rolls around upon its hard-sprung silvery surface while I take a can of frosty beer from the mini-bar and pick up the phone to call Robert. He sends a bunch of reassuring noises down the phone. Tells me that David Oakes is expecting my call and that he's been spun a cover story about how I'm investigating the Signal Thread's origins in California.

I let him know where we're staying which makes me feel better. It helps that at least one person on the globe knows where I am. After I've hung up I watch with a jaundiced eye as Philip tumbles about amongst the pillows, making the bed shake. I'm bushed. And feeling very strange. I have fled my country with someone else's child. I have stolen two passports. I have a limited amount of funds. I am basically in the shit.

'For God's sake, Philip!' I snap as he roly-polies over the bedspread. He sits up, startled, and then goes melty-eyed. 'I'm sorry,' he says. 'It's this age I'm at.'

Now it's my turn to apologise. Of course he has to let off steam. We agree that he should use the other furniture and he bounces happily on the hotel's blue settee, working off energy, while we watch a lot of TV ads which promise to help Californians make money, ease pain and get thin. Between the ads, game-show contestants whoop and holler as they win mountains of glittering cars, giant fridges and trips to Cancun. Every now and again Philip makes tut-tutting noises over the extravagance of it all. Eventually, he tires. I'm vaguely aware of him toddling over to switch off the bedside light and patting the sheet smooth under my chin before I sink into a twitchy sleep.

The sun is well hoisted when I wake up. Philip, of

course, is up already. 'Good morning,' he says, smiling brightly. 'It's a lovely day.' Grumbling in the glare, I see miles of marina berths bursting with boats. Morning breeze has cleared away the smog and the air looks sweet and clean. Candy-coloured cars hum beneath the window.

I order breakfast and take a shower before calling Oakes. He sounds crisp, not unfriendly, which I give him credit for considering I'm a nobody in his world. He and Robert must have been better friends than I thought. He even suggests lunch in Beverly Hills. 'I've got a crazy afternoon,' he says. 'Can't be late.' He suggests midday.

I take Philip for a walk in the morning to give the maids time to clean the room. The plan is to hang a Do Not Disturb on the door so he can stay behind while I check out Oakes.

I arrive early and sit in the lobby for a while, watching polished lengths of limo glide past the front door. David Oakes is easy to spot. He's a little shorter than he looks on TV. His head, with its short-cropped coppery hair, is alert, brown eyes watchful. He reminds me of a good keen dog, buzzy with a fine flow of adrenaline, ready to catch any stick that comes his way.

Doormen nod deferentially as he strides in. He pauses, looks about. Doesn't of course, know who to look for. Simply waits, comfortable within his own famous face, for me to approach him. I do.

'Miss Moon, I presume?' He draws out the vowels with a pursing of his lips. 'Sorry,' he apologises. 'You must get that all the time.'

We shake hands. His grip lasts no longer than necessary.

The maître d' finds us a table in a flash, ignoring patient tourists queuing at the door. They make thrilled noises at the sight of Oakes. Things proceed apace. Iced water sploshes into glasses, menus are flourished and salads arrive.

He offers wine but I'm still a bit lurchy. 'No, thanks. Jet lag. I feel some vital part of me is still struggling on over the ocean like a tired old duck.'

He smiles. 'More like a buzzard in my case.' Teeth shine. Eyes crinkle nicely. He's pale for a Californian, and has freckles which don't show on television.

His face is so familiar that I feel at ease. 'Robert was wildly jealous that I was going to see you. He says we have to have a drink on him.'

'Or two or three,' says Oakes.

'He said that too.'

'I find it so hard to imagine him as a domesticated kind of guy. We had some pretty wild times together. Has he really settled down?'

'Reluctantly. Only because of his boy. He's still very bitter about the way Kath left so suddenly.'

He makes no comment. A sour pull at the side of his mouth says it all. 'And is he happy in his work?'

'Tolerably. Sometimes I think he'd like a bit more excitement in his life.'

Oakes chases the last curl of lettuce on his plate. He eats very fast. 'I couldn't commit to a family at this stage of my life. I'd simply never see them. It's crazy here, you know. Hi, Jerry, how are ya?' he says to a passing suit.

I look around at the hubbub. 'I guess you know most of these people?'

'Some. This is a place where lots of deals get done. Lots of talk. Lots of hype. Lots of bullshit, too.'

Does he mind, I ask, never being able to go anywhere without being recognised? He runs his finger around the rim of his water glass. He has well-shaped hands.

'Most of the time it's not a problem. Fame's pretty addictive. But you crave anonymity, too. Couple of years ago I went off on my own. To Tahiti. I was doing radio talkback then. I sprawled under the palms for a week without a single person saying how the hell are you, Dave, and great show, Dave, and what you think about the President's latest budget initiative, Dave? It was *good*.' He spears a perfect red, round tiny tomato on his fork. 'Soon after that I got a crack at a TV show of my own.' He clenches his fist, a tiny triumphant gesture.

'And is it good?'

He emits a non-committal hum. 'The ratings rule your life.' His expression is a touch defiant. 'And mine haven't been so wonderful lately.'

'Should you tell me that?'

'Probably not,' he says. 'But you're a stranger.'

He keeps on talking, unburdening. 'It's a crazy world. I used to be irritable and frustrated over being stuck in my old job. I was desperate for a slot on TV. Now I've got what I wanted, here I am, still irritable and frustrated.' He changes tack. 'Rob said you're researching the Signal Thread?'

'Yeah,' I lie.

'We know it well,' he says. 'They need exposing. It's one weird outfit,' He sips coffee.

Now, Do it. 'There's something else you might be able to help me with.' I pause. 'Do you ever interview children? As in kids who are exceptionally bright and have worthwhile things to say?'

'Christ, no. There are enough brats waiting in line for my job without encouraging them.' He looks for the waiter, only half-listening to me. 'Why?'

It seems crazy here, amongst the clatter of china and idle chat, to speak of angels. 'Because I know an exceptional child who I think deserves international exposure.' Oakes looks at me neutrally. 'He's just a baby,' I add. 'A tiny tot. But he uses words like "lexicon" and "erudite".'

Déjà vu. I had this conversation ages ago, with Robert, who was not inclined to believe. Oakes isn't either.

He gives me the cold eye over the rim of his cup. 'So, what does he talk about?'

I cast about for the right thing to say. 'He's like a little guru.'

Oakes snickers. 'We've got plenty of them already in California. But go on . . .'

'I'm serious. Philip sits there in his tiny T-shirts with his pudgy legs and big eyes and shiny hair and spouts this stuff that sounds as if he's tuned into wisdom from another time.'

'So why hasn't he had any attention?'

'He hasn't wanted it.'

Oakes looks at me askance. 'You're sure someone's not going to pop up and tell me I'm on *Bloopers and*

Practical Jokes?' I let out a sigh. 'What about his parents?' he asks. 'How do they feel?'

'They're not a problem now.' I twirl the stem of my water glass.

'Now?'

'Philip's . . . arranged . . . to make his own decisions on his future.'

'Ho, ho. A forward-thinking lad.' Oakes leans on his elbows, amused in a superior sort of way. 'Why aren't you writing about him then?' he wants to know.

'I live in a small-cheese country. Philip wants someone like you, with a big network behind him.'

Oakes blinks. 'He's a one-man syndication expert too?'

'Are you interested?'

'Hell, I don't know. All I've got is your say-so.'

'I have a video of him.'

He looks askance at my bag and folds his napkin. 'I don't have time now. Later maybe. We're taping this afternoon. Why don't you come back to the studio?'

I hesitate, thinking of Philip, alone and waiting. 'Take as long as you need,' he'd said this morning as he settled down with a Gideon bible. (He'd looked quite taken aback when I told him he was probably the only person to take it out of the drawer in its whole life.)

'I'll be busy for a while,' says Oakes as he signs the bill. 'But there's plenty of Signal Thread stuff you can look through while you wait if you want.'

His navy BMW bears us to the rectangle bearing his name in the studio's vast parking lot. He whizzes me through security, conjuring up a visitor namecard for my lapel, and we go through dim cavernous studios and along a maze of corridors to a huge shelf-stuffed room where his researchers work. He introduces me to a thin, wiry-haired woman.

'Trix, this is Cynthia Moon, she's a magazine writer and a good buddy of mine from New Zealand. Can you park her in a corner somewhere and give her some background on that Signal Thread outfit?'

Her eyes gleam. 'It'll be my pleasure.'

Oakes is already moving away. 'How about I send someone for you?' he suggests to me. 'We're taping in a couple of hours. You could come and watch if you like.'

'I'll make sure she gets there,' says Trixie. 'You skedaddle.' He does.

Trixie sits me down in a partitioned-off cubicle with a desk, a PC, a VCR and a TV. Within minutes she's brought cassettes and a yellow folder full of newspaper and magazine clippings.

'All yours, babe. Have fun. This is the main file, but if you're interested in spreading your search, you can look for topics by subject on the computer.'

'I appreciate your help.'

'No problem. Anyone who's out to get those bastards needs all the help they can get.' She pauses, her face stiff. 'My niece. She got sucked in by them. Committed suicide two months ago.' My mouth makes an 'oh'. But she doesn't want sympathy, just stabs a finger at the file. 'Read,' she says.

The folder is fat with grief. On page after page,

people describe the hopelessness they felt as offspring, spouses, lovers and associates took to sitting around gazing blankly at spirals.

There's a lot of comment on the cult from psychologists. Declares one expert, 'It divides families, alienates parents from children and completely cuts off its adherents from reality.'

Not so, protests another, who vows she's seen the Signal Thread rescue people from acute depression. 'In this hostile world, where our future seems far from secure, everyone needs to find a rock to cling to. Signal Threaders believe very strongly that the spiral shape connects them with an all-powerful universal intelligence.'

'Sacrilege!' a fundamentalist pastor thunders. 'The Signal Thread is truly satanic. It is anti-love, anti-life, and anti-Christ!'

I watch a tape of the show David did on the Signal Thread. There's a mother who reminds me of Liz O'Keefe. She constantly fiddles with her fingers as she recounts her daughter's disastrous involvement with the cult. A sleekly confident analyst uses a lot of jargon and says the Signal Thread is a perfectly manageable aid to better living. Then a stream of callers come through. Many are emotional, some in ecstasy, others in despair. Oakes listens, sympathises, cajoles, pounces. He's clever.

Trixie's behind me. 'What was the level of response to this?' I ask. 'Did many people try to call?'

'Are you kidding? Like half the nation was trying to get through. It worked well for David, too. Gave his ratings a kick along. Do you want to go watch him? They're about ready to start.'

I'm taken to a dark studio to sit behind a gaggle of brontosaural cameras. Someone gives me an ear-piece so I can hear the questions from callers. David squints through the glare of lights and acknowledges me with a fleeting grin. He has candlepower.

His guest is one of Hollywood's top new stars, all Lycra-sheathed legs and chiselled lips, held in a taut grimace for a final delicate glossing from a makeup artist's brush.

It's time. 'Quiet, please!' bellows the floor manager. And Oakes and guest slide into gear.

'It was good,' I tell him when it's all over and he's leading me to his office.

'It was crap. She's about as quick on the uptake as a three-toed sloth. We had to rehearse most of that witty repartee.' He throws open a door that leads to his cluttered workspace. There are chairs, a low table, a bank of video equipment.

'So,' he says. 'Impress me.'

I give him Philip's cassette and he slides it into the maw of his VCR. There are streaks and blips and then the baby's beaming face. He speaks. Halfway through, Oakes emits a small explosion of breath and leans forward, intent upon the child. As the picture dissolves into snow, Oakes swivels around. Then he says, 'How soon can you get that child up here?'

Relief blossoms. And excitement. But caution niggles at me too. 'There are problems. Complications.'

'Which are?'

'Philip's in hiding. Officially, he's missing. But I've got him.' Oakes's eyes go narrow. 'He asked me to take him away,' I begin. And I tell him the story.

Oakes laughs when I finish. There's almost admiration in the sound. 'Christ, you're in deep.'

'I know. But you've seen him. Look at how he is! He drove me mad for days.' I haul in a breath. 'Philip says . . .' and I run it by him very fast '. . . that he's a sort of guardian angel.'

His lips twitch. 'You've kidnapped an *angel?*' The grin is unrestrained. 'The network'll love it!'

I feel defensive. 'That's what he says. And who am I to tell him he's nuts?'

But Oakes isn't listening. Already he's moving on, thinking, planning. 'Could what's his name . . . Jimmy? . . . bring the kid up here?'

'No. He doesn't need to. I already have.'

Oakes stares. And then slaps his knee. 'Even better,' he chortles. 'Have you talked to the kid about the legal difficulties in all this?'

'There's been no time. I get the feeling he assumes the big issues he wants to talk about will make small ones like kidnapping fade away.'

Oakes grunts. 'The FBI doesn't fade easily.'

'The point he'd make, I think, is that it can hardly be called kidnapping when he wanted it to happen.'

'And there are no precedents. It would come down to whether his parents own him and have the right to keep him in their home, or whether he should be free to follow his own destiny. Fascinating argument.'

He gets up and paces. 'So. He needs me.' He chuckles

cynically. 'God knows, I could do with an angel on the show. He's at your hotel?' I nod. 'And he's been there all afternoon, by himself?' There's a proprietorial hint of outrage in his voice which I don't like one bit.

'Yes, by himself.' He grabs his car keys and motions me out the door. 'There are other problems,' I call as he strides ahead of me. 'I've got hardly any money.'

He flaps an impatient hand at me. 'Don't even think about it.'

'And other things need thinking through. Don't forget all the crazies who'll think Philip's arrival is the Second Coming.'

He turns, walking backwards, voice heavy with suppressed impatience. 'That's why God gave us black-windowed limos and blocky guys with shoulder holsters.'

We're almost at the hotel when I ask him, 'Why are you helping? Is it for Philip? Or is it because he'll help your show?'

He swings the car with a slight squeal of tyres into the car-park. 'Why?'

'It's just . . . I don't know. I think it's important that when we deal with him, we're doing it for the right reasons.'

'How are we supposed to know what they are?'

Oops. He is stung. I open the door. 'What are you saying?' he presses, 'That I'm some callous bastard who'll wring out your prodigy and then cast him aside?'

'I'm not saying anything, David. But there's this purity to him, you know? You'll see when you meet him. Of course he'll pump up your ratings, and I understand

that's important to you. But in some ways he's incredibly
innocent. I want to protect him, that's all.'

'From me.'

Oh, hell. Bad move. 'You're getting this wrong. I'm not
attacking you . . . '

'That's not how it sounds to me.'

'I don't mean you, I mean the . . . system. Hollywood.
Producers. Money. All that stuff. Do you understand?'

'Yeah, yeah. You think I'm only interested in myself
and my own career.' His face is cold. 'I have to do it my
way. Or not at all. Understood?'

Obstinate jerk. We stare at each. 'Christ, Cyn,' he says.
'I'm not a cardboard cutout.' He sighs. 'Look, I'll do
this the best way I can. Okay?'

We take the lift in silence and I lead the way along the
corridor feeling grudging and sorry and justified all at
once. Hell, Philip can't handle hype and bullshit. They
need to know that. And there's a lot we haven't even
touched on yet. Like, what happens to him after this
is over? Will they send him home again? Will he even
want to go back to his cot and his stuffed toys?

I knock first to warn him, then press the card key
into the lock. Inside it's dark. Quiet. The child squats
on the floor, knees splayed with the loose, jointless
ease of infancy, chubby hands curled quietly in his
lap. His eyes are closed. But then the lids flutter as
he hauls himself back from whatever space he's in.
He smiles, acknowledging our presence, and hops to
his feet, extending his tiny hand up to the man who
stands gaping beside me. 'Mr Oakes,' he says jovially.
'Such a pleasure to meet you.'

ELEVEN

Callahan, the boss of Oakes's production company, is in an affable mood. He's called his top people for a Sunday meeting. He strides up and down his boardroom, punching his clenched fist into the palm of his other hand, bald head shining under the halogen downlighters.

'You're incredible. The world has never seen anything like you before!'

'Yes, it has,' says Philip. Despite the cushion on his seat, he can barely see over the edge of a very long expanse of hand-crafted mahogany. Seven other people are ringed around the table looking at him with various degrees of awe and nervousness.

'The ratings will go into orbit!' raves Callahan. 'Ah, pardon me?'

'The world has seen people like me before,' Philip repeats.

'What, you mean seers, prophets? But never on television!' He clasps his hands above his head, like a heavyweight boxer saluting the crowd. 'Dave's show is just the start. We'll get footage of you on every television channel in the world. Then personal appearances, a weekly phone-in show where you solve the world's problems, university lectures, videotapes, books. Think of the auction for the book rights! "The Philip Preston Prophecies",' he intones, his outstretched hand spreading imaginary words in a broad swathe against the room's giant windows.

'What about toys and video games, Cal?' says one of the executives. 'Little girls'd love an Angel doll and maybe we could look at developing a holographic video game where kids could act out various destinies with Phil as the hero.' The marketing and financial managers chirp with enthusiasm.

'I'm not sure that you understand me, Mr Callahan,' says the angel. 'I'm not interested in personal fame or in making money.'

Callahan halts in mid-stride. There is a shocked silence. The CEO slips back into his chair and leans towards the child, head cocked, eyes narrowed with concern. A small bead of spittle keeps forming at the corner of his mouth. He keeps on having to suck it in. *Phurp*, he goes. 'Not interested? But, Philip, you have come to us seeking a platform. You said you wanted to be placed upon the world stage. We assumed that you wanted maximum exposure. Are you saying now that this is not so?'

'I want the world to hear my message, certainly. But I am not here to sign autographs, star in comics or enter into personal endorsement contracts.'

There is a clearing of throats and shuffling of feet. Callahan dabs at his mouth with his little finger. 'Are you . . . declining . . . to take part in corollary commercial activities?' he croons. 'Remember, this is the modern world now, Philip. Taking advantage of marketing and public relations opportunities is absolutely essential if your personal integrity and the power of your message are to be managed properly. We're talking global media here. This is not the quiet scratching of quill pens upon parchment paper by hooded monks in a medieval monastery.'

'If my message has integrity, it does not need management,' says the baby. 'People will understand it without there being any need for analysis.'

Callahan's mouth stretches in a cold smile. 'I don't think, with the greatest of respect, that you understand the pressures you're about to be subjected to. You need protection. The whole world will be hammering at your door. We can keep those hungry and hysterical mobs at bay. Quite frankly, young man, there will be those who will want to tear you apart. You'll be shattering the illusions of millions of people.'

He laces his fingers on the shiny table. 'Keeping control of this thing is going to cost big money and take a great deal of effort. I mean, Pandora's Box – you're not just lifting the lid, more like blowing it with Semtex. Your personal safety and this network's integrity will be at stake. If you appear only a couple of times and then go your own sweet way, people will say you're a fraud, that it was a cute trick using computer-editing techniques, that you weren't really talking at all. That would leave us in a very invidious position.'

Callahan lets a short ominous silence fill the room. 'So?' he asks. *Phurp*. His round face is set in an expression of sweet reason. 'Can we make a deal? Understand this – if we give you the opportunity to have your say, we must ask in return for sole rights to the material which arises as a result. And we want an exclusive management contract. There's too much at stake for us to agree to anything less.'

Philip smiles. 'I have only one purpose. To talk to the people who watch television. I thank you for the facility you are offering me. Obviously, I will agree to listen to your advice afterwards as regards security. You're welcome to have "rights" if that is important to you. But I am not interested in money or deals. I do not want to sign a contract. I do not wish to encourage or endorse any commercial activity which attempts to capitalise on my name or my origins or my message.'

Cal's eyes go stony behind his expensively crafted spectacles. He gets up again and goes to look out through the filmy drapes at the cityscape below. He jams his hands in his pockets. 'We could tell you we're not interested.'

'You could,' agrees Philip.

'We could assume that you're just an exceptionally bright kid who's been manipulated by your grasping mother.'

'You could,' says Philip. 'It would not be a pleasant tactic, but you could.'

'For heaven's sake,' I snap. Cool eyes swivel to me, the stranger here. 'His mother doesn't even know he's here.' I'm ignored. It's as if I haven't spoken.

'Cal,' says the vice-president for public relations, 'our patronage of this boy will mark us as people who aren't afraid to take a chance. We'll be in *Time* and *Newsweek*. Even if we never make another cent out of it, the publicity we'll get is gold. Pure gold.'

The company's dour senior attorney throws his pencil on the table and shakes his head. 'How will our more conservative advertisers feel about this?' he asks, not for the first time, but no one seems to share his concern.

Callahan ignores the feeble clatter and swings about to look at Philip.

'So exactly what are you going to say to the world?'

'You're about to meet a most remarkable child,' says Oakes. His face is held in tight focus. 'This child is real. We are employing no smart computer technology, no ventriloquism, no trickery, no lip synching here tonight. And hard though it may be for you to comprehend that a child so young can think and speak and reason as he does – I assure you he can.

'Ladies and gentlemen, please welcome ... Philip Preston.'

Oakes doesn't usually work before a live audience. Today is an exception. There's a burst of applause as on to the set toddles the guest. He wears a white shirt and tiny white shoes and dark blue shorts. He waves and scrambles up alongside Oakes, using a small footstool they've put there to make it easier.

He's too small for the chair's ample curves, his chubby legs stretched before him. 'Good evening, David,' he pipes.

There is a collective gasp.

'Good evening, Philip. Are you comfortable?'

'Oh, quite, thank you. This is most commodious.'

There's a rustling, shuffling noise as the audience cranes to see better. The camera sweeps across the crowd. Some women have hands to their mouths.

'Can you tell us a little about yourself?'

'Yes, of course. I was born a little over a year ago in a country far from here, but in all truth I feel more like a citizen of the world. I have been here in the United States for just a few days and I came with the express intention of making an appearance on a show like yours, David.' The small one produces a winsome smile. 'That sounds very immodest, I know. I must say, I'm enormously grateful to you for the opportunity to speak.'

'It's our pleasure,' says Oakes. 'After all, you are a most remarkable young man. Most of us here tonight would call you a genius – an infant prodigy. Would you agree with that?'

'No, not at all.' Philip clasps his hands in his lap. He's looking more monkish by the day. 'Certainly, I'm an oddity. I slipped into the world somewhat by accident. But I'm not really so unusual. The subconscious mind of most babies is very aware, but the ability to express that awareness is usually veiled because the body is so busy bringing all of its component parts up to speed, so to speak, that verbalising comes later rather than earlier.'

'Why is it, then, that you can talk this way?'

'Well, I'm a special case. You see, you might call me an angel.'

A woman cries out. Mutters and whispers. Oakes holds up his hand for silence. 'Many people will find that hard to believe, Philip.'

'I know. But it is the truth. Normally, we do not show ourselves. Normally, we do not take on human form at all. In fact I find it decidedly inconvenient to be in this small frame. Still, I only have myself to blame. I inadvertently entered the body of a child about to be born.' He raises a finger. 'Mind you, I say it was inadvertent, but everything happens for a purpose. And as it happens, this is a particularly opportune time for me to be here, for it means that I can talk to millions of people through the medium of television. Such a wonderful tool! Just imagine, David, how much stronger Christ's message would have been had television existed in Roman times.'

'That's sacrilege!' someone shouts. 'How dare you take the Lord's name in vain!'

The camera zooms to an apoplectic face. A stout man stands in the centre of the rows of studio chairs, shaking his fist. 'Enough of this! I've heard enough!'

'But I . . .'

'Hush your mouth, young man!' cries the protester.

'Let him speak!' shouts someone else.

The studio erupts in bedlam. Oakes shoots to his feet, arms raised. 'Ladies and gentlemen! Please! Settle down!' The hubbub simmers back a notch. 'I respect your feelings, sir,' he calls. 'There'll be time for questions later. Now let's everybody calm down and listen.'

Slowly, with his hands still spread out, palms downward, as if mentally suppressing his audience, he takes his seat again.

'Philip, the gentleman up there seems outraged that you should mention the name of Jesus. What's your reaction to that?'

'I do not take his name in vain at all,' says the baby. 'I merely said that had he been alive today, the power of global communications, as exemplified by shows like this one, would have put an entirely different face upon early Christianity.'

'Are you saying then that you're here to found a new religion?'

'Heaven forbid.' Philip lets out his gurgling baby chuckle. 'There are far too many as it is. I am here to try to encourage people to take responsibility for themselves. That's all.'

Oakes turns to the camera. 'We're listening, ladies and gentlemen, to Philip Preston, an awe-inspiring child. A child like no other. One who wants us to believe he's a guardian angel come to earth with a message we all should heed. We'll be back right after this . . .'

There's a party after the show. Oakes takes my arm. 'Have a drink. I'd like you to meet some people.' He leads me through the gossiping throng in the hospitality suite.

I'm introduced to publicity and marketing people and give them duty smiles, still holding Philip. They show him great deference when he thrusts his small hand out to them.

'This is all just so wonderful!' gushes a PR assistant. 'How do you do, young man?'

'Very well indeed,' says Philip. 'Though I'd feel better if people wouldn't call me "young man". I'm well past the mewling and puking stage, thank heavens.'

'You know Shakespeare?'

'Yes,' replies Philip. 'Quite well. He's an intense sort of chap, but most engaging.'

The woman's eyes go very wide.

In a quiet moment I give Philip a warning squeeze. 'Stop showing off.'

He looks impish. 'I thought a little gamesmanship was mandatory in this town.'

'You want them to believe you, don't you? That means being serious.'

'I know,' he sighs. People sweep past with brimming glasses. They're very excited, slapping Oakes on the shoulder and shaking his hand.

'They're going to helicopter us to some secret place tonight where my fans can't find me.' Philip says the word 'fans' with despairing amusement. 'They seem to think assorted fanatics will be out with placards soon.'

'Do I come with you?'

'I hope so. I'd really like to go soon. I find the noise here a little debilitating.'

Me too, I tell him. We struggle through the throng to Oakes and Callahan falls upon us. His beefy hand engulfs mine, signet ring grinding into my knuckle. 'You've done a great thing, Ms Moon. Now don't you worry. We've got guards. We've got attorneys. While this boy is in our care, so will you be too.'

'Well, thank you, I appreciate your . . .'

'No problem! No problem! We have started something here tonight. Yes!' He punches a fist in the air,
while his eyes dart about the room. 'Great to meet you.
Just great. We'll talk again . . .' he says, and is moving
on to his next target.

Oakes sees my expression. 'Don't worry. He's always
hyperactive.'

A helicopter deposits us in the garden of a walled house.
It is grand yet warm, decorated in pale primrose and
white. Philip finds it curious. 'It's like wading in a bowl
of custard,' he says, bemused by its luxury. A pleasant,
unflappable maid named Rosie picks him up a mite
apprehensively, holding him as if he is a piece of rare
and expensive china, and carries him up the sweeping
staircase to bed.

'Breakfast at seven,' she says. 'I've left a snack in the
library in case you're hungry.'

The library is small and luxurious. Caramel velvet
and ivory walls. There is camembert, crisp crackers,
grapes, coffee and a dish of bitter chocolate pieces.
We sip and nibble. 'Are you pleased?' I ask. 'Is he
what you expected?'

Oakes pops a whole chocolate in his mouth. 'And
more. Though it's hard to know how to handle him.
He wavers between cute and Confucius. I'm constantly
tripping up.' He licks sweetness from his thumb. 'That
cuteness makes him endearing of course. We'll have to
get him to play on it more. People love that.'

I put down my coffee cup. 'Is that all you care about?'

'Pardon?'

'Fame, popularity?'

'Well, hell, it sure helps, Cyn.' His voice rises a little. 'This is a tough business. And fame and popularity translate into profits. I'm not in this just for the goodness of my heart.'

'He is.'

'But of course. He's the fucking angel, not me.'

'Don't talk about him like that!'

'Hey, come on, it's just an expression . . .'

'But it's utterly wrong for him, okay? You can't be casual about him like that. He's special. Different. You don't use words like that for him. Not around me.' Angry and sleep-deprived, I'm not up to arguing. I knuckle my face, trying to rub away some tension. 'I should shut up. We've had this conversation before.'

'You have. I seem to be the one who listens.'

I give him a mutinous look. Now it's his turn to back down. 'Sorry,' he says. 'I was crass. I promise to be suitably reverent in future.'

'It's not that either,' I try to explain. 'He doesn't need bowing and scraping. He's just . . . solemn, you know? And the world's so loose and jokey, so throwaway. I don't think he realises how much he'll have to fight to be taken seriously. And if we don't take him seriously,' I add, 'he hasn't got a chance.'

Oakes calls to me as I head down to breakfast. 'Quick,' he says. The TV's on. David and Philip are standing before it, riveted on the early morning news. It's footage from home. Shirley's on, glowing, pleased and proud

– but not as surprised as she might have been, she reports, because only today they received a videotape from her son telling her he is safe and happy.

Philip hears my puzzled noise. 'Jimmy and I made it at the same time as the one you brought up here,' he says quickly. 'He made sure it got to them.'

No, Shirley is saying on-screen, she didn't know her son was in LA and they have no idea how he got there. No, he'd never said anything to them about this angel stuff. In fact, they had no idea how truly gifted he was. She'd known he was bright but he'd never been *that* clever at home. Oh, yes, she still loves him. More than ever.

Just looking at Jeff makes me nervous. He's rigid, eyes darting, a twitch pulsing in his cheek. He wants to know who did this to them, who put them through this.

How does he feel about his son now that, suddenly, he's famous? Jeff shifts on his feet. 'Well, he might be our son but he's put us through hell.' His control slips. 'And, by God, when we get him back I'll be teaching him a bit of respect.'

The reporter says, 'But maybe he'll want to stay out in the world.'

'He's twelve fucking months old,' snarls Jeff, but because the news is in family time, the producers have put a *beep* where the 'fucking' is. 'I won't have him upsetting his mother like this.' (For 'mother', I'm thinking, read *me, Jeff*.)

'Oh, dear,' says Philip. 'Poor man.'

'Too late for regrets,' says Oakes. 'Come on. Breakfast.'

Around a table on the terrace, he outlines the day ahead. We're headed back to the studio for a press conference, plus a meeting to discuss personal appearances, touring and more TV shows. I spread marmalade on toast, without appetite, as I listen. 'If Philip goes touring, do you go too?'

'That's the plan. A global zap for two or three weeks. It'll boost the visibility of my show and help to get it on-screen in countries that don't yet buy it. Someone will hold the fort while I'm gone.'

'Do I figure in the plan?'

'Hell, yes, you're part of the story. You'll be on stage this morning along with Philip.'

Wonderful. Cyn Moon. Exhibit number two. I dread the thought.

'I'm looking forward to it,' says Philip.

'Don't expect too much intellect from them,' warns Oakes. 'This story is all sensation at the moment.'

Philip blinks. 'I was hoping for some serious debate.'

'Well, if you're serious, there's a chance they will be too. You'll get your best shot by being very dignified.'

'And cute,' I mutter, and he throws me a dark look.

Rosie comes out with coffee and ruffles Philip's hair, used to him now and unable to treat him differently from any other toddler.

'Hi, sweetie,' she says. 'My, you're a star today. You're in all the papers. The car will be here soon, Mr Oakes,' she says. 'You want your bags brought down?'

He nods. 'Philip's on tour. All we need now are the souvenir T-shirts.'

'Lord have mercy,' sighs the angel.

It's a big press conference. A room full of men and women with hard, curious faces. A bunch of mikes jostle at the rostrum like a clutch of snakes' heads. There's a tall box there for Philip to stand on. We wait in the next room.

Oakes, holding Philip in his arms, peers through a crack in the door. 'Are they happy or hostile?' I whisper.

'Hungry.' He glances down at Philip. 'Do you want me to carry you, or will you walk?'

'Down, please,' Philip says. Once on his feet, he tucks his little shirt into his shorts, smooths his downy hair and straightens his small shoulders. 'Good luck,' I tell them both.

At first, only those in the front row realise he's walked into the room. Then the people in the next row stand to get a better look, followed by the next line of chairs and so on. In seconds, the whole crowd is yelling at the people in front to sit down.

Then, just as quickly, the noise dies as Philip motions the front row down with his hands. They sit, stunned by his calm control. The second row subsides, and the rest, embarrassed to be still up and agitating, also sink to their seats.

Then Oakes bends over and picks up the child. There he is! Just a little snitcher of a kid. Oakes stands him on the improvised platform. The small face is just high enough to be seen over the ragged mass of microphones.

Philip smiles into the breathless silence. 'Good morning, ladies and gentlemen,' he says. There is the whizz-clack-shlack of dozens of camera shutters. Philip waits for the din to die down. Finally, there's nothing to be heard but the dense almost-silence of a crowd waiting.

'Am I a freak?' asks Philip. 'You probably think so.' He looks around, nodding sagely. 'It will sadden me, however, if your coverage is reduced to news of the most sensational kind.' He laughs. 'I imagine some of you already have headlines writ large upon your imaginations. Superkid, you'll be calling me. Or Wonderchild. Or Starbaby. But please do not focus on me.' He taps his small chest. 'I am merely an instrument. Celebrating me would be like listening to a great new piece of music and paying attention to the microphone instead of the song. That would be foolish, yes?' There is a vague burble of amusement.

'Let me tell you this very simple thing. An event will soon occur which will alert you to the fact that this Earth does not hang lonely in the void. This planet is one of many like it. It is but a tiny junction point in a vast web which links us with other peoples in the universe.' His audience shifts and mutters like a sleeping dog troubled by dreams.

'The event will prompt each one of us to make a decision about the world's future. Quite literally, ladies and gentlemen, the world will depend on all of us.' Suddenly he spreads his arms. 'What the world needs now,' he cries, 'is an outburst, an outpouring of love. What we need is for millions of people to open their throats and their hearts and cry, *yes!*' He shouts the short last word and then reigns himself in. 'If we can't do that – if the best we can say when we are tested is, "Oh, I don't know" or "It looks too hard" or "But what if?" – then we must take the consequences.' Philip takes a sip of water from a glass on the rostrum. He has to hold it with both hands.

'And what would they be?' someone calls.

Philip shrugs his small shoulders. 'That's difficult to predict, though it could mean the end of some things that we currently cherish. You see, if the best we can muster is an eruption of fear and negativity, then it will weaken the web's energy. Already it is fragile. I believe the planet would withdraw into itself for a time of healing. That may make it a hostile environment.'

'So give us the good news,' calls a caustic voice at the back. 'What happens if we, how did you put it, say yes?'

Philip laughs gladly. 'Ah! Then there'll be an energy alive in this world that we have never seen before. Knowledge will open up. Inspiration will flow. The power of the web will ignite our imaginations. We will find ways to solve the problems that beset us.'

'This event you speak of. What form will it take? And when?'

'It will be a natural phenomenon.' He grins. 'One you won't miss. More than that I'm not prepared to say. As to timing – well, within the next few weeks.'

There is a laugh from someone that skitters on the edge of hysteria. Another hand. Another nod. 'Judy Levy, *LA Times*. Where do you come from?'

'I was born in New Zealand.'

'No, I don't mean that. What ...' she struggles for a word that won't sound too foolish '... dimension?'

Philip's few pearly teeth gleam as he chuckles. 'I come from the same place we all come from. Out there. The place which exists in your imagination. It's very real. It has many names. Some call it heaven. Some call it hell. Some call it the other side. It can be whatever you call it.'

A portly man gets up. 'Sean Jury, *USA Today*. Your parents are naturally distressed about the way you, ah, left home. How do you feel about that?'

'Very sad.' Philip's voice wobbles for a moment, then strengthens. 'I love them. They did their best for me. But I knew I had to seek out people who could give me the help I needed most.'

'Philip!' comes a shout. 'Who else is involved? Who took you from your crib?'

He turns and beckons me forward. 'She's here. My friend, Cynthia Moon.' Cameras work again. Avid faces swivel and glare. He takes my arm. 'She's a magazine writer who came to my home to do a story about clever babies.' He chuckles. 'It wasn't easy to convince this one to help me. Like all of you, she is wary of fakes and crackpots.'

A thicket of hands shoots up. I pick one. 'What were your first impressions?' a lanky man asks.

I can't speak. It's awful being on this side of a press conference. I feel like a butterfly laid out for their scrutiny, impaled upon a board. Somehow my mouth cranks open. 'I was very . . . startled. I knew very little about babies, but I was overwhelmed by this one.'

'Did you write about him for your magazine? And what is the publication?'

'I work . . .' *Make that past tense.* 'I used to work for a monthly magazine called *Maggy*. I haven't been in touch lately.' I stumble on. 'No, I didn't write about Philip. He wasn't ready then. He asked me not to. You can see how he is. In the end, I became convinced that he is a very special human being. I thought it better to do what he wanted, rather than follow my reporter's instincts.'

'And did you arrange Philip's appearance on *The Oakay Show*?'

Oakes takes the cue and explains the sequence of events. Now the questions come faster.

'Do you fear arrest for kidnapping, Ms Moon?'

'No – as Philip says, he begged me to help him.'

'How do you feel about his mother?'

'I'm sorry she was hurt. I didn't mean for it to happen. But you see this child. He's not a normal baby.'

Callahan's waiting for us when it's all over. 'Great talking, kid,' he booms. 'And I've got some news for you. We're bringing your mom and dad to join you soon. Gotta show we care, huh?'

It's only later that I find out caring doesn't enter into it. The company needs parental permission so a proper passport for Philip can be issued to allow

him to go on the grand tour. And Jeff is suddenly
the beneficiary of a very impressive fee for helping
things happen in a hurry.

TWELVE

Faxes and messages pour in. It feels as if the whole world knows who I am, where I am, what I've done. There are hate calls, adoration calls, help-me calls, deranged calls. We're in a fortress. Bodyguards, PR people, secretaries, cooks, drivers. An army of protectors. The world's gone crazy over the angel baby. I'm merely a grain of rice in the crazy pudding. The nanny person. Carted along to interviews because Philip likes to have me there. Just another bum taking up limo space.

There's a two-word note from Lou. 'You're fired.'

A fax from Martin. 'So that's what you're up to. Bad move, Cyn. The brat's wrong. I'm right. You'll see.'

My sister Beth calls, shocked and tearful. We've always been different. She fell early into mortgage and babies while I was hungry for work. She's always disapproved. Now, more than ever. 'What's got into you?' she wails. 'How could you do such a terrible thing?' I try to explain but I know I sound unconvincing. 'I'm just so thankful Mum and Dad aren't here to see this,' she sniffs. Then, carping, 'You don't belong there. It's ridiculous.'

Yeah, Beth, I know. But I've no job at home. And stone-faced men in dark suits waiting for me. No, thanks.

I know I have to think about it sometime. But not yet. It's all too bewildering for me to think straight about anything.

I ring Robert, who's laughing. 'You should have seen Lou's face,' he chortles. And, more soberly, 'I cleaned your desk out for you. There's already a new writer there. Some slack tart. Can't talk to her like I could with you.'

He wants to know how I'm feeling. Shell-shocked, I tell him. Marooned.

'Ah,' he says, 'but what an adventure.' And then chills me by saying the police have had him in for questioning. 'They traced the passports of course. They were pissed off and didn't quite seem to know what to do with me. You must be having such a time.' He sounds wistful.

'Oh, Robert,' is all I can say. 'Look after yourself.'

I need soothing after that and try Jimmy's number. His serenity floats down the phone. 'Miss Moon,' he says, all calm affection. 'I saw young Philip on TV. My. Aren't you proud?'

'Oh, yes, I suppose. But it's nothing to do with me . . .'

'Everything to do with you. Without you, he wouldn't have had the chance to speak.'

He wants to know what's happening. So I fill him in on how we're besieged in a Beverly Hills hotel. The throng outside carries signs saying things like 'Behold the Anti-Christ' and 'Shove off – on Route 666'. Even, 'Damien Lives'.

'Who?' asks Jimmy. Never mind, I tell him.

'The Signal Thread people have been making a big

fuss here,' he says. I hear the scorn in his voice. 'Especially that Vortex fellow of yours.'

Not of mine, I'm thinking.

'Has Philip been critical of the Signal Thread?' Jimmy asks.

Only because people here keep asking him about it. I think he'd prefer not to mention it at all because he says we should be reaching out, not in. But the spiral meditation thing is huge here, Jimmy. Thousands of people are into it. Major cult status. Philip called it a psychic sinkhole the other day. Didn't do him any good. The Signallers hate him.'

'And you, Miss Moon, what do you think about it all? Which philosophy do you follow now?'

I flush. 'I don't know, Jimmy. He's the angel.' Exasperation fizzes on my tongue. 'I'm just his damn handmaiden.'

'Yes. So you are. Mind the Signallers, Miss Moon,' he says. 'They grow stronger. You do have your stone with you, don't you?'

I sigh. 'Yes. Why?'

'Keep it near. One day you'll have need of it.'

We head for New York the next day, with a posse of minders. First leg of an international promotional tour. The angel baby road show. By the time the cabin crew have served a plastic breakfast, we're settled in the cruise at 37,000 feet, heading north-east.

I flip through a magazine while Philip naps alongside me, curled up easily in his seat. For some reason I can't get comfortable. A pain nips at my middle. Ah! Again it stabs. I ease the seatbelt, leaning forward to ease the ache.

It returns, hard and grinding. Oh, please, not a case of the shits. Not now. What have I eaten? Just breakfast. It seemed okay.

The pain isn't letting up. I rub at my stomach. It feels rigid, muscles clenched. Suddenly my mouth fills with saliva and sweat pops out.

I rip the sick-bag from the seat pocket in front. 'Philip!' I croak and, oh God, drool spills from my mouth. He's awake now, saucer-eyed, as I lunge past him into the aisle, legs all awobble. Alarm flares on people's faces and they lean away as I totter towards the rear lavatories. Why can't I stand up straight? I'm fumbling at the handle and then there's a hand on my back and a voice saying, 'Honey, calm down now.' And I'm curled on the hard scratchy nylon carpet, knees drawn up, and, Christ I'm dying, it's *so hard to breathe* . . .

'Cynthia? Ms Moon? Can you talk to me?' Some woman's annoying me. I'm on my back. Floor, hard and cold. Yuck, foulness in my mouth. 'Cynthia,' the voice commands. 'Tell us how you feel.'

My tongue's fat and slow. I make it croak, 'Horrible.'

'Let's get you cleaned up a bit,' says the brisk voice. A warm, damp cloth is wiped and dabbed, unglobbing my eyes. Aah, the light's so harsh. A circle of worried faces looms, all squashed into a narrow space lined with aluminium. I'm on the galley floor. Oakes says, 'Cyn, can you talk?' His face is upside down with a groove of concern carving a cleft in his forehead, hands cradling my head.

'Looks like food poisoning,' says the nursey person. I squint at her. She's got the well-worn face of a woman who's flown many miles and seen everything. 'Raylene' is written on the metal stripe beneath the airline logo on her chest. 'It can hit really fast sometimes. But, lordy, I've never seen anything like that before.' She looks relieved.

'I'd like to sit up,' I tell her.

Oakes helps me sit up as Raylene waves the others away. 'Have you ever had an episode like that before?' he asks.

I shake my head. 'Is anyone else sick?'

'No, praise be. One's enough,' says Raylene. She gives me a paper cup of water ('Just a few sips now') and watches as I swallow. Feels my pulse and seems satisfied. 'You should go see a doctor after we land. You had such a flood of saliva and a whole bunch of spasms. It was really odd.' Thoughtfully, she screws the cap back on the water bottle. 'It reminds me of a school camp I went to, years ago. One of the kids got bitten by something poisonous. A spider, I think. You looked like he did.' She shrugs, dismissing the thought. 'Now let's get you comfortable. Can you stand?'

On my feet, just, I feel a hundred years old. My blouse is disgusting, saliva-sodden. Someone brings a clean sweatshirt I had tucked into my cabin bag. That helps. Raylene tucks me up in my seat next to Philip with a blanket, while he pats my hand, shocked and silent. I'd love to clean my teeth but it can wait.

'She's all right now,' Oakes tells the anxious ring of faces around my seat. 'Best let her rest.' After some solicitous patting of pillows they leave me alone. Exhausted, eyes closed, I can still hear a sweet, breathy whisper. And then I feel the squeeze of Philip's small hand on mine and I realise he is praying for me. In a way, it helps. In a way, it makes me want to scream. I pull away from him and sink into a dream-filled funk, sore and scared.

Next day I'm pacing a bitter New York street, trying to walk off my misery. I'm haunted by how I felt just before collapsing in the aisle. There was the pain, sure, but there was a dark swooping giddiness I've felt before. '*We're going to journey together, round and round, down the spiral, Cyn . . .*' And I remember Jimmy scolding. 'You are in thrall to him now . . .'

The taste of nausea rises at the back of my throat. I swallow hard, walk faster.

Philip and Oakes have gone off to yet another interview. I've got this glassy numbness in my head. Planes, hotel rooms, no fresh air. I had to get out. I'm fine on my own. Scarf and dark glasses. Hell, it worked for Jackie Onassis. And she was mega-famous. Not me. I'm the face in the background, in the crowd, just before the ad break. A nobody. The hotel has many exits. It is easy to slip out and slog off down a lumpy strip of sidewalk, hands rammed in pockets.

They made me see a doctor to check out my health. Nothing to be found, of course. It was just some bug.

Rest, he said. A small godsend. For the others took off for some studio on their own, leaving me free.

Except I'm not.

Will I ever be free again? How long is the public's infatuation with Philip going to go on? And when it's over, then what? Back to Jeff and Shirley. They're meeting us in London tomorrow. The big reunion for the cameras. I'll be required to smile tremulously as I hand him over. Cal is of the opinion that it looks bad if we don't get Philip back into the bosom of his family. He's right of course. From the PR point of view. Even Philip understands that. 'But I can't go back to the playpen, Cyn,' he told me. 'Not back to lying awake at 2am watching my clown mobile spin in the dark. Hearing them fight in the room next-door. Hearing the thumps.' Woeful, was he.

The ribbon of sky overhead hangs grey and sullen. People rush by, bumping me sometimes, never stopping to say sorry. A police car accelerates away from the kerb, its siren bursting into a howl. Across the street two men argue over a taxi. 'I gotta have it, man!' one of them hollers. 'Fuck you!' shouts the other. And as they stand there bellowing, the driver, fed up, takes off. Suddenly the two antagonists are allies. 'Motherfucker! Asshole!' they howl after the retreating cab.

The ground shakes as a subway train rumbles by below. Puffs of steam eddy from the gratings. I feel as if I teeter on a brittle crust over murky soup. One crack and I'll topple through. In a rush I remember the dream of the purse-web spider, and the knife that sliced up through the surface by my feet. I shudder.

A man lurches at me as I turn to go back to the hotel. He burps rancid beer in my face. 'Got a cigarette, lady?'

'No! Piss off! Leave me alone!'

'Jesus, lady,' he mutters, 'you'd think you'd been bit.'

I cling to the pole on the corner and cry. The Walk sign flashes and a human tide washes past me. Crazy women who weep on streets in New York are best avoided, so fortunately nobody stops. I'm left to wring myself out, on my own. It works. In a little while I'm feeling clearer, more steady.

I blow my nose vigorously and head back the way I've come. And stop, wary. A small group of protesters is outside the hotel's front entrance with banners and signs. One reads, 'It's Blasphemy, Baby.'

There are police cars, the giddy spin of red roof lights. But they're chanting even as they're moved off. 'One-two-three-four! Time to show the kid the door! Five-six-seven-eight. He's the messenger of hate! One-two-three-four! Time to show . . .'

Keeping my head down I turn the corner and veer round the block to get in through a side door. But there's a different group here and no cops in sight. In costume this lot, grey Lycra, top-to-toe, printed with black spiders' webs.

They're shoving pamphlets at passers-by. One of them spots me, pushes his piece of paper into my hand. I grab it and slip by him, eyes averted, but he's already double-taking.

'*It's her*!' he shouts. And they're all around, jostling, pressing, hooting.

And then the hotel's security guards wade in, wrenching at my arm, hustling me inside. And Oakes is running out of the elevator, coming at me, furious. 'What the hell do you think you're doing out there on your own?'

'Trying to have a life!' People are turning and pointing as they take in the famous talk host and the rumpled woman having it out in public. Oakes sees. Clamps on a polite face, steering me by the elbow between the elevator doors, crunches his thumb on the button.

Silence seethes between us as we rocket smoothly to the thirty-ninth floor. As the doors open there's a rush of corridor babble from other crew members who are all hanging around, awaiting my reappearance. The stupid missing woman. Oakes waves them away, gets me into my room, slams the door, and starts scolding like a fishwife. Fish-husband? Fishperson? I laugh which makes him even more mad. 'Never go off alone like that again,' he grates. 'It's unprofessional. It's inconsiderate. It's goddamn dangerous.'

'Okay, okay, I hear you. Dammit! Just give me space.' I fling my coat down and glower. The pamphlet they gave me downstairs flutters to the floor and lies face up. It's headed 'A Web of Lies'.

Oakes is backing off a little. 'You just have to hang on for a while,' he insists. 'Right now, we're stuck with this. We're a team. And what would you do if you dropped out? No money, no job. You need the network and its protection now.'

I feel stiff. 'I know, but you're a star, you're used to all this. I hate the feeling of being surrounded all the time.'

Oakes cracks a grey smile. 'It goes with the territory. This is different though.' He stoops to pick up the pamphlet. 'Want me to read it?'

'No,' I quaver. 'Just give me a hug.' He does. Quite a nice one. I don't stay in it for long though. Long enough for comfort. Not for complications.

'Shit,' I sigh. 'What a mess.' We sit side by side on the bed, not touching. I can feel him looking at me.

'You're a bristly sort of woman, you know that?' he says.

'Not all the time. I'm just careful.'

'No you're not. You've just been very careless out there.'

'I mean personally. Personally careful. I don't like making mistakes.'

'Would I be a mistake?'

I dart him a sideways look. 'I don't know. It's just, you're so . . . Californian. So sure of yourself. So much part of the whole damn international television blot.'

'Blot?'

'Yeah, you spread like an ink-stain, you and your network. The whole world's turning into the same animal, sucking on the same cultural tit. Manufactured by you guys.'

Remarkably, he stays calm. 'Have you finished insulting me now?'

'Yes,' I tell him in a small voice.

'And with all my faults and the terrible system I represent, is there anything you can like me for?'

'Yes. You've kept me on, letting me be with Philip, even though I'm no damn use for anything. You could have offloaded me by now. Maybe you still might.'

'Is it important for you to be with Philip?'

It's curious to hear my voice say, 'Yes. Damn him. Silly little tyke. I'd worry about him.'

'I guess we keep you on, then,' he says reasonably.

He brushes the tangled hair back from my face. His touch is rough and affectionate. 'Fix yourself up, Moon. You look like hell.'

London is hell too. Worst of all is the big reunion. They give us about two minutes in which to confront each other, bury hatchets, pass Philip over and gather ourselves for the press conference.

Shirley weeps at the sight of her son. He hugs his mother tenderly but there's no mistaking his woebegone look as Jeff snatches him away. There's a sharp, proprietary look about the man now. He's wised up to the potential. As he grips the baby to his chest, the grasp reeks of 'gotcha'. The last few days have tenderised Shirley; toughened him.

I hold out a conciliatory hand to Shirley and she grasps it in her damp one. But only for a moment.

'It was a terrible thing you did,' she quavers. 'To think that when you came to see me, the next morning . . . all that time you had him, and you never said . . .'

'But Shirley . . .' I begin, and she sighs. 'I know, I know, it was Philip really, wasn't it?' She slides her child a yearning hopeless look. 'Why did you want to leave?' she whimpers. 'Was it so awful with us?'

Philip shifts in his father's arms. 'You loved me well. It was just . . .' and he waves his hand at the small mob of tour organisers who stand all around '. . . I needed to do this.'

'We'd have done it for you, son,' says his father. 'All you had to do was ask.' He's trying to sound reasonable but anger seeps out like blood stains through a rough bandage. Philip's customary confidence withers. His eyes are huge and sad. This is how an angel looks guilty.

'It was very confusing,' he whispers. 'So hard to know what was best. And Cyn was there.'

He reaches out a hand to me and Jeff very firmly presses it back, clamping Philip's arm in his palm. 'Yeah,' he says. The thin lip curls as he gives me the look that says *bitch*. 'So you were.' And he explodes: 'What makes you think you had the right, the *goddamn right*, to take a kid from his parents!'

Oakes steps in like referee between boxers. 'Come on, Mr Preston, now's not the time. We've got a room full of media next door. They want to see some smiles. This is big, huh? Great moment? They're all waiting. You're *news* now, guys. We can work all of this out later, okay? Okay?' And even as he's speaking, cajoling, persuading, and Jeff's muttering, and Shirley's sniffling, and Philip's all ajiggle on Jeff's shoulder, pale with distress, Callahan's heavies are hustling us through the doors and into the cameras' sights.

Aah, I don't like it. Too many faces, too avid, too frenzied.

But Jeff likes it. He perks up as the shutters fly. A proud dad expression now. Even Shirley works up a timid smile or two. The photographers are shouting, This way, love, hug 'im tight. Yeah! Smile, Philip! A big googly one . . . oh, come on! Closer please, Mr Preston?

Give us a happy one, angel! One more, now, one more. Beeyoodiful!

Philip is hidden from my view by Jeff and Shirley's backs. The three of them have been pulled forward while Oakes and I, ignored for now, stand back. But the angel seems to be struggling. Jeff's elbows and shoulders are working as he fights to contains his wriggling child. I catch just a flash of the panicked baby face over his shoulder as Philip fights to get free.

And then he lets rip. Philip doesn't just cry. He roars. He shrieks. He bellows. He shouts to heaven. The flashlights stutter and die. The noise so rips at people's composure that the cameras drop, and all the eyes that have been screwed up behind lenses emerge opened wide with shock. People sway. It's as if the banshee wails have physical force. Jeff is half-turned towards us now, away from the crowd, hunched over his struggling, sirening child until finally, with disgust, he thrusts the kid into Shirley's arms.

Pale and frightened, she hustles him off our little rostrum and into the back room. Jeff brushes by me, furious, and slams the door closed behind him. We're marooned, stunned, our star turn gone from sight. We can still hear faintly the wails, reducing now. I'm desperate to go too, to see what's wrong. But Oakes grips my elbow.

The faces before us that were curious have now gone hostile and wretched. Deprived of their prey, the pack turns on us. 'Ms Moon,' someone yells. 'Have you seen this?' He's holding up a tabloid. CYN'S SINS! blare the headlines. Oh, yes, I've seen it. Learnt all about my shortcomings over this morning's break-fast table.

Oakes read it out to me while my poached egg went cold.

'*Cynthia Moon, the woman who helped starbaby Philip Preston escape from his cot, has some kinky habits,*' he intoned as he sipped his coffee. '*A former friend, hairdresser Martin Vortex, says he was shocked by Moon's sexual appetites.*

"She's voracious," said Vortex in an exclusive interview with Maggy, *the glossy magazine Moon used to work for. "On one date, she drank heavily and then tried to talk me into heavy sex involving satanic rites. When I refused, she ran out, screaming. I knew she'd get involved in something bizarre one day."*

Moon is currently in London and scheduled to appear tonight with baby Philip Preston, the toddler who's taken the world by storm. Turn to page seven for more.'

He flipped the pages and read on in a heavy sing-song: '*Martin Vortex says he's not surprised at Moon's attachment to Philip Preston – the gifted baby who claims the world is in for a shake-up. Some call the toddler a great teacher while others claim he's a child of the devil. Vortex, who dated Moon only a few weeks ago, believes the child lives in a fantasy world and is being manipulated by Moon.*'

'*"She's got a hunger for fame. She told me she was after the big time. Sure, that kid's bright, but she's got to be coaching him."*'

'Creep,' I said.

Oakes bored on. '*Vortex admits he and Cyn Moon didn't see eye to eye. He is a local leader in the Signal Thread movement, the booming international form of meditation whose followers are bitterly opposed to the baby's teachings.*

Vortex claims he tried to teach Moon the Signal Thread path but she was not receptive. "She's in a black place in her mind," he said. "I feel sorry for her."'

'Patronising prick,' I said.

'Moon's former boss, magazine editor Louisa Williams, describes her as unreliable. "She needn't bother coming back to work," she says.

Oakes shoved the paper away when he'd finished. I felt sour inside, all pain and gall. Vortex's newsprint grin torched up at me from the table and I slammed the paper over so I couldn't see the handsome shit. 'Why should people believe me and not him?' I said. 'I'm the unreliable one, remember? Martin's the smart guy.'

Oakes looked at me, bewildered. I was damned if I was going to tell him any more, so Philip did. 'She had a bad experience with Vortex,' he explained. *Out of the mouths* . . . 'He drugged her. When she came to and realised what was going on, she fought him off and escaped.'

'Satanic rites?'

I squirmed, hating the memory. 'He had this huge spider. He wanted to watch it run over me.' And I shot Philip a hot glance. 'How do you know all this anyway?' I carped, embarrassed that all this X-rated stuff has been absorbed by his shell-pinks.

'Jimmy told me,' he said. But that was then, in a quiet hotel room with friends. And now I'm surrounded by what feels like the enemy. The assembled hot breath of the London press corps is in my face and *they* all want to know it too.

So in my usual fashion, I do the wrong thing. I go all don't-care and jokey, make my hands into claws. 'Evil spiderwoman,' I snarl, grinning. 'Terror of the tabloids.' Of course, the cameras go crazy.

I am saved by Philip, who suddenly reappears on stage in the arms of a bewildered-looking Shirley, who is steered once more before the cameras by an urgent PR man. He thrusts her none too gently to the microphone, elbowing me aside. 'Ladies and gentlemen, our apologies,' he smarms. 'Everythings's fine now. Philip is happy to continue.' And he steps aside, hand extended palm up like a magician's assistant coaxing us all to focus on the rabbit emerging from the hat.

The rabbit blinks, pale and subdued. 'My apologies for the commotion,' he says. 'I suddenly got frightened. Sometimes it's hard being a baby. It was all the flashes, all your . . . energy.' A tremulous smile. 'I felt somewhat swamped by it all.'

In seconds he melts their rage. Their faces soften, lips curving into smiles. 'Now,' he says quietly, 'you may have your photos and I'll answer your questions, but can we take it quietly?' They take it like lambs. Next, I'm thinking, they'll be kissing the hem of his garment.

'I don't think that was quite the right strategy, Cyn,' David Oakes says coldly later on as we watch ourselves on the news and get to my spiderwoman crack. I look gaunt and hunted in the black dress that I thought would make me look sober and elegant.

I flush, feeling wounded. 'I'll wear pink gingham and frills next time and just stand there and simper.'

'I wouldn't bother,' he says. 'They'd only call you Miss Muffet.'

THIRTEEN

I wake early the next morning before dawn, exhausted
yet yearning for exercise. Cal's people have put us in a
small, exclusive hotel, all Persian rugs, antique clocks
and shuttered windows draped with chiffon. It's stifling,
but at least secure. Just one front door and a walled rear
garden, inaccessible from the street.

I put on jeans and a sweater and, dying for fresh
air, I slip out on to the brick patio which faces the
rear garden. Philip is there in the half-dark. He is
squatting in the garden, dew soaking his pyjama pants,
feeding cracker crumbs to three small squirrels. The
animals hop up on to his rounded knees, bright-eyed,
begging for morsels. For the first time in days he
looks happy, face glowing as the squirrels tumble
around him.

I watch for a long, tranquil moment, my own heart
easing, and then at last he sees me, smiles with gladness.
'Aren't you freezing?' I ask, but he puts a finger to his
lips. There's a bench seat so I sit, hugging myself to
ward off the chill. It's going to be grey again. I crave
sun. Bright, clear, Pacific sun.

For the longest time it seems I've seen nothing but

television studios and concert hall 'green rooms' and the backsides of old warehouses and office buildings as we speed in cars from one interview to the next. Today, we're supposed to be leaving for Paris and then on round the world back to Los Angeles, stopping off all the way for more cameras, more questions, more avid faces. Shirley is miserable and homesick, Jeff is growing more preened and self-important. I feel ill at the thought. It's a meagre but definite pleasure to sit now in the quiet autumn garden, watching Philip play. He shoos away the squirrels and gets to his feet, pulling wet fabric away from his behind.

I pull up my knees, refusing him my lap with exaggerated distaste.

He allows me a bleak smile and perches instead on the step at my feet, chin in hand.

'How's it going?' I ask. We keep our voices low in the early-morning stillness.

'Hard,' he whispers. 'Jeff hasn't forgiven me. Nor you. He likes the publicity, sees dollars in it, of course. Keeps on haranguing David about the contract I wouldn't sign. Now he wants to sign it on my behalf. Legally, of course, he can. But he wants appearance money. Thousands of dollars every time I set foot anywhere. It's awful. Just . . . anathema.

'He wants to be in charge. He's used to being in charge. Used to owning the road in that big truck of his. Used to running the marriage. He's being unkind to Shirley again. Not so that it leaves any marks. It's like when I was at home. And he looks at me, eyes pained. 'I could always hear them through the wall. And it's the same here. He nudges at her with his fist. Nudge, nudge. Push.' Philip motions with his tiny, rounded fist. 'Knuckling her, hurting, but not quite enough to bruise. He enjoys her fear. The other one had that streak in him. I could see it right from the start.'

I'm puzzled. 'What other one?'

'That soul I displaced. The turbulent one. He and Jeff would have been disastrous together. A child full of overwhelming ambition and greed, coupled with Jeff's resentment. I thought I was doing the right thing, warding it off. But look what I did.' And he looks at me over his shoulder, his eyes haunted. 'I gave Shirley misery anyway. It just goes to show that you should never meddle, never attempt to thwart the natural course of events.' His small shoulders slump. 'I'm starting to wonder if I'm doing the right thing.'

I stare at him, appalled. I've been taking all my assurance, all my confidence, from this child.

He talks on. 'This trekking from country to country. The waving at the crowds. What impression do you think I'm making?' He swivels to look me full in the face.

Cold and anxious, I dig my hands deep in my pockets. 'You're a sensation,' I begin.

'What else?' he presses.

'I think . . . you scare people. They don't understand your message. Don't want to listen, lots of them. They'd rather think you're predicting the end of the world than hear what you're really saying.' He's looking stricken, so I try to cheer him up. 'But they adore you, though. All those tears and smiles.'

'That's not right either,' says Philip. 'It's worship. I don't want that.'

Then I think of the people with the placards. The ones whose faith he threatens. And the Signal Threaders who dog us everywhere we go. A group of them got uncomfortably close to us yesterday. They set up a hideous hum as they crowded around – a discordant noise that churned my stomach.

There's a bang in the street outside and I flinch. 'You see,' says Philip. 'It was just a truck back-firing. But I've put fear in your life.' I press my hands between my thighs. 'Let's go away,' he says quickly.

'What?'

He gets up and hugs my knees, face tip-tilted up to mine. 'Please, I can't stand this. You've no idea how I felt yesterday. When I cried – it wasn't just the crush and the flashlights. I felt suddenly overwhelmed. A blackness. A haunting. I think we need to remove ourselves for a while.'

My mouth is dry. 'You mean hide?'

He laughs. 'Oh no, there's nowhere to hide. But I need a place where I can work at full strength. Right now, I'm feeling diminished and that's not good for any of us.'

I squint at him. 'What do you mean, haunting?'

'The Signal Threaders. It was *their* energy I felt around us yesterday. Those press people weren't the problem. They were just confused and eager. I can cope with that. But malevolence is growing. Cyn. I represent the web's radiance, the outreaching energy of its spokes. The Signal Threaders don't want that – they want the dark side of ecstasy, the energy that spirals inwards. They realise I'm trying to get the world to recognise my way. They want *their* way to rule. They want control, they want only their message thrumming along the Signal Thread.'

I'm back in the tube, hearing its electric babble, succumbing to its fierce, seductive pull.

'I want people to reach out and think for themselves,' Philip is saying. 'They want people to sink mindlessly into the current and do what they're told. There is no more important conflict on earth, Cyn, than this.' He stands straight-backed, strong-eyed now, past doubting. 'I nearly faltered yesterday. This circus we've created . . .' And he has the grace to look apologetic as my mouth opens in protest. 'I'm sorry, I've created it, I know. I thought it was the right thing to do, the television, the big impression. I was wrong. All I've done is awaken the spider. I must do things quietly now. Discretion is of the essence.'

Rage fizzes up some chute inside me, acrid as cider. I want to shake him. 'Philip, you're supposed to be the angel, all-bloody-knowing and wise. How come you didn't know this *before?*' My jaw is jutting, mouth all mean and crimped, but I can't help it. 'For Christ's sake, doesn't some frigging archangel blow a trumpet in your lug-hole or something when you're stuffing things up?'

He blinks. 'No, Cyn. I'm human. I have to make my own mistakes. I can't rely on calls from some angelic counselling service, any more than you can. Well, only in extremis. Dire emergency. That happens for all humans, of course.'

Things seem kind of dire for me right now, but no comforting messages come my way. My head is packed with wadding. Flatly, I ask, 'What do you mean, you want to go away?'

'These cities sap me,' he says. 'I need green. I need to feel earth-energy underfoot without hundreds of people all around. Could you? Please?'

'When?'

'Now. It's still early. Quiet. You could leave a note.'

'Oh, sure.' And my lip curls. '"Dear Shirley, I've done it again. Love, Cyn."'

'No, no,' he says. 'Just, "Philip needed to get away, to contemplate".'

I lean forward. 'These people don't understand the word, Philip. None of them. Not Oakes, not Callahan. Not Jeff. They only know action and they're all on a roll. We have bookings, tickets, schedules, commitments.'

'*They* have commitments,' Philip corrects me.

I talk slowly at him, pronouncing each word as if he's a dunce. 'There-is-nowhere-to-go, Philip. I have no friends here. I've got hardly any money. I don't even know where the nearest train station is. You just happen to have the best-known face in London right now. And I'm not exactly incog-bloody-nito either.'

He looks at me with an expression I'd call sly on anyone but an angel. 'We could go to Jimmy,' he says.

'I *beg* your pardon?'

'Jimmy. Your friend. My friend. One James Lightbody. I rang him from LA once I knew what our schedule was.

He said he'd come here too, just in case he could help. He sold his pink car, Geraldine, to pay for the ticket. She was worth quite a lot.'

Cold air in my mouth. I'm gaping. 'When?' Shock makes the word come out all feeble. 'When did he come?'

'Arrived about the same time as us, I imagine. He's staying with a friend – some old naval shipmate. Apparently we can trust him. I have the address.'

I can almost feel my shoulders slump. 'Oh God,' I sigh in defeat.

We sneak into Philip's room for a jacket and hat. Sneak into mine for my bag. Tippy-toe past people's doors. God smiles upon us (or maybe Archthingy Gabriel, noting our extremis, sends the receptionist off on an urgent trip to the lavatory) and there's no one at the front desk. Apparently no one to see us slide into the revolving door to be spat out into the raw London dawn. There are lots of people outside but no one says boo as we climb into a cab with a grumpy driver who's been working all night and is too tired to care, who looks at us not once, the woman and her kid, as he drives us out of the city to a village near Gatwick airport.

'There,' whispers Philip as we sit on the worn back seat, mutually stunned by our audacity. 'That wasn't so scary, was it?'

But it is. Now that we've fled, it seems like an extraordinarily stupid move.

'How do we know Jimmy's at this place you say he's at?' I fret. 'What if there's no one there?'

Philip's face smooths into one of his irritating fond-uncle looks. 'I phoned him last night. He's expecting us.'

'Last night,' I grit at him, 'you had not even *mentioned* this to me.'

'I know I can always rely on you,' he smiles. 'Except when you want to plan things. Some events are better left to happenstance.'

'Come *on*. I've planned nothing in my life lately.' I twist round to peer through the rear window. 'Do you think they'll have missed us yet?'

'Probably. P'raps you should phone when we get there and let them know we're fine.'

'Why me?'

He smiles benignly as we come to a stop outside a modest, pebble-fronted cottage with lace-curtained windows. 'You do that sort of thing so well.'

Jimmy's alight with excitement as he opens the door.

'Isn't this grand?' he beams. Philip opens his arms so he can lean from my embrace and wrap them around the old man's neck. Jimmy takes him from me, stepping back into the gloomy hall. 'Come and meet Daniel.' He gestures with his head. 'No sense in standing out here in view of all and sundry.'

Daniel is stooped and lantern-jawed, with fierce blue eyes. His face is thin and lined beneath the bony verandah of his jutting cheekbones. His smile charms me, though, and his handshake is strong.

He fusses us into armchairs and goes to make tea. His walls are cluttered with paintings of ships and

browning wartime photos. Jimmy points to a framed
shot of two young uniformed officers. 'Recognise anyone?' Hopeful and sunny are the youthful faces, lit with
eagerness, eyes unshadowed by doubt or loss.

'Look at you,' I tease. 'Ladykillers. When was that?'

''Thirty-nine. Dan's the only one I knew then who is
still alive.'

'And he's all au fait with Philip and Oh Two and
everything?' I ask. The old military man hardly seems
the type. Jimmy twinkles at me, nodding. 'When you
get torpedoed in the North Atlantic and drift alone
on a liferaft for three or four days, you get to know
something about angels.'

On the low table between us stands a polished brass
ship's bell, mounted in a frame. Philip squirms to get
down. Delicately he touches the clapper to the inner
side of the bell's gleaming roundness. It makes a quiet
sonorous *ping* and he smiles with delight.

'We had a fire in this building once,' says Daniel as
he comes in, tray-laden. 'I rang the bell like billy-ho
that day. You never saw a place empty so fast. It can
wake the dead, that bell.'

Philip strokes it. 'Angels love a good bell, you know.
Sweet and clear they should be . . .'

'It came from a frigate Dan commanded,' Jimmy
explains. 'Long gone to the wrecker's yard.'

The old gents slurp at their hot drinks, crinkled
mouths tremulous over hot china rims. A clock ticks,
brittle and slow, on a bookcase. There is not the slightest
sense of urgency. 'So what now?' I ask.

Jimmy sighs lightly. 'Don't fuss, Miss Moon. We'll go

soon. Dan will take us to a place that's just right for Philip's renewal.'

'A cottage in the country,' he says. 'No one will have the slightest inkling that you're there.'

'Why? What's so special about it?' I'm good and grumpy now. Hiding out doesn't sound like a way out of the mess we're in.

'It's quiet. Leafy. A place where you can breathe. And . . .' Daniel considers for a long moment and then smiles. I see a split-second of the boyish grin that gleams in his old pre-war photo. 'There's a special place there. You'll see.'

Two hours later I'm in the fusty back seat of Daniel's ancient Daimler, bouncing gently in its soft leather embrace. Jimmy and his friends seem to specialise in museum-piece cars. This one has a real walnut dashboard. And a radio with only an AM dial. Out of which is twittering the news that the angel baby is missing. A taxi driver (apparently not as tired as I'd thought) reports having dropped off a child and a woman at an address near Gatwick.

'We must have just missed them,' says Jimmy.

And the old blokes chortle to themselves. They apparently haven't had such a good time since 1945.

'We didn't ever phone them,' I say to no one in particular. 'They mightn't chase us if they know we're okay.'

'But we're away now,' says Philip. 'They don't know where to look.' He sits hugging the old ship's bell, which he has insisted that I bring along, despite its awkward weight.

turn with the steaming mug she's done mopping her face, is composed again.

'I wish,' she says.

'Will he make it difficult for Philip to choose his own future?'

She smiles wryly. 'He never got the nursey peptalk. As far as he's concerned, he's the father, Philip's the kid. He owns him. "He can't fucking vote for another two decades," he said to me this morning. "What makes him think he can leave home yet?" Trouble is, the law's on his side, he reckons. Philip might be forced to come home because the law's not made with angels in mind.' And she peers at me across the rim of her mug and whispers. 'Do you *really* think he's an angel?'

It's the first time someone's ever asked me that straight-up ever since this all began. With other people I might still have been cautious, unwilling to expose myself to derision. Might have said something like, 'Well, he *says* he is,' and left it at that. But I have told this woman too many lies before. 'Yes,' I say quietly. 'I think he is.' And she nods to herself. I have the feeling she has made a big decision.

'What are you going to do, Shirley?'

'Shirley,' she sneers. '*Shirl*, they called me at school. 'It sounds so dumb. A put-down sort of name for the sort of girl who's too stupid to do anything with her life but get knocked up by some stupid bastard and spend the rest of her life regretting it. I could have got an abortion, you know, 'cos I knew I didn't love Jeff. Not really. I'd got one before. Didn't even think about it. Never regretted it. But I knew with this one that it just wasn't an option. It was as if he was whispering to me all the time, telling me to just keep on hanging on to him in there while he grew, not to do him in. Mums and babies are often sort of psychic like that, did you know that?'

She sees my neutral look and smiles. 'Nah, 'Course you don't. You don't find that out till you've had one of your own. Anyhow, I knew with this baby I had to go on with it.'

'What are you going to do?' I ask again.

'I'm going to hug him and tell him I love him and then I'm going to leave. He doesn't need me.'

'Shirley . . .'

'No, he doesn't,' she says, fierce now. 'Jeff and I are just window-dressing here. The sappy parents brought along to make it look good. Philly's got you and David Oakes and that old man Jimmy he keeps talking about, and all this crew,' she argues, waving her hand overhead to indicate the sleeping troops all about the house. 'You can all decide better than me what should happen to him. I won't take part in any wrangling. Haven't got the money for that, either. Jeff has. He's been *raking* it in lately. Totally obsessed with the dollar signs. Book and movie offers and all the rest. He's going to court to make sure we keep Philip, he says, but I want none of it. Philip would end up hating me. And I'd rather he loved me from a distance than hated me up close. I've already asked Margot. She's given me a plane ticket home for tomorrow. Think she's pleased to see the back of me actually. I'm one less mouth to feed.' She eyeballs me. 'I'm not telling Jeff I'm leaving him. I'm just going to do it.'

I reach a hand across the counter to take hers. 'Good luck,' I tell her. 'You're amazing.' And I laugh. 'D'you know what that means? I looked it up the other day after all that tearing round in the maze. "Great beyond expectation" is what it says in the *Shorter Oxford Dictionary*.'

She's not listening though – is already planning her new life, reaching out, saying yes to something better.

'My vocab's not much chop,' she admits. 'I listen to Philip talking and realise I don't know what he means half the time. When I get home I'm starting again. My mum said there was no point in going to school. But I want to go back. I'll see about student loans. I might even go to university.' And she smiles, luminous with hope.

'Your son,' I say, 'is going to be very, very proud of you.'

'I'm going to go up and tell him now,' she says. 'I was putting it off but you've given me the push. Then I can just slip away tomorrow while they're all at the press conference. It's easier that way. Will you come and see me, back home, sometime?'

'Of course,' I tell her. And I mean it. I realise that the girl I used to pity can teach me lots about living that I never even knew I was ignorant about. Suddenly I feel immensely weary and more than a little ashamed. And that niggling pain doesn't go away. I totter off to bed, climb into the stiff sheets and manage to achieve a sort of stupor.

Oakes fusses over me like an old hen in the morning and insists that I miss today's show. 'Sorry, Moon. You look grisly. And you don't need to be there,' he points out. 'We'll be making it short. No question time. And you know what that's like.'

He convinces me. Public meetings are getting grimmer. The jostling's worse. The clutching hands grow stronger. People are grabbing at the angel-baby as if he's a human lifebelt. And while we've been on this trip it has seemed that the world's become a more unstable place.

I've watched the news on CNN with an increasing sense of foreboding – seeing new outbreaks of diseases once thought to be conquered and some they still can't put names to. Heard scientists lamenting new signs of environmental destruction. Watched bomb-blasted grannies lying in dirty streets ruddy with blood. Is it any worse than it ever used to be, or is it that I'm extra-sensitive to it all now?

No one objects when Shirley suggests that she stay behind too. If she gives her baby a longer cuddle than usual, it attracts no attention. If there's extra strain on Philip's face, and a tad more love in his eyes as someone takes him from his mother's arms, then I'm the only one who notices. They leave in a flurry of car-door slamming and goodbyes.

Shirley doesn't dawdle over her own departure. She's down with her suitcase ten minutes later as a taxi rolls up the drive. We hug each other tight, suddenly frightened – Shirley of sorting out her life, me of sorting out her husband, who will surely never believe that his wife has planned her defection all alone.

'Off you go,' I order. 'You're doing the right thing.'

At last she's bundled in and driven away, waving all

the way down the long driveway and until the car slides out of sight. It feels strange to be here in the empty house. Well, almost empty. Jean the cook is in the kitchen, rattling up lunch. I go out to the patio and sink into an overstuffed lounger beneath an umbrella. A few puffy clouds idle overhead. I can hear the sea slapping at the beach beyond the wall.

My eyelids droop. In a minute, I might take a swim in the pool. In a minute. I doze for a long, indeterminate time and then become aware of a phone ringing inside somewhere. Check the time. Three-quarters of an hour? Don't need to get up though. Jean's there. She'll get it.

'Ms Moon? Are you awake? There's a call. He says it's important.'

It's Jean in her apron, wire whisk in one hand and cordless phone in the other. Still dozy, I take it from her and she ambles back to the kitchen, pausing for a moment to ask if I want Thousand Island or French for the salad.

'French,' I mouth, swinging my legs off the lounger so I can put my feet on the patio. I figure it's Jimmy. I've left a message for him with Daniel's housekeeper in England, so he'll know where to find me if he wants to get in touch. 'Cynthia,' says a male voice, younger and lighter than the old man's.

Silence. I can actually feel the flesh move down the length of my spine. It's a soft, tense creep, like a cat's paw withdrawing from an object that has suddenly been perceived to be an object of potential menace.

'Surely you haven't forgotten my voice this quickly,' Vortex says.

I struggle to keep my voice firm. 'How did you know where to find me?'

'Well, Louisa ... dear Louisa, she's such a good friend now ... she has friends all over the place, even in Honolulu. And media people somehow get to find out things like the phone numbers of exclusive rented houses. My, we are living high, aren't we, Cyn?'

'What do you want?'

'I've been sending you warnings for some time, Cynthia. You're really not very good at taking notice.'

'I've no idea what you're talking about.'

'Well, Miranda tells me she certainly let you know my displeasure. And Louisa, I know she gave you a very clear message – so clear that any dunce ...' and he spits out the word with such ferocity that I flinch '... would have been able to understand it.'

'And I wouldn't be at all surprised if you've had some sickness lately. And a little bleeding. Dark, heavy stuff, seeping out, Cyn, very messily, draining you dry.'

A strange whine has started up in my head – a piercing noise that runs over the top of my skull to lodge in an agonising buzz behind my eyes.

I rub at my face, knuckling the eyeballs. The pain gets worse. I've been staring at the ground in shock and note distantly the trembling of my knees and the fact that I can't stop it happening. My mouth is flooding with saliva. It's like that time on the plane all over again. But worse. I'm unable to impose tension on anything – knees, thoughts, lips. There's too much menace oozing from the earpiece.

'Let me make it even clearer for you, Cyn,' Vortex

says. 'You're a spoiler. A destroyer. You're a bumbling stupid fool in a garden, thrashing around with her hedge clippers and killing the webs. You and that fucking baby. Raving about balance, putting down the Signal Thread, gabbling about the fork in the road. There is no road, Cyn, not for you any more. There is only the spiral and we can't have you tearing it apart.'

There's a terrible weight on my chest now. Can't breathe. With a tearing gasp I roll off the lounger on to my knees, elbows on the seat. The voice grinds on and on.

'You have something very powerful close by, don't you? Two things, in fact. For a while there was only one. A real little goer of a lighthouse, this object you're carrying around. Although sometimes you didn't keep it close and then we couldn't *smell* you any more. But now there are two of the things, well, you're not hard to detect. You're pulsing,' he growls. 'Loud and clear. And to make things even easier, I have a very precious part of you here with me that gives me special access. It's in my hand, right now, so shiny and pretty, and I can stir it around and reach right within your very core.'

And a pain scorches within me, twisting and burning. My mouth gapes with a soundless, in-drawing gasp. I watch my fingers go into a wide, starfish stretch. The phone clatters to the paving stones. But the voice still oozes from it, compressed and tinny, pouring out evil as my back arches and my heels drum and the pain overwhelms me . . .

SIXTEEN

You know those stories that people tell about how it is on the brink of death? About slipping from their bodies, smooth as a finger from a satin glove, and seeing everything from above? The doctors. The ambulance people. The shocked loved ones. That's how it is now for me. I am here but not here. Watching, but not involved, as the white van bears away the shell of me, my husk.

Oakes and Philip and Jeff Preston, returning from their press conference, pass the ambulance screaming by, lights aflash, as they round the corner close to the house. They take little notice for they are still shaken by the disappointed howls of anger that went up when Philip said just a few words, adding nothing new to anything else he'd said around the world, and then refused to answer questions. I can see how the scene unfolded, for the words are still abuzz in their heads.

'You can't just walk away,' a blonde TV reporter screeched at them. 'What about the bombing in Los Angeles? Don't you feel responsible?'

'No!' Oakes cried. 'You can't blame him for that.'

'But what about the ozone hole – bigger than ever!' yelled someone else. 'And the famine in Liberia!' And

247

the oil fires in Alaska!' Angry questions had ripped at them like black birds, beaks agape, as if the baby, by bringing all these things to the forefront of their minds, had conjured up all the misery in the world and would somehow now have to fix it. Margot tapped at Oakes's shoulder. 'We've lost it,' she shouted over the hubbub. 'Can't control this rabble.' They'd fled out the back of the building. Nobody had followed, but it wouldn't be long before they were besieged again, thought David.

Now they are turning into the driveway. And he sees Jean sobbing at the front door. A security guard is running towards the car, skidding to a halt at the window. 'They've taken her to hospital! She's sick!'

'Who? Who's sick?'

'Miss Moon, she's had some sort of turn.'

The cook is stumbling towards them. 'I'm so sorry,' she wails.

'Where's Shirley?' demands Preston. No one answers him.

'Jean!' shouts Philip. 'What's happened?'

His small ringing voice is like a slap. Her eyes clear and she pours out her story. 'I came out again five minutes later. I could have left her here for hours! And there she was.' Jean clamps down a fresh upwelling of sobs. 'I've never seen anyone so sick. She was all moaning and stiff as a board, and lots of, I don't know, *gloob* . . . strings of saliva stuff coming from her mouth. I screamed for Gary here,' she says, nodding at the guard, 'and he came running. And then I remembered the phone. It was under the lounger – and when I picked it up it was still switched on.' She shudders. 'And someone

248

was still talking on it, funny sort of talk, raving on. And I screamed, "Get off the phone!"'

Jean presses a hand to her heart, recovering now. 'I thought she was dying . . .'

'Where's my wife!' Preston demands, struggling to get out of the door.

'Who gives a fuck!' yells Oakes in an agony of impatience and boots him out on to the driveway so that he stumbles to his knees. Oakes slaps the back of the driver's seat. 'Go!'

They race after the ambulance, passing the car bearing Margot and other staff members, not heeding their puzzled faces as they fly by. 'Has Cyn said anything to you about feeling unwell?' Philip asks.

'No, she's just seemed tired, like she was this morning, but this sounds entirely different anyway – more like poison or a snake bite.'

'We all ate the same meal last night and this morning. And there are no venomous snakes on the island. Or spiders,' adds Philip.

'So what is it?' Oakes asks. His voice comes out in a croak.

'We are dealing here with ancient forces,' Philip says. 'Currents that are deep and dark. In the modern world, it may seem ridiculous to you that someone can fall foul of malevolent spirits, but I fear that Cyn may be in that sort of peril. And maybe we should consider whether she was right to fear the presence of those stones. Maybe they do make her vulnerable.'

'Oh, come on,' protests Oakes, but echoes of the crash of London lightning boom again in his head.

Poor things, I think, as I feel their pain. They shouldn't worry so. I'm fine, up here. So peaceful. Though I can see that my discarded body is labouring to survive.

'She's latrodectic, Mr Oakes.' The doctor is a porridge-faced young woman with wiry hair who had been on duty for too long. She is still sharp enough to note his bewilderment. 'Reaction to a black widow bite,' she explains.

Oakes stares into the room where three nurses are working on the patient. 'I thought there were no spiders like that in Hawaii?'

The doctor shrugs. 'Hundreds of aircraft land on this island every day, Mr Oakes, carrying thousands of tourists, all with God knows what in their baggage. Accidental bites are rare, but not unheard of. The symptoms are fairly unmistakable. Extreme pain ...' David feels Philip tighten in his arms '... which builds to maximum intensity about thirty minutes after the bite. That would have been about when she arrived here. There's nausea and vomiting, a great deal of salivation, the muscles become rigid, breathing is difficult.'

'Can she be healed?' asks Philip.

'Sure, we have anti-venom,' she soothes. It seems appropriate to give the baby a comforting stroke, but she is damned if she knows how to act around this child. She retreats into professionalism. 'A bite like this isn't usually fatal, though if she hadn't been found so quickly it might have been a different story.'

She glances at the group around the bed, duty calling her back. 'There's a waiting room just down the corridor. Get yourself a coffee. We'll call you when it's okay to see her.'

Oakes hovers, unwilling to leave. Philip pulls at his arm. 'They'll look after her,' he says quietly.

The doctor turns on her soft rubber soles and whisks back into the room. Oakes trudges along the corridor to the waiting room and finds a stiff vinyl couch. He sags into it, letting Philip scramble down alongside. 'Shit,' he says. 'What a shambles of a day.'

They sit in silence. Waiting. 'You know my mother's gone,' says the baby. 'She has freed me.'

'That's nice,' says Oakes.

'But my father doesn't know that,' Philip adds. 'Not yet anyway.'

'Jesus,' says Oakes. 'That's all we need.'

They hear footsteps coming along the corridor, lots of commotion, urgent whispers. Margot slips into the room shutting the door behind her to keep out prying eyes. 'How is she?'

'Don't know. All right, I guess. They say she'll be okay.'

'Thank God for that.' She sits, looking weak-kneed. 'Oakes, are *you* all right?'

He gives her a caustic smile. 'Don't panic, Marg. We don't need any press releases.'

'I'll have to, I'm afraid. The media are setting up in the car park. *Majorly.* I'll get some official info and go give them the glad tidings.' She heaves herself up. 'Oh, one more thing. There's some guys out at the nurses' station. They say they're friends of yours. Want me to have them kicked out?'

Oakes looks at her with scant interest. People are always saying they're friends, mates, cousins, buddies. You learn about ingratiating bastards in his business. 'Names?' he says.

'Lightbody, of all things. Had no trouble with that one. And . . . Finian. I thought of rainbows. You know, that trick when you're lousy with names and so you think of something that will remind . . .' But even as her sentence trails off he is brushing past and pelting down the long shiny passageway.

He wastes no time with hellos. One look and already heads are turning, recognising him, in the rows of bucket seats in the huge waiting area. 'Come,' he says. 'Out of here, quickly.' And he hauls them back to where Philip waits.

Jimmy is trying to hurry, trying to talk all at once. 'Is Miss Moon all right?' His voice is sharp, edged with anxiety.

'No,' says Oakes as they reach the little room with vinyl seats, shut away from all the curious eyes. And unaccountably, for it is many years since he's cried, Oakes is suddenly unable to continue speaking. He sits down, feeling like a fool.

Philip reaches up and takes the old man's hand. 'Jimmy, it's so good to see you. Cyn's so ill. We were at a press conference and she was gone by the time we got back.'

'Gone?' Jimmy breathes with horror.

'Gone as in taken away,' he explains.

'Oh, my lord! I thought you meant . . .'

'No, no, she'll recover. They think it's a spider bite.'

Philip hesitates, then adds, 'The housekeeper says that when it happened Cyn was talking to someone on the phone.'

'Vortex,' grates Jimmy. 'Has to be. Have you seen her yet?'

'No, but soon, maybe.'

At last Oakes finds his voice. 'Finian, you old reprobate. What in God's name are you doing here? And Jimmy. This is all . . .' And his hands drop into his lap because for once the famous talkshow man can find no words.

'They gave me back my passport,' says Robert. 'I guess they figured that if Philip hadn't technically been kidnapped then technically I hadn't done anything too terrible either. And when I heard you were headed this way I thought I'd come along for a few days. Sophie was okay about minding Billie. Jimmy and I arrived at the reception desk out there at the same time, both asking about the same patient. She is going to be okay, isn't she?'

The doctor's at the door, hears the question. All faces turn to her. 'She's hanging in there,' she says. 'But she's not responding much. It might help if you see her for a little while. Just a few moments, mind.'

I watch them curiously as they file in and stand around the bed. All at once I'm aware of a floating translucent cord which links me to the body lying down there, so flat and still. I know that once it's cut we'll be parted for ever. It's odd to think of that shell as me, the Cyn person. I am sad for my friends for they're so shocked and fearful. But I can't feel sad for the body in the bed.

It feels nothing. Its head looks moist and puffy, like a mushroom after rain, the nose a bony pyramid pushing up under the skin. Hair lies in limp strings, dark snails' trails on the hospital linen. The eyes flutter open, dark and wet, prunes afloat in egg white, but they do not see. How can they, when the seeing part, the me part, is up here on the ceiling?

The shimmering cord shifts in the air, a sinuous seaweed stem swimming in an undersea current. It tugs at my gut. And suddenly I'm giddy, balanced on some irrevocable brink. There's a light! And hands outstretched, holding the stones, the precious ancient stones. There's a roaring in my head. Go back! And then I'm falling, whooshing into my skin. *Ooph!* Hurtling down the cord into dark, aching squelchiness. God, I hurt. But I'm behind my eyes again, seeing beloved faces above me. 'Hello,' I say in a high treble. And they smile. Great, beautiful smiles. Oakes. Jimmy. Robert. Philip. I feel for Jimmy's hand and hang on tightly. He's a liferaft in my cold heaving sea. He lowers Philip to the edge of the bed. The baby leans over and kisses my cheek. 'Dear Cyn,' he says. 'You gave us such a fright.'

'Not as big a fright as I got.' My speech is slow and bumbling – it's a huge effort to get mind and lips to work in unison. 'They say I was bitten, but it was Vortex.' I squint fiercely. 'It was him. He bit me. In the head.'

'Shush now,' says Oakes. 'You're okay now.' He strokes my hand. I didn't know he could be so tender. 'Just sleep. We'll talk about it later.'

My head's wobbling, left and right. I'm scared, don't want them to go. 'What if he comes back?'

'Miss Moon,' Jimmy says. 'You don't have to say anything. I know how tired you are.' I lie listening, eyes closed. Small teary pools ooze out from under my lids as I absorb the comfort of his presence. 'Do not fret or worry,' he says, speaking in the lilting voice he might use to a small, sick child. 'Just lie there. Get well. Go to sleep. You can sleep, I promise you,' he soothes. 'You're under my protection now. I know it was him. I have already thrown my blanket of love around you. He cannot penetrate it. Do you understand that, Miss Moon?'

'Yes,' I sigh. 'How did you know to come?'

'Oh Two gives me far more than dreams, Miss Moon. She's good at warnings too. I was about to fly home but I knew I had to be here.'

'Who the hell is Oh Two?' Robert whispers to Oakes, who gives him a bewildered shrug.

I'm still focused on Jimmy. 'Why does Vortex want to hurt me?'

'Because through you he can hurt Philip. He and his kind want the Signal Thread to speak through them alone. Philip's stopping that from happening.'

'But how is it he can make me sick like this?'

'I don't know yet, Miss Moon. But I intend to find out.'

I'm almost asleep in their circle of warmth when I remember something else that seems important. 'We've got the stones, Jimmy. Vortex knew. Somehow he knew about them.'

'I thought he might.'

I force my eyes open. 'This isn't going to end, is

it, until I've done what they want? What the stones want.'

'What's she talking about?' Robert mutters to Oakes.

'Miss Moon, don't talk now . . .' Jimmy's saying.

'No, no,' I protest, 'I want to. We have to. I was damn near dead just now . . . but the stones sent me back. We have to act out that dream of yours, Jimmy. Me on the mountaintop, with Oakes. Locking the stones together.' Jimmy says nothing but I can feel his slow smile.

I swing my head to Oakes. 'Do you think I'm crazy?'

'Hell, I don't know. The word's taken on a whole new meaning for me lately.'

I still want Jimmy's blessing. 'Is it right for us to do it now?' I ask him.

'Of course,' he says. 'Why do you think I've come all this way, an old fool like me, stuck in his ways?' I make a faint snickering noise. Jimmy seems pleased to see me smile – the severe look is leaving his face. 'Mind you, I'm not sure about hill climbing. Perhaps I can stay at the bottom with a cellphone and just talk you through it.'

'How do you know about cellphones?' I manage a mild tease. 'An old man like you, stuck in his ways.'

'I do read about technology,' he says mildly.

I'm feeling sick and drained. 'Oh, Jimmy,' I sigh. 'This mountain of yours. It seems like a nowhere place.'

He gets stern again. 'Certainly not. It's an everywhere place. This is all one world. Any high spot will do. Those stones are creatures of the air, so you need wind and space. And of course, it needs to be a place of power.'

'How are we going to find that?'

'It will speak to you. You'll know. And then you and

Mr Oakes must join the talismans together and spark off
the moment of truth which Philip has been warning the
world to expect. Not you alone. It needs the mix of male
and female energies.' My eyes slip to Oakes who stands
by the bed, looking dubious.

'Remember,' Jimmy is telling me, 'a long time ago,
when we first met, I perturbed you by interpreting
your name. You thought I was being ridiculous. So.
Here we are again.' Jimmy's speech is slow and clear.
Two-and-two-make-four tones.

'You represent the moon, the weaver, the nurturer,
the female side of all existence. You need a partner to
stand for the sun, the maleness of all creation. That's
why Mr Oakes is playing a part in all this. It's a matter
of balance. Of duality. Sometimes,' he adds, 'knowing
why things happen doesn't help you in life. Sometimes,
you just have to cast yourself off the edge, like those
little airborne spiders that stand on tippy-toes and let
the wind take them where it will, trusting they will land
in a safe place.'

I don't want to cast myself adrift. My feet like solid
ground. But I hear myself say, 'I know.'

Oakes hushes me then. 'We'd better go now,' he says.
'Nurses are giving us black looks.'

Jimmy touches my arm. 'Miss Moon, did Vortex ever
cut your hair?'

My hair? And I remember. The orange lilies and
the glass table. The shreds of hair vibrating under
his tattoo.

He reads my face and sighs. 'Ah. He has a piece of
you then. That's what it is. He can't affect Philip or

David but this connection between you – it's made you vulnerable.'

And I suddenly remember a conversation with Louisa, so long ago, when we talked after my meeting with Miranda Lewis. Louisa had a message for me from Vortex – that strange sentence. 'Tell her I have her here in my hand.' Ah. Not 'here'. *Hair*.

'Don't worry,' Jimmy is saying. 'The stones may be a beacon for men such as him, but believe me, they are a shield as well. They've protected you, not exposed you. They are why you're still with us. Why you'll still be here tomorrow. Safe and sound.'

I let myself slide at last into sleep.

The next day, Oakes spoons me into a nondescript rental car and takes me back to the house by the beach. On the way, I tell him about Shirley's decision to drop out. 'Smart lady,' he says, 'with a creep like that for a husband.'

Margot's in a snit. 'Jesus,' she bitches after giving me a perfunctory greeting. 'Why's it all gone so sour?' She's sitting scanning the morning papers. The post-press conference reports are derisory. One story suggests our whole tour was just a giant promotion for Oakes's show. ('Well, of *course* it was,' she mutters with disgust.) Another commentator has me as an ambitious manipulator – and the starbaby as bright but bulldozed putty in my hands. There's a smattering of stories about my collapse, all alluding to food poisoning and exhaustion – the story Oakes asked the hospital to release.

'All this trouble,' she mutters, 'and we only get page

five. Cal will be spitting,' she adds darkly as she goes off to phone him.

A glance at the front page is enough to inform anyone why we're not on it. Philip is last week's news. The world has bigger scandals and crises to mess with now. A major bank has collapsed in the States, leaving people heaving and shoving outside the doors. A strange blight is decimating crops in Russia. There's rioting in Germany between fascists and black immigrants. Whole blocks are ablaze in Frankfurt. A minor member of the British Royal Family has been lacerated by shrapnel from an anti-monarchy bomb: England is stunned.

A little wobbly still, I sit on a cane settee on the breezy patio. Oakes joins me and we're quiet for a while, listening to the burbling of pigeons on the arid lawn. Philip's inside, alone, in meditation. We've learnt to leave him alone for long periods. Lately, he's withdrawn more and more.

I'm brooding on Vortex. Oakes, reading my silence, turns my chin with his hand, making me look him in the eyes. 'He can't hurt you again. Jimmy's promised. Remember? He told you that yesterday.'

'Did he?' I don't remember much. Except for his voice. It was like wrapping myself round a hot-water bottle when I was a kid in bed on a stormy night. 'Where is he anyway?'

'He and Robert are sharing a hotel room on the beach. Robert and I sat up really late last night. Drinking. Talking. We had a few years to cover,' he says with a fond grin. 'I guess they'll be here soon.'

'How did they know where to find us?'

'Not hard. It was on the news. Robert was watching TV in his hotel room. Jimmy was in a cab on the way in from the airport. They both went straight to the hospital.'

I watch palm fronds wipe the sky clean. It seems strange to be able to sit here without worrying about the next interview, the next press conference, the next goddamn flight. We don't go on to LA for two days yet. Cal's keeping us at arm's length, letting things simmer down. We're free for a whole glorious forty-eight hours. It's also a relief to be free from the glowering Preston presence, but I know he's bound to want to confront me over Shirley's departure. 'Where's Jeff?' I ask reluctantly.

Oakes makes an irritated noise in his throat. 'Dismal jerk,' he says. 'Shoved off in a temper this morning. Whining that we've turned his wife against him, destroyed his marriage, alienated his son. And it's all my fault of course for luring Philip on to primetime and ruining Jeff's entire miserable, pathetic life.'

Oakes sounds relieved. Me too. But there's a small cold corner of concern in my head too. 'Where's he gone?'

'Oh, that's partly why Margot's in a lather. He threatened to run to the media and tell them bad little Philip drove Shirley away. Won't *that* make great copy?'

'Can't we stop him?'

'Oh, sure. With a payoff. Asked for a mill, the greedy bastard. He didn't have a hope. Cal's not got much stomach for this any more. He's being pressured to call the whole thing off, Cyn. Our promotion of Philip is no longer politic. The conservative lobby are heavy dudes and lots of them are big advertisers. They don't take kindly to uppity kids who call themselves angels. So, I suspect our whole juggernaut is about to come to a halt. And an antsy truckdriver who wants to try a little blackmail is going to get no-fucking-where.'

'So he's gone off in a rage?'

'Yep.'

'But where to?' I don't like to think of him out there. Brooding. Plotting.

'Don't know. Don't care. Just as long as he stays away.'

Jimmy and Robert turn up then and there's lots of hugging for me and shoulder-slapping between Oakes and Robert.

Jean brings coffee and cookies and we all sit around gabbing. It feels so good. I can feel the tightness inside start to ease, even hear myself laugh. These three men supply me with a cocoon that feels safe and secure. And David's news that Cal may soon pull the plug on our operation doesn't upset me one bit.

Jimmy and Robert are bursting with something, I can tell. A satisfied small smile keeps sliding on to the old man's face. So I ask him what's up. 'When you told me last night that Vortex had pieces of your hair, it got me thinking about whether I could diminish his power. So I asked Robert if he knew anyone who might have access to his domain.' I try not to react, but can't help the quiver that comes on at the sound of the name.

I close my eyes, seeing again the long expressive fingers pushing my brown clippings into a compact pile on the glass table.

'His salon, you mean?'

'No, his private quarters. He's gone away, as you know.'

I frown. 'I don't know anyone who . . .'

'But you do,' interrupts Robert. 'Louisa. She and Vortex really had something going for a couple of weeks.' I make high, disbelieving noises. 'Yeah, really,' he insists. 'She was staying overnight, even had a key.'

'Whaaat?' I'm guffawing now, trying to imagine how Lou took to spider-enhanced meditation sessions.

'I phoned her this morning – with some trepidation. I had no idea whether she was still seeing him or not.' Robert takes an irritatingly slow munch at one of Jean's cookies.

'And?' I prod.

'She loathes the guy. He's taken off with a heap of her funds. They were planning a trip together and he went without her.'

'So,' Jimmy chimes in, 'I got Robert to ask her to go to his apartment and have a look around, see what she can find that may be of help to us in fending this man off.'

'I told her we'd call her at his number around now,' Robert goes on. 'She wants to talk to you anyway. So why don't you do it?'

I didn't think I'd ever be having telephonic heart-to-hearts with my old boss but soon I'm going 'Mmm' and nodding sympathetically while she grizzles about her ex-lover (and mine, though I'm not about to remind her of that). I put her on speakerphone so we can all hear.

'I organise the holiday, I buy the tickets, book the hotel, get cash to play with, do every damn thing. And then the creep takes off without me! With *my* money. Leaves me a note saying it's over. Tells me I don't please him any more.' There's acid in the way she mouths 'please'. 'Cyn,' she adds gruffly, 'sorry I bawled you out about taking off the way you did. Guess you had something bigger on your plate than I could ever offer.'

I string some never-mind phrases together. The sorries can wait.

'Louisa, I gather Robert's told you I was really ill yesterday?'

'Sure.'

'I've got a friend here called Jimmy who thinks Vortex might be . . . oh, I don't know . . . hexing me. Vortex phoned me and that's when it happened . . . when he was talking.'

She lets out a hiss. 'Godammit it, I'm sorry. Soon after you left I gave him some things from your desk. He . . . kept asking. Jesus, it was such stupid stuff. A couple of lipsticks, a comb. It was all so trivial and he made a sort of *game* of it. Said it helped to have your things in his possession. It didn't seem serious, you know?' For the first time ever I hear a bit of a crack and wobble in her voice. 'The bastard flattered me. And it had been a long time since anything like that came my way. You'd think I'd be too bloody old, wouldn't you? Too cunning. Too well used by all and sundry to fall for that.' Her voice is tight.

'Lou, I'm not talking lipsticks. Where are you now?'

She chuckles. 'In his living room. You remember those big leafy trees in pots he had growing there? Not quite so big now, actually. I've been pruning them. Right down to tiny wee stumps. Martin's haircutting scissors don't make bad secateurs.' I have to grin, imagining his gleaming floor knee-deep in tattered foliage. 'Very expensive those scissors. Hundreds of dollars a pair,' she adds in by-the-by tones, and she lets me hear down the phone the tiny gnashing snicky-snick sound of Martin's blunted blades.

'We're looking for hair clippings, Lou,' I prod her. 'He might have them hidden somewhere.' She sounds a bit puzzled. 'Well, there's his cabinet in the other room. Where he keeps all his samples. Just a sec.' I hear the shushy swell of static as she carries the cordless phone further from its station. 'Okay, I'm in front of it now,' she reports. 'It's a cabinet, lovely old thing actually, with lots of narrow shelves. He has little plastic bags stacked inside in alphabetical order, the sort with zip-up tops. They're his colour samples.'

Jimmy breaks in and introduces himself. 'What are these samples?' he wants to know.

'He keeps clips of his clients' hair, for quality control,' she explains patiently. 'So that when someone wants the colour she had last year he can match it exactly. I asked him once why he kept them up here and he told me there wasn't room downstairs. These are back files, not current ones.'

'Pull one out,' he orders her. 'Any one.'

'Okay,' she says, puzzlement in her voice.

'Whose name is upon it?' he asks.

'Patricia Shelley,' she reads.

'Well then,' says Jimmy. 'Pity her, for with her hair in his possession, an evil man like Vortex can do great mischief to her.'

Louisa sounds amused rather than shocked. 'Oh come on,' she scoffs. 'Patricia? I know her. She's from one of the wealthiest families in this town. And she's a friend of Martin's. She even financed him when he upgraded the salon. Lent him thousands . . .' Her voice trails off.

'Jimmy's eyebrows rise. 'Ask her later,' he says. 'Ask her if Martin has yet paid back any of the money she lent him.'

'I can't. She's . . . in a hospital somewhere. They say she had a nervous breakdown.'

'Poor woman,' says Jimmy. 'What colour is this hair of your friend's?'

'Grey,' quavers Lou. 'Well, you know, pepper and salt.'

Suggests Jimmy: 'Most women dye their hair to cover up the grey, do they not? The so-called sample you hold would appear to be uncoloured. There is no dye to match, is there?' We hear only the hush of Lou's silence. 'He's a user,' says Jimmy gently. 'A manipulator. Don't feel ashamed.'

'I'm just feeling . . . so *abused.*'

'Relish that feeling then. There's nothing wrong with regret – it shows you have a heart.'

She bites back, sounding more like the Lou I know: 'Who the hell are you to be making assumptions about me?'

'I'm just a friend of Miss Moon's.'

Louisa's voice sharpens. 'You warn her to stay clear of Martin then. He's mad as hell and dying to get even. His business has done a freeze since all of this began. He thought being famous would help, but when you're famous for being weird . . .' She expresses herself with a choking noise and I hear the old familiar rattle of her bracelet as she apparently makes a chopping movement across her throat.

'It's hardly her fault,' says Jimmy.

'Hah. Try telling him that. Cyn, are you still there?' she asks. Yes, I tell her. 'There's something I want to know – why didn't you level with me about the baby when this all started?'

'The time wasn't right back then.'

'But you're a reporter!' she complains. 'It was the best story in the whole world. How could you have turned it down? You were out there on my time! Where were your journalistic ethics?'

Robert chimes in: 'In a different place from her human ethics, Lou. Sometimes, there's a divide.'

She barks her dry laugh. 'We could argue *that* for hours, Finian.'

'But we don't have time,' says Jimmy. 'Vortex is off on the loose somewhere. He's addicted to control, and the dark side of the web is giving him the strength to be very good at it.'

'So what do you plan to do?'

'Not me. We. You can get back at him by getting rid of every last shred of those hair samples.'

'I guess you're looking for Moon?' she suggests and

we hear her flicking along the tabs. 'Molloy, Maynard, McKay, Mottford. No Moon.'

'Ah,' he says with a disappointment that makes me uneasy.

'What do you want me to do with all this stuff?' Lou is asking.

He tells her and we wait while she goes to the kitchen to find a big rubbish sack and then, following his instructions, removes the little bags and tips their contents into the sack. All we can hear as this goes on is rustling and the sound of her breathing. I close my eyes and can imagine how the hair drifts into the bag's rumpled walls – blonde, brown, honey, black, auburn, crinkled, straight and wavy – discarded packets forming a slippery plastic moat about her feet.

'Uurgh,' she says. And then, 'Sorry, just found my own.' Then her voice gains strength. 'Okay, nearing the end, guys. Wah Lee, Walker, Woodley, Wright, Yarmouth, Young. That's it. Hang on, there's one more.' The quaver is back, her voice deeper. 'It's different from the others, stuffed in the corner. I almost didn't see it. Oh,' she whispers. 'It's Martin's. Not just a snip. All of it. Christ, he's lopped it all off.' In my mind's eye, I see it held in her hunter's fist – long and thick, hanging heavy like a dead black rabbit strung up by its ears. 'Do I throw this away too?'

'No,' growls Jimmy. 'Keep it. It's a prize.'

And he tells her what to do with all the rest.

We hang up soon after that so she can get on with the job. Bone-weary, I ask to be excused for a while to go take a nap. Still tuckered out after yesterday, I'm quickly asleep and immersed in a dream in which I see Lou as clearly as if I'm there, thousands of miles away. She throws a sack into the back seat of her car and turns its sleek nose towards the west – heading for a lonely beach where massive waves hurl themselves upon black sand and steely winds blow so constantly that the trees crab sideways up the grey-green hills.

She parks as the sun sags towards a leaden horizon, and trudges over the deserted iron-sand dunes. Kicking off her shoes, heedless of her stockinged feet, she hitches up her skirt and wades knee-deep into the ocean's surging grip. It tugs, testing her, but she stands firm.

'You're not going to get me, you bastard!' she howls as the cold wind roars in from the Tasman Sea to buffet against her. She opens the sack and a gust sucks and plucks at it and a storm of hair whirls about her head. And then it is gone, ripped away by the wind. Creamy foam churns about her ankles.

She whoops out loud, letting out a scream of release, and with both hands she stretches the bag over her head and it too is whipped from her grasp, leaping away along the beach, round and stiff, like a tumbling brown turtle shell.

SEVENTEEN

I wake up feeling dry and itchy as if there's hair inside my clothes. There's no more bleeding today, thank God, but I feel I need cleansing. I have the strongest urge to immerse myself in clean ocean water. Swimsuit? I'm sure I threw one in . . . yes. As I pull it out I graze a knuckle on a corner of my spiral stone and decide, without really thinking about it, to throw it in my shoulder bag too.

When I emerge from the house the others are sitting round the remnants of a lunch that's come and gone while I've been sleeping. Philip's with them now and he stretches up for a kiss.

'Hey.' I give Oakes a poke. 'I'd love a salt-water swim. Will you take me to a beach?'

No one can think of a good reason why not, especially when we check the street outside and find there's no media lurking out there. We might even be able to play tourist, be real people. Oakes insists on security though, so Gary the guard is dragooned into driving us in yet another dark-windowed limo, different from the ones we've used before. I'm finding the plush affluence oppressive after all these days of being chauffered.

The car reeks of money and status and some leather-preserving polish. It makes me nostalgic for Geraldine's blowsy comfort.

Robert insists on taking the rental Ford that Oakes used to bring me home from the hospital. 'Might as well use the car while we've got it,' he says. Fancies himself as a bit of a wheel man, does Robert. And the rental's quite snappy.. He can't resist a toy to play with, especially a nice new shiny American one.

We discover, past Diamond Head, a pocket of sand where there are few other swimmers. A ridge of volcanic rock makes a tiny lagoon which is sheltered from the inky swells that chug past the point. I splosh into the tepid calm and roll over to float on my back, sea water making a tickly circle around the island of my face. Bliss.

Oakes carries Philip out into the water and tows him along with a lazy kick. 'My,' Philip's saying dreamily as I stroke over to them, 'I can't remember when I did this last.'

'No swimming pools at the monastery, I presume,' says Oakes dryly.

'Good Lord no. We didn't even wash very often. You deodorised twentieth-century types would have found the ambience most distasteful.'

Philip makes fluttering sea-horsy movements to keep his body stable. 'We should search for a suitable summit for the stones,' he announces. My contentment ebbs fast. 'I've been musing on it,' he says. 'Margot did some scouting. Got me some local tourist guides. What-to-do-in-Honolulu stuff.'

'And?' Oakes looks discomforted. There's a look in his eyes that says 'Do I really have to play this silly game?' He changes the angle of his kick and heads for the beach where Jimmy and Robert wait on the sand. Robert hates swimming. Jimmy said he was content to watch.

'There's nothing in the brochures labelled spiritual hot-spots.'

'Surprise, surprise,' says Oakes.

'But there are various waterfalls and clifftops – it depends on how far we want to go,' Philip glances at me, 'and perhaps how much walking you can do. Your strength must still be low.'

'I don't need smothering,' I comment crisply as I wade out.

'Diamond Head's a possibility,' muses Philip as Oakes puts him down on the beach. 'It's supposed to be the old home of Pele, the fire goddess. There was a place at its base for ritual sacrifice. The missionaries destroyed it. They wanted the natives to have no reminders of their former barbarous ways.'

I wrinkle my nose. 'Good on them. It sounds hideous.'

'Don't forget though,' argues Jimmy, 'that European life wasn't so benign when Captain Cook first came here. Misbehaving sailors had their backs flogged to a pulp. The Hawaiians were horrified. Justice was brutal everywhere.'

'I know.' I turn and gaze up at the peak. 'It just gives me the creeps. It's so barren and bony. And all those dry trees around it – they're like scruffy old pubic hair.' The others laugh. I fling up my hand, sending sand flying.

'Look at this place. Hula girls in plastic skirts. Fake luaus on the beachfront. The stink of suntan oil all over. How can the mountain possibly have any spiritual power now?'

'Let's go check it out,' says Jimmy.

'Now?' says Oakes.

'Why not?' Then, 'Have you got your stone?' Jimmy wants to know.

'Yes,' Oakes admits. 'But it's just a look-see, right?'

'Sure.'

So we turn our backs to the sea and drive inland. Oakes decides to keep Robert company in the smaller car. It's only after we're under way that it occurs to me that this is a silly idea. Jimmy and Philip and I are hidden from the world behind black glass, while the famous Oakes face grins cheerfully at us as we glide past them to take the lead. The traffic's heavy and soon there are several cars between us, but they keep us in sight. We drive by the house on the way. All seems quiet on the street. No TV vehicles lying in wait, just a big yellow truck paused by the side of the road.

I look anxiously back as we approach the turnoff to the Diamond Head crater, but, no people problems loom. The sunflower yellow truck is grunting along, heavily laden, behind the Ford but it pulls over to the side of the road and we leave it behind as we make the right-hand turn to Diamond Head. Scrawny trees grow in a grizzled sort of way along the narrow road. Their branches are hung with dessicated brown seed pods. Through my open window I hear them rattle in the hot breeze. They give me the creeps.

A semi-circular tunnel mouth looms and then we're into the hill, cruising through a claustrophobic curve to emerge into a flat crater. Its walls are shallow at one side but swoop up to thousand-foot ramparts at the seaward end.

'We'd need to go up there?' My voice sounds hollow. The flat saucer of land is dry and stony with a scatter of exhausted shrubs. There's a sprawl of sterile National Guard buildings lying coralled inside a tall barbed wire fence. Gary pulls into the car park and turns off the engine. Robert pulls up alongside and in a couple of quickfire moves, Oakes is out of the Ford and slipping into the limo. 'Better,' he says. 'It's kind of public over there with Rob.'

'Let me out,' says Philip. 'You don't have to show yourself. I just want to see how it feels.'

I open the door a crack and lower him to the ground. No one's looking so, very cautiously, I ease outside too, slowly standing up. There are a few dozen other cars and a couple of tourist buses, air-conditioning units rumbling.

Family groups mill around their cars. A toddler cries. Long-legged teenage girls in fraying denim shorts and halter tops are sprawled in the back of an open wagon, drinking Cokes. Giggles overlay the electric thump pounding from their stereo.

Around seventy-five yards away a slender man in well-cut cream shirt and trousers is kicking at the ground, doing nothing in particular. Sometimes he picks up a stone and throws it into the dry brush. He throws well, with ease and power. He is bald, his pale scalp glowing dully, like old ivory, in the filtered sunlight.

I'm just about to turn away when he dips easily to the side, showing his profile for just a second before pulling back his arm to throw another pebble.

In a numbing rush of shock I recognise his grace. Know his face. My hands are claws gripping the top of the car door for support as I shrink back into the car.

My cringe makes Philip reach for me.

'It's him!' I hiss. 'Vortex!'

'Where?' says Oakes.

'The bald one!' *God what's he done that for?* I haul Philip on to my knee and cringe behind him, not willing to risk another look. I prod at Philip's back. 'What's he doing now? Tell me!'

'Nothing. Just standing there.'

Oakes reaches in front of me to pull the door shut. My pulse is crashing in my neck. 'Look again,' he orders. 'He can't see in here. You have to be sure.'

I inch an eye past Philip's small shoulder. Bald Vortex (*but his hair was so precious to him!*) still stands on the wasteland. He is quite still now. Too still.

'Christ, what's he doing here?' Panic is seething inside me again. 'It's as if he's listening.'

'We're in a closed car, Miss Moon,' says Jimmy patiently. 'There's no way he can hear.'

A strained quality in his voice makes me pay attention. He's not sounding surprised enough. He flashes me a fierce shamed/sorry look. 'Louisa told Robert he was on his way here. But we thought it best not to worry you after what happened the other day.' He keeps running his hand down the skin of my forearm, as if by doing so he can smooth away my dread.

I jerk my arm away and grate, 'Get me out of here.'

'But what's the problem?' says Gary. 'Who is that guy?'

'Just go!' snaps David. Robert's staring at us from his seat, puzzled as hell, so Gary nudges down his window and signals that we're heading back to the house. Robert mouths okay and we pull out of the parking space and head back towards the dark gaping tunnel. For a moment or two we're blocked by a gum-chewing blonde in a halter top who backs her sports car into the gap. Robert, in the clear, eases by us, indicating that he'll go first.

My brain is fizzing as we follow him out, leaving behind the oppressive black mouth and the clacking trees. What's Vortex after? Me? Philip? *All of us?* I'm feeling not just frightened but furious, a total idiot, for it hadn't occurred to me that he was here in Hawaii. How did he know where to find us? Sure, I knew he'd taken off but I thought he'd have gone to ground with a coven of his friends. When he'd called he'd sounded so long-distance, so removed from real life, that I was sure he was half a world away. Somewhere. Anywhere but here. Is he so angry that he'd follow us all this way just for revenge? Out of jealousy?

Robert makes a careful turn out on to the highway and we follow, passing the yellow Mack truck that I noticed before. It's still parked, engine running, diesel fumes hazing from its smokestacks. It's a nuisance sitting there, because when I twist round to see if anything's following us, it's in my view.

'Gary slow down,' I plead, 'just for a moment, just so we can see . . .' We slow to a crawl. I feel a need to pause for a moment, to make sure that all is well. Perhaps it wasn't even him. Perhaps I'm panicking without cause. We're all swivelled in the back seat now. A few cars come down the road behind us and a bus. The bus lumbers by us. The cars turn off and disappear in the opposite direction. Robert's car is almost out of sight up ahead now.

'Come on,' complains Oakes. 'Let's move it.'

At which point the limo's engine dies. Gary curses. 'Damn thing, he grumbles. And as the starter motor grinds without firing, the parked truck spews exhaust smoke and noise and rolls past us, slow but accelerating. I just happen to glance up and catch a glimpse of the driver's cab as the huge rig rolls by. See the pale, set face, the slit of the mouth as he stares forward, not seeing us, unable to see us through the darkened glass even if he did look.

'It's Jeff,' I yell. And at last the limo's pistons are pumping. 'Go, go!'

Gary turns to me, an agonisingly slow swivel of his head. 'You mean follow the truck?'

'Yes!'

'What the fuck's he doing in that thing?' demands Oakes.

'He said he had a friend here in the trucking business. He said he wanted to go and see him. Oh, God save us,' says the angel in a long drawn-out quaver.

Up ahead, Robert is driving steadily, seemingly unaware of the menace looming behind him although now we're all shouting and pleading for him to look behind, *look behind*!

'He thinks I'm in the Ford,' groans Oakes. 'He must have spotted me before. It's me he's after. I'm here you crazy bastard!' he roars in vain.

'But you're not there in the car now,' reasons Jimmy with maddening logic. 'Why should Jeff be so focused on Robert?

None of us answers because we can't bear to voice the fear that Jeff's so full of rage he'll lash out at anyone. He hasn't seen us in this black-walled limousine, hasn't recognised it as ours for we haven't used it before. But he's seen the Ford, he knows whose it is, and he wants it.

Up ahead there's a long, right-handed curve. Robert's brake lights are glowing for the T-intersection that's coming up. I can see the back of his head as we follow him around the curve. Window down, elbow on the ledge, he's gnawing absently at the knuckle of his forefinger.

The truck behind him is squatting fatly on its wheels as big rigs do when they're carrying a load. Robert's brake lights are coming on and he's indicating a left turn, slowing now for the traffic lights are turning orange.

And we see it all in minute detail.

Robert is stopping and Jeff is not. Insulated in our air-conditioning we can't hear the truck but we see the belch of smoke from the exhausts. And we can tell that Robert has seen the hulking Mack at last because

there's more smoke, from Robert's tyres this time, as he
floors the accelerator, hauling on the wheel, trying to
wrestle the car round the corner and put some distance
between himself and the looming eighteen-wheeler
before the lights go red. Robert nearly makes it. But
then a girl steps out from the sidewalk, toting sports
bag and tennis racket, head down, ears muffed with
tiny headphones, absorbed in her own world of noise.
I see the flash of pale legs striding out confidently, the
rumpled socks and Reeboks.

Robert's brake lights flash. In front of us Jeff, travelling too close behind Robert, is forced to brake too.
The giant rig slews and – oh, Jesus God! – it's over
the top and the car is suddenly a mess of ragged
metal and torn fabric and shattering glass, squeezed
beneath the truck's chassis. The Mack powers through
the intersection, crunches over the kerb and smashes
through a low brick wall into a timber yard stacked with
piles of four-by-two. As the screechng tangle batters its
way through the jagged breach in the bricks, we feel
the thud of ignition, see the bright orange flash.

'Oh my God. Oh my God,' I'm wailing as Gary
pulls the limo round the corner. We roll past the
tennis player, who stands shocked and screaming in
the road. Drivers who'd been stopped at the lights
sit gripping their steering wheels, gaping, frozen with
horror.

'Robert . . .' I howl, punching at the door. Boiling
rubber-dark smoke stains the pale sky. Jimmy stares
back, eyes wide and tragic, and Philip's face is buried
against Jimmy's chest, hands making tight white balls

as he clings to the old man's shirt. 'Cyn, stop it,' says Oakes over and over, stilling my flailing fists.

We drive on. 'We can't stop, Miss Moon,' Gary says. 'My instructions are that if there's trouble, we get out. No waiting. No involvement. Anyway, there are plenty of people there. And we can't help them. They need paramedics, firemen . . .' And his voice trails miserably away. 'We can't stop,' he says again.

I find out, much later, from Robert's sister Sophie that at that precise moment she was feeding Robert's little Billie back at home, watching him chase his cereal round and round his plate with a spoon. It wasn't a windy day but a door slammed in the house with a great crash, making the two of them jump, and she felt an icy draught. 'Oooh,' she giggled to her small nephew to comfort him. 'Wasn't that a big bang? We'll have to tell your daddy about that when he comes home.'

No one says anything much for the next few minutes. Gary drives on, I whimper a lot, David curses, Philip trembles and Jimmy prays. Soon Jimmy's had enough of my noise and David's profanity.

'Please be quiet,' he says. And when we don't take much notice he says it much louder. 'None of this can help Robert now!' he roars. It shocks us into comparative stillness and Philip raises his head, face wet with tears.

Gary breaks the silence. 'Where to, sir?' he asks. 'Back to the house?'

'No,' says Oakes. 'I'm in no mood for cameras.'

Neither am I. The barracudas will be upon us when

they know what's happened. And they'll all know in no time at all.

'But we can't just drive around,' I protest. 'We have to *tell* somebody.'

'Tell them what?' says Oakes. 'We saw it but we don't know why it happened. Whether Jeff meant it to happen. Scare tactics or intent? If he hadn't seen us in the car, would he have rammed the house instead? We'll never damn well know.'

One thing we all know. The angel-baby tour is over. There'll be no more rapt audiences. Not with the angel's daddy dead. Not when the angel's driven away his mother, wounding his father so deeply that he goes crazy in a borrowed or stolen truck. Not when famous celebrity David Oakes has missed being incinerated by the skin of his teeth, leaving his friend to burn instead.

It's shock, I suppose, but I'm dry-eyed and numb and very clear about all of the above. That's the way all this will be reported. There is no place for us to go where we will be greeted with warmth.

'It is my belief,' the baby says, 'that we must carry out our small ceremony now.'

'What?' I gibber at him.

'You both have your talismans with you?' Jimmy asks. Oakes and I stare at the old man. 'Philip is right. Now is the time for the mountaintop. If we simply return to the house now – to the world, if you like – we'll be immersed in a maelstrom of questioning and enquiry and doubt and recrimination. We won't have peace or time to ourselves for many days.

The point of Philip's speaking out in the way he has done will be lost. We must act now. Gary?' And the driver's eyes flick uneasily in the rear-vision mirror. 'We have a rather special thing that we must do. We'd be grateful if you'd leave us now and let Mr Oakes drive.'

Gary starts to protest but Jimmy won't be swayed. 'Please tell those in authority that we'll be back to answer all the questions. But we have witnessed a terrible thing. We want to have some time to ourselves first.'

'Do as he says,' orders Oakes and the man pulls over. He leans in the window as Oakes settles behind the wheel. 'God knows what you're up to,' Gary says, 'but whatever it is, do it well.' And he slaps the limo's flank like a cowboy urging on a wagon.

We pull out into the traffic. 'Right,' says Jimmy. 'Take us to the highest point you can think of.'

The day is going grey with fine rain blurring the sky. Lumpen clouds clog the hills ahead. 'I know,' Oakes says, 'the Pali Lookout. It's up on the spine of hills that divide the island. We can drive all the way up there.' And he puts his foot down.

I glance back once or twice as we clear the city but the traffic's too thick to read. If we're being followed from a distance there's no way of knowing. And anyway, was it Vortex back in the crater? Or was I just being paranoid? And if he did follow us out of the crater, he'd have been blocked at the crash scene. I catch Philip gazing up at me, all knowing eyes. 'Stop worrying,' he says.

At the top of the mountain divide, the rain is heavier. Oakes turns on the wipers. Thwack, thwock, thwock, thwock. We peer through the gloom.

'There it is!' says Oakes as he spots the Nuuanu Pali sign. He swings the car off the highway on to a narrow climbing road. Here, the rain-fed jungle grows juicy and dark. Shiny choking vines with elephant-ear leaves strangle the trunks of tall dripping trees.

We arrive at a circular parking area. It's little more than a paved space between rocky peaks. Another car is leaving, pale children's faces smudged behind wet glass. The driver of an ice-cream truck, eyes slitted against the rain, is closing his doors. He waves his hand in disgust, as if to tell us we're wasting our time coming up here to see the view. And then he drives away.

We are alone.

Oakes switches off the engine.

'Nice weather for it,' he says, his face pasty in the gloom.

'Do we have any coats?' I ask plaintively.

'Nope.'

'Umbrellas?'

Oakes pulls a mouth. 'You wouldn't want one in this – not unless you wanted to go parasailing.'

A gust of wind rocks the car, thrashes at the reedy grass on a nearby bank. I screw up my nose as rain smacks against the windscreen. 'It's disgusting out there. Where've the tropics gone?'

'Does it feel like the right place?' Jimmy asks anxiously. 'It must feel right.'

'I don't know. How are we supposed to know that?'

'Get out and see. Just the two of you, with Philip, without me in the way. Go see if it speaks to you. Where are your stones?'

David's is in a camera case on the back seat. He reaches over, finds what he's looking for and slips it into his pocket. I've got a waist-bag so I slip my talisman into that and clip it on before scrambling out with Philip and slamming the door. We both gasp in the chilly blast. Up here, on the island's windward side, the trade winds are anything but balmy.

Oakes grabs my hand and we struggle, heads down, along the path to the lookout, moving out of the car park's comparative shelter into the squall's full blast. Philip clings like a bear cub, legs around my waist, his bottom perched upon the bag slung around my hips. I'm sure I've read somewhere that babies are extra-vulnerable to wet and cold. Hell, he might get hypothermia.

'Okay?' I ask, hugging him tight. He nods against my chest, his small face pale and serious.

Out in the open now, we stand on a two-tiered concrete platform at the rim of a range of mountains, facing the ocean. This upper level is fronted by a waist-high wall. I grasp its edge to keep steady as the gusts buffet against us. Broad steps to the left and the right lead down to a lower viewing platform where another wall is topped by a metal pipe railing.

The face-whacking raindrops thin for a moment and I can see why people come up here with their cameras.

The view is stupendous. Sunlight shines on a distant bay far below and there's a blue arch of sky on the horizon. This storm will soon pass. But meanwhile we're being chilled to the bone. My teeth start to chatter. Away to each side stretch the mountains that form Oahu's backbone. The stony cliffs are riven with deep vertical fissures, carved out by centuries of exposure to wind and rain.

I'm having the strongest sense of having seen this place before. I turn my back to the wind and squat down behind the concrete bulwark, cradling Philip, sheltered from the blast. Oakes drops too, knees up, his back hard against the wall. 'I hate heights,' he says and gives me a weak grin.

Above our heads the boiling clouds shred in the turbulent updraught like salt foam smashed on the shore by the beat of a stormy sea. Why is this eyrie so familiar? Images wash and niggle in my head and then I remember. The dream. That blasted goddess dream. The floating hair and the strange flying over the deep-creased cliffs. These cliffs.

'This is it!' I shout. 'I've been here. Long ago, in a dream. 'Don't laugh.' But Oakes isn't laughing. He gives me a long, steady look.

'I'll go get Jimmy,' I tell them. I hand over Philip and scoot back to the car park, head down against the rain, wrench open the passenger door. 'Come on!' I cry. 'We're here!'

But the car is empty. For a second I stare stupidly at the yawning seat. And I stand up and notice for the first time, now I'm not squinting against the wind, that there's another car up here. Red. Shining wet. Its windows fogged.

Terrified suddenly, I duck back inside the limo and crouch down on the floor, slamming the door shut after me. Foetal, panicked, not thinking straight. Where's Jimmy? Who's out there? I wait. There's no sound but for small creaks as the wind bullies the vehicle, rocking it on its tyres.

One forearm is pressed against my chest. I'm conscious of the drumming pulse beneath the skin at my wrist as my heart gallops. I hear a car door close. Kthunk. Fear bathes me with heat. In my wet clothes, it's like I'm steaming. Some small voice in my head is saying, 'Careful Cyn, stay low, don't move, don't show yourself.' But I can't stay here for ever. David and Philip are still out there. They'll be cold, wet, worried. Do something.

It's still quiet. There's been no sound of an engine restarting. Would I hear that anyway above the wind? Perhaps someone just poked a head out, felt the cold wind, and retreated inside again, slamming the door. That's what made the noise. And now he's just sitting there in comfort eating a sandwich. Reading the paper. Listening to the radio. Growling at the kids. Doing something ordinary. Something harmless.

And then, oh Christ, the front door's wide open and icy air is rushing in and a shadow looms. I am a mouse frozen beneath a hawk's outspread wings. And I shrink before the smile. Twist my head up to see that handsome awful mocking face.

'Why, Cyn,' says Vortex in a tone of wonder, 'isn't it

strange that whenever we meet you're always in some particularly ungainly position?'

Oh, those teeth, the eyes, the pale shocking skull. Bone and chalk. Death colours.

'Fuck you,' I snarl.

He reaches over and grabs my wrist in his talon-like fist. 'Well, I only wish we had time, Cynthia,' he says wistfully. 'I still think fondly of that first evening when you fucked me most successfully. Shall we talk a while?' He slips into the passenger seat and closes the door with his other hand, never letting go of my wrist. I wrench and twist in vain.

'Stay,' he says. 'I really do want to talk.'

He lets go and I snatch my hand away, sitting up on the back seat now to ease my cramped limbs. The skin burns where he's been gripping.

'Where's Jimmy?'

'The feeble old guy? Oh, I've taken care of him. No worries, Cyn.'

'What have you done with him?'

'You're very unobservant, Cyn,' he says, and inclines his head in the smallest of casual movements outside the car. I scramble over the seat to the window and see Jimmy lying face up on the concrete, face waxen, raindrops dribbling down his cheeks in cold tears. He'd been hidden from me as I ran to the car, lying there all the time on the far side of the vehicle. I grab at the door handle but Vortex beats me to it by snapping down the central locking switch.

'Let me out,' I plead, slapping at the glass, flailing uselessly at the handle.

He sighs with exaggerated despair. 'You're such a drama queen.'

'But he needs help!'

'He's of no consequence,' he snaps. 'Listen, Cyn, we have so much in common. We both believe in the power of the web. We both know its strength. Why are you so set against me? Why do you take that poxy little kid's word against mine?'

'Don't you *dare* call him that!'

'Temper, temper,' Vortex taunts, and he throws back his head and laughs. Last time he did that, his hair swung and rippled. Now there's just the stubbled blue-sheened skin flexing over bone. Everything in me wants to fling myself out of the car and run. There's a blankness to his eyes. He looks sane and mad all at once and it makes me very, very scared.

I've got to keep him talking, give the others time to get sick of waiting and come back here, away from the dizzying cliff. The windows are all fugged up with breath and sweat now. There's just a chance, if David sees the closed car, that he'll spot the danger and sneak Philip past into the undergrowth without Vortex spotting them.

'Where's your hair?' I ask him, inching back, wary of his next lunge.

He rubs his hand across his head, caressing the stubble. 'Tomorrow,' he sighs, 'I'll start growing it again. Losing it was like a death, do you know that, Cyn? Every pull of the razor, a small death. But I had to do it to fight you and your little friend. You have to be stopped. All those lies you've been telling ...

we Signallers won't stand for any more. You've turned the whole world against us and so you have to pay.' He smiles, the grin bright and savage. 'But,' and he wags his finger, 'the spiral will reward me for my sacrifice, I know that.'

The sun visor is down on the passenger side and he turns to admire himself in the little mirror there. 'Ancient warriors used to shave their heads before battle, did you know that? It was a symbol of self-lessness.' His lips pull back from his teeth. 'And it made a man more lethal too. No enemy could grab him by the hair and bend back the head to bare the throat. I couldn't risk that, you see, so off it came. In a way I quite like it,' he muses. 'There's a purity to it. The wind prickles that strange clear space around my skull.' He tilts his head to and fro like one of his salon customers inspecting her highlights. 'My physical and mental readiness are at peak,' he informs me pleasantly.

And like lightning he lashes at me. I see it coming and rear back but there's no room and he manages to grab my arm again and he's got a cord and while I struggle and thrash he's wrapping it round and round my wrist, yanking my arm painfully between the front seats, lashing it to the steering wheel.

'So where are they then, your pretty angel and the dork from Hollywood?' he asks as he pulls the knot tight. 'Looking at the view, I suppose.' He clambers out of the car and bestows a polite smile upon me. 'I might just go and join them. But don't worry, Cyn,' he adds. 'I'll be back.'

He waves like a small cheeky boy just dropped off at school and then slams the door. His gleaming, rain-wet head shines egg-like for a moment against the dark glistening rocks. And then he's gone, leaving me trapped in the car, squeezed between the two seats, right arm tied forward, the rest of me scrunched painfully in the back seat.

For a second or two I scream after him, scream at the others, scream for help. But there's no one to hear. 'Jimmy!' I howl but I hear nothing and can't see him now from where I'm pinned. One shoulder is wedged between the veloured slit between the bucket seats, my knees on the carpet between the seats. I'm about ready to cry when I get the strangest feeling that Robert's sitting on the back seat scolding me. 'For Christ's sake, stop blathering, Moon,' he says in my head. 'You're flapping about like an old chook.' But he's not here at all, of course. I know that. *You watched him burn, Cyn. Doesn't that make you mad enough to do something about this situation?*

I twist and stretch awkwardly with my free hand, tearing at the knot which ties me to the wheel. Vortex was careless, I discover. Didn't tie it tight enough. *So much for your peak bloody performance, you creep.* I keep plucking at it and suddenly I'm free, scrambling out and on my knees now beside Jimmy, patting his face, calling to him. His head wobbles loosely under my hands at first but then there's a tiny flicker of response and he mutters, struggling to talk. I hover in an agony of indecision, desperate to get out to the others on the cliff. There's a rough blanket that we used on the beach in the back of the car. I haul it out, wrap it over the old man's sodden clothes, wad it under his head. The rain's easing. It's all I can do. And then I'm running for the path.

EIGHTEEN

This is what's going on while I'm penned in the limo.

Oakes pulls the round bone-white stone out of his trouser pocket to make his lap more comfortable. He lays it on the ground, and then hugs Philip to him for mutual warmth, drawing up his knees to surround the boy with as much protection as he can.

'We have to get you back in the car soon,' he says. 'You're going blue around the gills.'

'First things first,' says the small one. 'It won't be long now.'

They wait then, in silence, Oakes steeling himself for the moment when he'll have to get to his feet again and face the void. He hopes he won't have to go down to the outer platform where the land falls away and the emptiness shrieks.

He glances down at the boy curled within the shelter of his arms and thighs. The small face is beatific, eyes closed, lips moving in some soft small murmur. Gradually David feels his unease subside. They seem enclosed in a circle of peace. He closes his eyes.

And suddenly he is shocked into awareness, staring at the well-shod toe that is nudging at his own foot. Oakes twists sideways, scrabbling with his legs to push them both away from the bald man who is smiling down at them. The smile drips ice.

He hates being on the ground, at a disadvantage. He wants to be upright but he also knows with certainty that Vortex should not see the rock that he is half-sitting on, digging into his hip.

And then Philip squirms from his arms. 'Stay back!' David yells, off-balance, groping for him, but Philip slips out of reach. Vortex falls into a predatory crouch before the child, balanced on toes and fingers, swaying.

'I suggest you leave,' says Philip without fear. 'This is no place for a man like you.'

Vortex barks with laughter. It makes him look like a hairless dog, snappy teeth agape. 'And why not?' he sneers. 'Little squirt! Such a piddling creature to have such a big mouth.'

'Touch him and I'll kill you,' warns Oakes.

The bald man laughs again. 'Ah. Bravado from the TV star – the former star, perhaps we should say. Cyn has stuffed your life up nicely, huh? She's good at doing that.'

'I told you to leave,' the small boy says.

'Did you?' The voice is a grotesque wheedle. 'Did the itsy-witsy liddle boy want the nasty man to go away then?'

'Philip, come here,' Oakes pleads, and is ignored.

'This is a sacred place. You defile it,' the angel tells the spider.

The bald skull tilts as he regards his foes, the eyes narrowed with cunning. The weight of his body turns his fingers into bones. 'You don't know about this place, do you? I don't think you'd be here if you did. It's a dark place. The souls are thick here and angry. Three hundred warriors died here once, butchered in a great battle. Some were speared where they stood. Some were thrown over the cliff. Some jumped, they say. And their souls linger still. Can't you feel them? Can't you see them up there, making the clouds boil?'

The man points up but Oakes won't look, afraid of the mass of bloodstained faces he might see howling at him from the sky.

'They're my kind of people,' says Vortex. His eyes gleam. 'They're on my side here. They know that goodness is an illusion. They believe in winners. They know I'm a winner.'

With appalling speed, his hand lashes out and grabs the boy. 'I want the stones!' he shouts.

Leaping up, he dashes down the steps to the lower viewing platform, dragging Philip by one arm. The child is scraped and jarred, legs flailing, as he is jerked past the corner of the wall.

Oakes scrabbles after them and judders to a stop. Vortex is standing at the edge, leaning against the metal pipe railing that tops the outer wall. His right arm is outstretched and Phlip dangles from it, held by one foot, head down over the howling void. The small body sways as gusts of wind slap against the cliff face.

I get back from the car park just in time to see Vortex bundling Philip down the stairs. Appalled, I dash to the parapet as David follows them down, so intent on saving Philip that he doesn't even see me. Below me is the dreadful tableau – Vortex with arm outstretched quivering with the strain and Oakes, outraged, rooted to the spot.

Oakes's voice comes from deep down within him, engorged by dread. 'Put him down!' he roars.

'Tell me where the stones are,' Vortex bellows back.

I scream at him, voice cracking with horror. 'Bastard! Let him go!' My hair blows back and then smacks dripping in my eyes. I dash it away and stand there frozen, chilled hands pressed to my cheekbones.

Oakes looks back at Vortex. Slowly, the bald head turns so its eyes can see the child's expression. The spider hopes to see terror there, he wants to hear pleading. But the face swinging upside down, so close to his, is untroubled.

Unbelievably, the kid smiles. Vortex seems to swell with rage. He looks up at me. 'Put him down?' he says. 'Certainly.' And opens his outstretched hand. The small body plummets without a sound.

'Philip!' My howl swells and is lost in a shriek of wind.

Oakes goes the colour of putty under his ruddy hair. He leaps at Vortex, teeth bared. Feral.

The man manages to sidestep as Oakes comes at him, and the first blow skids off his shoulder. They grapple and slip. Oakes spins to attack again and Vortex catches him off-balance, grabs his hair and cracks his forehead on the railing. I see his knees sag. He collapses at the waist and Vortex gives him a heave to push him partly over the wall. His feet scrabble.

Vortex holds him in place easily by gripping the belt

at the back of his waist. 'Your menfolk are having a high old time today,' Vortex calls to me conversationally. He leans over Oakes, presses against his back, crooning in his ear. It looks obscene.

My toe nudges something heavy. A rock. A weapon. I dip and snatch for it without looking, and my arm goes back. I don't even aim. My anger is enough. The stone arrows straight and true.

A crimson crack opens down the pale skull. Vortex staggers and reels, letting Oakes go. His hand goes up to the wound, presses, and comes away smeared with scarlet. By then I'm over the wall, dragging desperately at Oakes, who is dazed but on his feet at last.

Together we stagger to the steps, trying to reach the path before Vortex can recover. I slip and my knee cracks on a concrete stair and I can't get up. The knee hurts but so does my stomach, cramping pains, awful pains, and nausea. Oh God, not here. Not now.

On my back, mouth gaping. Oakes squats, trying to pick me up, but I'm flopping and twitching and he can't gather enough of me at any one time to be able to make the lift. He hauls, panting, as Vortex stands there grinning. Rain and blood are trickling down his head, making a road map of red lines on the grey stubble of his scalp. As he smiles, a scarlet dribble slides over his lip and smears his teeth. He's holding a small plastic bag, something dark inside. Smiling steadily, Vortex rubs the bag between his palms. It's my hair. His weapon. My precious hair. I let out a wail.

In the car park Jimmy hears me. Even with the wind

thrashing at the trees and the rain still smacking on his fingers and the back of his neck as he hunches on all fours, sick and dizzy, trying to clear his head, he can still hear my cry. His head is throbbing where Vortex hit him and he can feel the distended flesh there above his ear but it is of no importance because Oh Two is scolding him to wake up and pay attention and *do something*.

There is no time for prayer except as a beseeching flash. He clutches at the door handle on the driver's side, hauls until the door pops open and then, painfully, he scrabbles up into the seat where he knows there is a phone. He's seen Gary use it, watched what he did. Then, working slowly so as not to make any careless error, Jimmy presses the long series of digits that will connect him with the shabby old homestead perched above the grey and glistening waters of the Hokianga Harbour.

Louisa is sitting barefoot out on the rose-laden verandah when the phone rings. She drove straight to the cottage on the knoll after she disposed of all the horrid hair. The old man told her to. She had no idea why it was required but he was most adamant about it. 'Please, Miss Williams,' he said. 'Your presence there could be crucial to us.' And so, with uncharacteristic meekness, she'd agreed and the old couple, Norm and Alice, weren't at all put out when she turned up unannounced to wait for whatever it is Jimmy needs her for.

'I'll get it,' she calls, and pads inside.

It is Jimmy. Under stress of some kind, his voice strained and thready. 'Vortex's hair,' he says. 'Destroy it. Right now.'

'How?'

'Any way you can think of,' he says with exasperation. 'Just get rid of it. Hurry!'

She's been keeping the coiled shiny black hank in a bowl on the polished hall table. Now she drops the phone and snatches up the slithery stuff, dithering, unsure what she should do with it.

Alice has welcomed Louisa to her home. Of course it is fine for her to stay if Jimmy thinks she should. It does your heart good to see someone bury her glammed-up city clothes in a drawer along with her lipstick and rouge and all that flim-flam, and get into jeans and a sensible sweater. And it is just fine to see the strain and urgency wash from someone's face like it has from Louisa's. But Alice doesn't like that hair that Louisa insists on keeping in the house. It looks like a dead thing. Something rotten. Alice's tabby keeps hissing at it. But Louisa insists that Jimmy says she has to keep watch over it. Just in case. So Alice has put up with it, though the table it sits upon has stayed undusted.

And now, while Louisa is making such a ruckus out in the hall, Alice is in the kitchen making pikelets on her old wood stove. She has a new-fangled electric one but she likes the old wood-burner better. She clicks her tongue as she tries to ignore the commotion, and then she nearly jumps out of her skin as Louisa bursts into her kitchen waving that horrible hair. She runs to the stove, opens the door to the fire box and thrusts it in.

Disgusted, Alice flaps her hand as the acrid stench and hiss of burning hair fills the room. 'You're ruining my pikelets!'

But Louisa pays her no heed, snatching up the poker to push in the last strands, stirring them around, making the firebed glow hot and red.

Up on the clifftop, far away, a most peculiar expression starts to spread on the bloody face of the man with the plastic bag. The smile thins, quavers and is wiped out. Then Vortex screams. The plastic bag flutters to the wet concrete.

Oakes squats and pulls me to him. I am shivering, my eyes wide now. We cling together as Vortex bends and shudders, both hands clapped claw-like to his head, ripping at his scalp as if trying to rid himself of something that burns and stings.

He howls as the wind gusts again and a shriek of air funnels up the cliff face in a twister laden with shredded sticks and leaves and clods of earth. It turns tighter and darker now, a destructive blast-furnace chimney of wind that hovers, roaring, above the reeling man, and then plucks him from the ground, whirling him high.

The flailing body disappears into the maelstrom. For a split second, we see it spin from one cloud's tendril to another. And then it is lost as the vapour rips into ribbons over the jungle.

We gape upwards. 'Miss Moon?' comes a voice from behind us. 'Are you all right?' We whirl and see Jimmy, pale but upright, holding a cellphone to his chest, his other hand clutching the blanket around his shoulders.

Oakes hoists me up to help me over to the old man. 'I'm okay,' I tell him, shrugging him off. Together we coax Jimmy to the ground, sheltering from the wind behind the wall.

A reedy noise is coming from the phone. 'Jimmy?' a voice is saying. 'What the hell's going on? Can you hear me?' I grab it, recognising the voice. 'Vortex has gone, Lou,' I manage to say. 'The storm got him. Can you believe that? It just came and took him away.'

Louisa sounds baffled. 'Took him away where? What do you mean?'

Jimmy is motioning to get the phone back again so I pass it over. 'Miss Williams, you've done us a great service,' he says. 'But please,' he adds, 'we can't talk now. We'll ring later.' And he switches it off.

'What in God's name happened just then?' asks Oakes. 'Did you do that?'

'Miss Williams did. She destroyed Vortex's hair – the thing which he believed gave him his dark powers. All his signal threads burnt at once, so to speak. His whole foundation torn to shreds. Helped along, I might say, by a few hundred old souls lurking around here who were only too happy to help in his demise. Vortex, in his arrogance, assumed they'd be on his side.'

He smiles wanly but all the time he is speaking he is looking about, his expression changing quickly to one of alarm. 'Where is Philip?'

I have to tell him. There is no gentle way to do it. The old man lowers his head and makes a long low keening noise, rocking from side to side. 'Oh, Miss Moon,' is all he says. And then his voice strengthens with resolve. 'You must take the stones now and touch them together. Philip would want that. And Robert.'

A feeble patch of sunlight flutters over our patch of concrete. The wind is dropping. The tourists will be back soon, mutters Oakes. He looks odd. Numb. Shocked. But I can tell from his eyes that he's resigned to doing what Jimmy wants before we can be gone from this place. Two of the people we've loved best in the world have died to make it possible. And then we'll need the police to start a search for two bodies. A doctor for Jimmy as well – who is looking grey and sweaty, shivering now despite the blanket – and somewhere quiet to call Cal and report this latest disaster.

'Let's do it,' he says. He turns, looks, feels behind him with his hands. *Nothing.* 'I can't find the stone,' he says. 'But it must be here. It's where we sat, next to the wall.' His hands pat the concrete uselessly.

My gut shifts, a sick lurch of realisation. 'Oh my God,' I whisper. 'I just picked up whatever was there. I didn't think.'

Now we're all on our feet scanning the lower platform. Nothing. I run down the steps to the rail and peer over, afraid I might see Philip's small body on the rocks far below. There is no sign of him.

There are a few boulders protruding from the cliff face and a narrow ledge perhaps seven or eight feet from the top. I look . . . and shriek.

There the stone sits, round and squat, directly below us. So near. So far.

I stretch towards it. 'Don't do that!' Oakes snaps, grabbing at my clothes. Jimmy comes to join us, unsteady on his feet, reaching for the rail.

'Jimmy, be careful,' I plead. 'Come away from the edge.' And we lead him to the rear wall, coax him to lie down in the fitful sunshine. His pallor is even worse. 'We'll get you some help soon,' I promise.

'Don't fuss,' he argues. 'I'll be all right. Please, just try to get the stone.' And his eyes flutter closed.

'Oh, shit,' says Oakes. 'He needs an ambulance. I'll get the phone.'

And he makes to go and retrieve it from the upper platform but Jimmy calls him back. 'I'm not dying,' he says with asperity, his eyes still shut. 'I'm praying. This action needs prayer. Just get on with it.'

Oakes allows me to take him back to the cliff edge. 'If only we had a rope,' I fret. 'You could anchor me and I could go down and get it.'

'But we haven't.' There is a hint of relief in the way he says it.

'We do!' I remember. 'In the car. Vortex had some. We could tie one end to my wrist. Look – the ledge is wide enough for me to stand on as long as I've got something to hang on to. And see? At the end of the platform the ledge goes up higher. I can hold on to the railing there. Then as the ledge drops away . . .' Oakes's skin seems to crawl at my choice of words '. . . you can hold me with the rope.'

He swallows. 'Why don't I do it?'

'It has to be me. I'm lighter. If I slip, you're strong enough to hold me. I know I couldn't hold you.'

He knows I'm right. We go back to the car and disentangle the length of cord from the steering wheel. It's about four feet long. Long enough. Working together, we each tie one end of it to our right wrists. I'll be clinging to the cliff-face, moving to my left and so

I'll need my left hand free to bend down and pick up the stone. Oakes decides on his right arm because it is probably stronger than his left, he reckons. The rope offers no guarantees, but at least it gives us a little assurance that should I slip . . . but we don't want to think about that.

We go back to the lookout and check on Jimmy. He is prone still and unmoving. His blank face seems oddly ecstatic, and by some mute consent we neither look long upon him, for he seems privately engaged in some inner communion, nor attempt to make him talk.

I put my stone safely by the wall so I can drop the other one in my waistbag once I've retrieved it. The bag I leave gaping open, unzipped, across my stomach.

'Right,' I say. Oakes nods severely, tips my chin. 'Take care,' is all he says.

I climb over the rail to stand on the ledge below, facing the wall. Then I move sideways step by step, both hands on the metal pipe.

'Does the ledge feel firm?' he asks.

It's okay, I nod. Then my narrow foothold begins to slope downhill, and gradually, step by step, I descend. Soon my arms will be at full stretch on the rail. Oakes wants me to take hold of the cord before the transition becomes too difficult. 'Cyn, change your grip now. I've got the rope firm.'

I do, and feel my face go pale.

'It's wobbly,' I complain. 'Hold still.'

'I am. It's okay. Keep the strain on and I'll gradually lower it with you. You're doing great. Just fine.' I'm staring at the concrete outer skin of the wall now, knees scraping on the rough rock face below it. My left leg quivers. I stop and take a few deep breaths. The sun is warm on my back, the wind light and steady. No horrid gusts. No surprises. I think of Philip and want to weep but push the emotion away. It would be dangerous here.

'Are you all right, Cyn?' Oakes's even voice floats down from above. I'm surprised at his calm as he hangs over the wall where he recently came so close to dying. 'Just taking a rest,' I say. I sound calm, too. Even more amazing.

'You've only got about six steps left to go. One,' he intones. I push my foot leftwards, following with the other. 'Two. Three. Four. Stop now, Cyn.' I obey. There is still some play on the rope but my fingers are locked solid on it, my arm almost at full stretch. Everything is starting to ache with the strain. A green grass stem sprouting from the cliff face tickles my nose.

'Look down to your left now, Cyn. It's only about two feet away.' I peer under my armpit. There it is, tiny crystals within the rock sparkling prettily in the sunlight.

'I see it!'

I attempt a sideways bend. It doesn't feel good. It means crouching with my bottom in space, knees knocking against the cliff. It means having to look down into the dizzying void. 'Can you give me any more slack?' I shout. 'I don't think I can reach it otherwise.'

Slowly the strain of my arm lessens. I glance up and am shocked to see an alarming amount of Oakes

leaning over the railing. Veins are standing out on his
face and neck as he holds on. 'No more!' I cry, suddenly
panicky.

'It's okay,' he grits. 'Bend now, do it.'

One chance here, I tell myself. Just a reach, a touch.
Now my fingers are under it. I scoop up the stone,
straighten my knees and sway with relief. 'Done!' I yell.
And I drop it into the belt-bag and zip it up.

'Fantastic!' he calls. I can hear the strain in his voice.
'It's all easy from now on. Back up the path. Go.'

Legs and arms atremble now, I take one step and
another . . . having to place my toes closer to the edge of
the ledge because the stone makes a hard lump between
my body and the cliff face.

The ledge inches higher. I look up, can see his face
wet with sweat. No handholds here on the smooth
cement wall but soon I'll be able to touch him, soon
I'll be there.

And then my right foot falls into space through the
crumbling edge of the path. I fall only a couple of feet
before being brought up short by our improvised safety
strap, just long enough to start to scream before my body
slams against the wall. My fingers have lost their grip and
now I'm hanging by the wrist from the knotted cord. It
bites into the skin and my shoulder is on fire.

I'm dangling with my back against the wall. 'David!'
I shriek.

I strain to look up and wish I hadn't because I can
see my fall has almost pulled him over too. My weight is
suspended from the knot around his wrist. His hand is
swollen and turning purple. He is straddling the metal

railing, his right shoulder and half his body on my side of the wall, his left arm clamped around the pipe, his face scarlet with effort. 'Christ!' I hear him say. Then something tears inside my shoulder.

'Cyn!' Oakes groans. 'Talk to me, damn it!'

I can only make a high, squealing noise through clenched teeth. His muscles and tendons must be shrieking, the left arm starting to burn. I'm a limp weight pulling his mass to the wrong side of the wall. Soon the law of gravity will kick in. Should he just wait or should he let go? Even through the agony, I know what he's thinking. Which is worse – the going or the knowing you are going to go?

Then someone says. 'Hey, look out buddy. What're you doing down there?' And meaty hands grab him around the ribs and cling on.

'Clarence?' calls a woman's voice from the upper platform. 'Oh my God! Waylon! Brodie! Go help your dad!'

More hands take hold, but he can't be pulled up because his arm is still strained over the railing. He groans. 'Sheeit,' a man exclaims. 'There's a woman danglin' down there. Haul her up, boys!'

Soon I'm on my back on blessed concrete, staring up at a circle of the bluest sky surrounded by a ring of concerned faces. There is Oakes. There is Jimmy, head all lumpen on one side, but awake and all abrim with relief. A very large woman with rosy cheeks, outrageous earrings and a blonde haystack of hair and three lookalike men, tummies straining the fabric of their

shirts that are asplash with palm trees and rainbows –
all looking worriedly down at me.

I smile. I'm alive. 'Praise the Lord!' cries the woman as
Oakes starts to unknot the rope from our bruised wrists.
And at her cry a barrage of cheers goes up. The sun
has brought out the tour buses and the upper parapet
is lined with a row of grinning tourists, their cameras
clacking. It's all utterly surreal. I'm past caring.

'Say, haven't I seen you on TV?' the big woman asks
Oakes. She looks around. 'Where are the cameras?'

'Hidden in the trees,' he says wearily. 'Smile. You're
on *Candid Camera.*'

Her hand flutters to her throat. 'Oh my! Boys! Go get
the camcorder. We gotta get this.'

Oakes helps me sit up and then reaches for the stone
I'd put down for safekeeping. He hands it over. 'Let's
do this before someone carries it off as a souvenir,'
he says.

I unzip the bag around my waist. My shoulder still
burns, but first aid can wait. The camera-snappers watch,
puzzled, as Oakes dips into the pouch and pulls out the
other stone. We face each other. Something – perhaps
it's the presence of our audience – makes us bow. The
watchers hush respectfully. Jimmy, arms raised, smiling,
surrounds us with his love. It's like a cloak, warm and
palpable.

With great delicacy we raise the two stones and move
them close. Closer. Even closer. There is the tiniest click
as we join them together, face to face, groove on groove.

The audience cheers and whistles, puzzled but
delighted.

But then the applause dies. There are gasps and whimpers. A single cry of awe. A giant collective intake of breath. For a streak of gold rockets across the heavens from left to right, leaving a shimmering seam slashed across the fabric of blue.

And then the thin line seems to waver and split and a second line arrows down, forming a great V suspended under the first so that now a great golden triangle is etched above their heads.

And then from the low point of the V emerges yet another shimmering streak. Straight down this one zooms, so that the triangle became a vast Y-shape.

'Oh God, David,' I breathe. 'It's the web.'

Now radial lines zip out from the centre and new golden streaks speed in from the horizon to link up with the others, and the web grows and grows in perfect geometric spokes, each centre joining up in perfect alignment with its neighbours. All over the world, all at once, the Earth's great invisible energy field comes alive for all to see.

As the enormous force surging through the web gathers strength, the glittering net lights up the night on the globe's sunless side and cuts laser-like lines through daytime clouds.

It crackles and sings as the power of the universe charges through it and a resonant hum booms around the planet and the very earth shakes with its song.

People feel it through their feet and their skin. They cower as it aches in their ears.

Callahan looks up, startled, as the Venetian blinds

begin to shimmer at the windows. 'Fuck, it's the big one . . .' he says to his empty office and, well-trained Angeleno that he is, dives under his desk.

In monasteries and ashrams across Asia, the monks rush to prayer, their heads ringing with the sound they've sung for thousands of years and which they can now actually hear booming in the sky. 'Ooommmmmm,' they chorus in ecstasy and wonder. 'Oooommmmmm!'

Afloat upon the oceans of the world, fishermen, deckhands and sailors gape as, all around their craft, ranks of gleaming dolphins hurtle from the water, leaping and diving in a synchronised dance of joy.

In her garden Shirley sits on her lawn, dazed. She's been planting a few flowers by her cracked front path. Beginning her life again. And she feels a touch on her arm and turns and her baby is there. Philip! Real, so alive, his face aglow. 'I'm sorry,' he says to his mother. 'I love you. Please forgive me. But this is why I had to leave, you see . . .' And he points over his head and she looks up, puzzled, and then back at him, and he's gone. Just like that. And now she sits, her face, wet with tears, and gazes at the blazing lines of fire ruled across the sky. 'Yes,' she whispers. 'Oh, yes . . .'

Louisa is driven to distraction by waiting for the others to call back. They do get beside themselves, these city folks, Alice is telling Norm, just as the strange thrumming noise begins under their feet, over their heads, everywhere. The roses tremble and on the far side of the harbour the gaunt dunes shudder and avalanches of golden sand rumble down to the sea. 'It's Jimmy,' cries Norm. 'Yes, you old bugger!'

On the far side of the world, Daniel stands on his hill above the swirling green maze. He holds a shining bell and pulls mightily on its clanger so the sound of it sings along with the holy roar from the sky. 'D'you hear that, angels?' he shouts with joy. 'Listen to that!'

On our clifftop on Oahu, the tourists shout in confusion. The big Americans stand and gape. Waylon is bewildered. What sort of TV show is this? 'What in tarnation's going on?' he demands to know.

Oakes and Jimmy and I take no notice. No notice at all. We stand entranced, hugging each other, gazing upwards at the glittering strands. And we lift our arms to the searing sky, fists clenched, and let out a ragged and mighty shout. 'Yes!' we all cry.

EPILOGUE

And so Philip drifts and watches while the Earth teeters in its free zone at the hub of history.

It may still go either way. The web is fragile, barely stable. It's been newly nourished with love, but needs more, and soon, if the world is to flourish.

Anxiously, the angel patrols the web's outer perimeters, sometimes twanging the filaments like a harp string. Other angels tell him it's mischievous, but he likes to remind people of their duty by setting the occasional vibrating fibre aglow in the heavens.

'I am merely waving a celestial flag at them,' he says, 'reminding them of the choice they've made. It's all up to them now.'

Every now and again, he visits his friends. Only Jimmy can always feel his presence. They talk, taking pleasure in each other's company, just as they did before.

Shirley's grief begins to ease, which pleases him. There is a new serenity about her, despite the great uncertainty that stalks the globe. She still keeps her baby's picture in a frame beside her bed, but her heart is healing.

And Miss Moon and Mr Oakes? Love blooms between

them. They declined to complete the last leg of their journey back to Los Angeles. There was little point with the city, and the world, in such chaos. Oakes resigned with no regrets. They said farewell to Jimmy as he journeyed back to New Zealand and promised to go and see him soon. Meanwhile, they've settled into a small house high on a hill from where they can see the creamy curve of surf upon the coral reef.

They don't notice as Philip shimmers by. Not surprising perhaps as Oakes is just telling her how important she is to him. It makes the angel's heart swell with joy. He watches, fondly, as they lie together.

She touches the hollow where his collarbones meet and then flattens her hand just-so against the broadness of his chest. 'You know,' she says, 'you and I are just like spiders. And like those stones, too.'

He shakes with laughter. 'Crazy woman. What *are* you talking about now?'

'Spiders,' she says: 'Philip told me. They have these amazing sexual bits that will only fit when two spiders are ideally mated. Two of a kind. We're like that, you and I. We fit together. Just like that. Snick-snack. Perfect.'

'And will you spring at me afterwards and eat me up?' he asks.

'Only if you ask nicely,' she says. They stay in close embrace for long moments and then she adds, 'One of the reasons I love you is because you're so strong and straight. You're like a big old tree, my very own god of the forest.

'Did you know that lots of people's names go back to

the trades their ancestors had? I bet your great-great-great-grand-daddy and his family used to live amongst oak trees. You can be my very own oak. You can shade me from the sun. You've got lovely foliage,' she grins, tugging at his thick hair. 'When I'm feeling playful I can climb right up you,' she goes on, winding a naked leg around his. 'And when it's stormy,' she giggles, pulling him on top of her, 'I can hide underneath.'

Philip moves on, contented. There are times when even angels shouldn't eavesdrop.

Then, rising high above the Earth, he swoops with slow pleasure along the length of a golden filament, enjoying the way the web gently curves before him, cupping the planet in its embrace.

Below, mighty swirls and platters of cloud partially veil the turquoise and indigo seas and the continents bright with emerald and russet and chocolate and ice. He sighs. It is so very beautiful.

Playfully, he gives the strand another thrumming, setting it asparkle.

And he laughs out loud. Is it his imagination or do the colours down there seem just a little richer than before?